By moonlight or candlelight. . .
discover the joy of
Christmas love.

CHRISTMAS
Dreams

Four Inspirational
Love Stories
from
Christmas Present

Rebecca Germany
Mary Hawkins
Veda Boyd Jones
Melanie Panagiotopoulos

BARBOUR
PUBLISHING

Published by Barbour Publishing, Inc., P.O. Box 719, Uhrichsville, Ohio 44683, www.barbourbooks.com

Our mission is to publish and distribute inspirational products offering exceptional value and biblical encouragement to the masses.

 Member of the
Evangelical Christian
Publishers Association

Printed in the United States of America.
5 4 3 2 1

CHRISTMAS
Dreams

Evergreen

Rebecca Germany

Chapter 1

T he thud created by Nora Daniels's loafers didn't begin to reflect the frustration pounding through her whole body. As she maneuvered through the maze of reporters' desks cluttering the newsroom of the Winter Haven Tribune, all she could think about was finding the nerve to hand in her resignation. The *Tribune*, with a daily circulation of 15,000, was a typical small-town central Florida newspaper, filled with homespun stories that were generally shunned by the more cosmopolitan press of nearby Orlando and Lakeland.

A groan escaped her lips as she marched through the door to the employee lounge that also served as the photography department. The room, filled with mismatched furniture, adjoined the darkroom and photographers' supply closet. If only she had a really interesting story assignment, she thought dejectedly, maybe the Christmas season would pass quickly.

Nora had just filled a Styrofoam cup with stale coffee when the darkroom door slammed into her shoulder, sending the cup flying and its contents running down the wall and onto the floor.

"Oh, Nora, I am so sorry." A giant hand grasped her shoulder as Nora struggled to regain her balance. "I wasn't thinking when I came barreling through that door."

"I'm fine, no damage done," she assured him as she eased herself away from his warm clasp. She had to smile at Rick Thompson when she noticed his straight brown hair drooped over one eye, strands of film draped over his broad shoulders, and bottles of developing chemicals held precariously in one arm. "It looks like you're the one who could use some help," she said as she reached out to rescue a bottle that was dangerously close to falling onto the tiled floor.

"Thanks. I just need to put these away."

After Nora followed Rick into the large closet where she deposited her bottle on a low shelf, they returned to the lounge and he began mopping up coffee with paper towels she had located beside the sink. Although she had known Rick for the two years she had worked at the newspaper, their paths didn't often cross. Still, she admired his friendly attitude and had duly noted his obvious Christian faith. She hadn't let her thoughts about him extend beyond that.

Though she longed to have a family of her own someday, she just didn't have the desire to get into a dating relationship at the time. *Besides*, Nora thought sadly, *even if I were looking, he wouldn't be interested.* Although she received many compliments about her cornflower blue eyes and layered ash-blond hair that perfectly framed her round face, she was painfully aware that her weight and reserved demeanor didn't turn many heads.

"Sorry about your coffee," Rick said again as he

raised his large, athletic frame from the floor.

"It's really okay. This weather is too hot to drink coffee anyway," she explained weakly.

"I suppose you'll be heading north for Christmas in a little more than a week," Rick said as he held a strand of newly developed film toward the fluorescent ceiling light.

"No."

The silence that hung between them was heavy with the weight of that one word. Then Rick ventured to ask, "Do you have family visiting Florida over the holidays?"

"John and Gary, my brothers, have made plans to stay home with their families. Last year we all made a point of being together for Christmas, but it wasn't a pleasant time." Nora could still remember the tension that developed as she and her brothers tried to re-create all the Daniels family traditions without their parents.

"I'm sure your parents' sudden passing was still fresh on your minds," Rick offered in an attempt to ease her obvious discomfort.

"Nothing was the same," Nora continued with a shaky breath. "The fire that took Mom and Dad also took all the material reminders we had of them and our Christmases together. And now we can never really go home for Christmas again."

Embarrassed by her uncharacteristic revelation, she moved to brush away a tear that had managed to slip down her rounded check. The slow motion of her hand triggered something in Rick's expression.

"Just wait until Horn finds out that you'll be around for the holiday rush. He'll have a number of little assignments to fill your time," Rick offered with a smile.

"Mr. Horn knows, and he has already given me a story assignment that should keep me busy. . .not to mentioned bored."

"Well, you can always count on Horn." Rick's laugh was warm. "What funeral or dog pound is he sending you to this time?"

Nora didn't need to be reminded of the dull stories that were showered on her as the string reporter. "He feels the *Tribune* should cover the role of the local homeless shelters in helping the less fortunate through this Christmas."

Rick laughed again at her dry tone and proceeded to mock her, saying, "I'm sure the shelters are full of interesting stories about people who are struggling to overcome their circumstances."

She made a face at him.

"Really, I am serious."

Finally she smiled begrudgingly. "I don't mean to sound unsympathetic or even above the assignment. It's just that. . . ," she said, pausing for a moment, "I guess I wish my work could be more challenging or rewarding."

"If you're not careful, you may find yourself enjoying your interviews with the volunteers who make those shelters run, not to mention the people who use their services. I'm sure there are hundreds of stories to be told."

Nora appreciated his sincere attempt to help her look at the positive side of her job. His blue gaze had settled on her face and seemed to be willing her to see things his way.

"Has Horn scheduled a photographer for the assignment?" Rick probed.

"Why? My stories are hardly front-page material."

"Need I remind you that a good picture—by a good photographer—can make the whole story?"

"Do I have a volunteer?"

"Well, if the boss hasn't ordered pictures, it would have to be on my own time," Rick reasoned, "but I would enjoy tagging along and seeing what the camera can find."

"It's really not necessary," she said, but she began to enjoy the idea of having some company on the assignment.

"I'm free Tuesday afternoon. You'll want to get started as soon as possible. When is the story due to release?"

"December twenty-sixth," Nora said as she reached for her planner near the coffeemaker. She quickly flipped to December and jotted a couple of notes.

"Great," Rick said, turning his attention back to his strands of film. "By the way, I haven't seen you lately at the singles' Sunday school class at Oakgrove."

Nora could feel the heat in her cheeks. "No, I haven't been in quite a while," she admitted, "but I intend to get back soon."

"Good, maybe I'll see you tomorrow then." He

gave her a brief smile as he walked back toward the darkroom.

Nora retrieved her purse from the coffee table and tucked her planner into its depths. She almost hated to admit it, but she felt better than she had upon entering the lounge. At least she had the prospect of Rick livening up some of the time around the holidays.

Past a thriving grove of orange trees, Nora pulled her compact car into a drive alongside the small house she rented with her friend Carmen. Nora could just pick out a slice of sunset over the lake that was one block behind her place. The view from the carport was the best she could hope for from her yard, but the aroma of onions and fresh peppers drew her to the back door.

Carmen had pulled her dark, curly locks into a thick ponytail, secured with a bright red bandanna. With her cutoff jeans and polo shirt, she resembled a college student more than a career woman with a twelve-year-old son.

"Something smells wonderful," Nora complimented as she crossed the kitchen to lay her purse on a chair.

"Oh, hi," Carmen said, smiling. "I'm cooking enchiladas."

"Move over, Taco Bell!" Nora joked.

"Yeah, yeah," Carmen said, laughing. "My grandfather, who was born near Mexico City, taught me everything I know about cooking." She then deftly changed the subject to Nora. "Did you have a good day? How many obituaries will we see in tomorrow's paper?"

"Only three." Nora sighed as she pulled a chair away from the small oak table and sank onto it. "I told Mr. Horn that I would be staying in town for Christmas and he was more than happy to give me an assignment."

"Oh? And what will you be covering?"

"Just the local homeless shelters, but I get some help. Rick Thompson, one of the *Tribune*'s two full-time photographers, has volunteered to come along even though Mr. Horn obviously didn't plan on photos."

"Very interesting," Carmen murmured as she reached into the oven to pull out a steaming pan heaped full of enchiladas. "I hope I made enough. Chris is growing so fast, I can't seem to keep him full these days."

Nora laughed, thinking of the boy who had always been small for his age. In the last few months he did seem to be going through a growth spurt.

"Now, tell me," Carmen continued, "is this. . .Rick. . .is he single?"

"Yes, not that it matters," Nora hurriedly added. "He goes to our church but I don't think you've ever met him."

"Has he worked at the paper long?" Carmen quizzed Nora.

"At least two years." Nora shrugged. "He was there when I started."

"I can't believe you never mentioned this guy before. And he's single! Is he engaged? Good-looking?" Carmen continued to drill.

"He is not engaged, at least not to my knowledge," Nora said crisply. "He's in his late twenties, I'd say, around six feet, brown hair with a lot of natural blond highlights, blue eyes, broad shoulders, large hands, and a funny little scar that can barely be seen on the tip of his chin." Nora ticked off each quality on a finger. "He is rather average, but I suppose he could be considered good-looking."

"What? You noticed that many details about the man and never bothered to mention him? No wonder you're not married," Carmen said, shaking her head. "But as I always say, better to never marry than be unhappily married."

Nora knew Carmen was referring to her own stressful marriage of fifteen years that had ended when her workaholic husband suffered a fatal, premature heart attack. Nora had met Carmen at college when she was getting her teaching degree, and now Carmen was halfway through her first year as a second-grade teacher. Despite their age difference, Carmen and Nora had formed a common bond, with Carmen becoming the older and wiser sister Nora never had. Though Carmen remained wary of marrying again, arranging marriage for Nora was a different matter. Carmen still loved fairytale endings.

As Nora ripped lettuce for a salad, Carmen continued her tactical assault. "You'll have to bring this man of many qualities by here sometime," she said with a mischievous smile lighting her eyes.

"I can introduce you to him tomorrow at church, but he's just an acquaintance from work. I don't think he'll have any reason to visit my home." Nora's tone warned Carmen not to pursue her attempts at matchmaking. Nora had in mind the kind of man she wanted as a husband and she didn't want anyone pushing her to settle for less.

When Nora finished, she wiped her hands on a dish towel. "I think I'll change into shorts before we eat. If it cools off, maybe we can all go for a bike ride later." Walking out of the kitchen she added, almost too casually, "Oh, by the way, remind me to set my alarm for early tomorrow. I want to try and make it to Sunday school."

Nora felt bad that she had let herself slip into a routine of avoiding the singles' class at Oakgrove Community Church. She couldn't explain why, really, but some of the lessons from a series done last summer had made her feel uncomfortable. The teacher had focused on trust in God, incorporating the virtues of peace, patience, and forgiveness. Since her parents' death, these virtues had been in short supply in Nora's life. She was ashamed to admit—and she knew better—that she blamed God for the way her life had turned out.

Nora had anticipated meeting the man of her dreams in college and marrying right after she received her degree. When she graduated with no prospects of marriage, she fully intended to move home to upstate New York to be near family and friends. Then a job with the *Tribune* had been offered and, with college bills waiting to be paid, she couldn't pass up a steady paycheck. Now her childhood home in New York was burned to ashes, her parents were gone, and she was stuck in a dead-end job in a state where the seasons never seemed to change. . . where everything was perpetually green.

Rick had given her a casual wave when she entered the crowded Sunday school class, but Nora was strangely disappointed to see him sitting next to a young woman she didn't know. She didn't see him again until he filed into the sanctuary choir loft. Thankfully, Carmen wasn't one to pursue the introduction.

Chapter 2

When Nora didn't see Rick on Monday, for the first time in her two years of working at the *Tribune*, she felt a void in the office. Her time, however, was more than filled with making calls to various local shelters. Most of the people she talked with were helpful and willing to schedule an interview along with a tour of their facility. One shelter director was even interested to know if Nora's photographer would be willing to do some extra pictures for the shelter's brochures to generate contributions. Nora said she would have to ask Rick, but somehow she knew he wouldn't turn it down.

Nora decided to focus on four shelters and prepared her schedule for the next week. She rounded out her day with the usual grim task of preparing the obituary column, and she made final edits to her brief piece on the Christmas shopping turnout at the mall. Only nine shopping days remained and Nora had yet to buy one present. She shouldn't procrastinate any longer, she reasoned, as she still needed to prepare boxes to send to her brothers and their families. There was a story that day about the abundance of mail that the post office was having to sort and ship this year.

On her way out Nora flicked the tinsel that someone had strung around the door frame. As the humidity wrapped around her and the sinking Florida sun hit her squarely in the face, she knew she wasn't in the mood to shop for gifts this year. All the elements of a traditional Christmas were missing. If she didn't have to fight cold and snow to get to and from the stores, it just wasn't Christmas.

❧

Rick was at her desk promptly at two o'clock Tuesday afternoon. He was free for the rest of the day, so they loaded his camera bag along with her tape recorder and notebook into his little pickup truck.

"Sorry for all the clutter," Rick apologized as he opened the door to the passenger's side. "I seem to be always on the go, and the truck collects all the things I may need: Bible for Bible study, songbooks for choir practice, camera equipment for job shoots, candy bars for the munchies, and I have even been known to carry a change of clothes for the gym."

Nora had trouble suppressing a laugh as he tried to explain his reasons for having each item that he was tossing behind the seat. Then he proceeded to dump the sand from the floor mat.

"My personal sandbox," he joked, and Nora's laugh broke loose.

When they were both finally settled in, she gave him rather roundabout directions to their destination. The interior of Rick's truck had a rather welcoming scent, piney and purely masculine, and Nora was clearly distracted.

At their first stop, the Good Shepherd Mission, the director, Mr. Gray, showed Nora and Rick their newly renovated strip motel that could temporarily shelter up to twelve homeless families. As the motel was no longer drawing customers, the aging owner had donated the property to her church, which in turn donated the building to the mission.

Nora could already see an angle for her article developing around the many people whose contributions of time, money, and more made the work of the shelters possible. She could highlight what each of the four shelters had to offer the community, and she would point out what the readers could do to ensure that the important work done by the shelters would continue.

When their tour was completed, Nora sat down with Mr. Gray to ask him questions while Rick roamed the shelter's grounds looking for potential pictures. When Nora finally slid into the truck, she was more than willing to call it a day.

"Mind if I put in a tape of Christmas music?" Rick asked as they pulled out into traffic.

"No, maybe it will help me get into the spirit of the season," Nora said. "If you don't mind my saying so, I don't look forward to spending Christmas in Florida. I know we can celebrate Christ's birth anywhere, but. . ." Nora was ashamed by how shallow her words sounded to her own ears.

"I'm sure it's hard on you not being able to be with family this year."

"Every Christmas I can remember has been spent in New York. My brothers and I would always anticipate having snow on the ground for Christmas morning." Nora found herself smiling at the memories. "It didn't even matter how much snow we had as long as there was enough to make the lawn white."

As Rick merged onto the highway, he said, "I can still remember Christmases as a boy in Ohio."

"Did you grow up in Ohio?"

"Yes, we lived in northeastern Ohio until I was about eleven and then my dad got a job down here," Rick said. "I remember some great Christmases when we had so much snow that we had to stay home. We loved having mounds of snow to play in, but I'm sure it caused my parents many headaches trying to get all those last-minute gifts. Our first Christmas here the weather gave us no indication that Christmas was coming. We bought the first artificial tree I had ever seen, and we laughed at our neighbors who strung their outdoor lights on palm trees and pool fences."

"Like that?" Nora pointed toward lights that were just beginning to show up as the sun sank below the flat horizon. On the left side of the highway mobile homes were packed close together as far as the eye could see. The elaborate fountain at the entry to the park reflected red and green lights.

"Yeah, and have you seen the Santa that the Citrus Hotel has floating in their pool?"

Nora laughed, remembering how silly it looked.

Most people pictured Santa sled-riding or ice-skating, not sun-bathing!

"Hey, it's time for dinner! Do you want to grab a bite?" Rick asked.

The last time Nora agreed to have dinner with a man had been on her first—and last—date with a guy she had met through some old college friends.

Rick picked a small family-owned restaurant on the shore of one of the area's many lakes. They both ordered the catfish special and waited in comfortable silence. Nora appreciated the fact that Rick didn't insist on trying to make conversation, and she allowed herself a few minutes to gaze out the window and admire the black silhouettes of palm and pine trees against the last magenta glow of the sunset.

Rick was the first to break the silence. "Do you have all your Christmas shopping done?"

"I haven't bought one gift yet," Nora answered with a small groan. "I haven't even been in the mood to help my roommate and her son pick out a tree for our place. Just call me Scrooge."

"No tree?" Rick exclaimed in mock horror. "We'll have to do something about that."

Nora felt completely at ease laughing and talking with Rick. She was surprised that she had never really noticed that at work.

As they ate, they made plans for visiting the three other shelters on Nora's list. They would have to work Saturday, but Nora felt confident that she would be able to visit the shelters and gather all her research by Monday. She would be able to get the bulk of the article prepared before the holiday. She planned to drop in at one of the shelters on Christmas Day to add some holiday details to her piece.

"Oh! I nearly forgot," Nora said. "Mrs. Nickolson at County Relief Services is looking for a photographer to take some pictures. They will use the photos in a brochure to promote their services and drum up contributions for the new year. I told her I would mention it to you, but you would be expected to donate your time."

"I could probably fit that in," Rick said between bites. "I could even start taking shots while we're there tomorrow."

Nora looked at him in amazed wonder. "You are so willing to volunteer," she said. "How do you ever fit it all into your schedule?"

"I love my golden retriever—Pete's his name—but it can still get pretty lonely if I don't keep busy." Rick shrugged. "Besides, we are told to 'do unto others,' and I try to do what I can."

Nora grew quiet. She was remembering how her father used to say something very similar. He had been the man everyone at their little church had looked to when something needed fixing, the youth group needed a van driver, or a Sunday school class needed a teacher. He never complained about the work and always kept a cheerful attitude.

"I hate to cut the meal short," Rick said suddenly, "but I have to lead a men's Bible study tomorrow morning at six and I have a lot of preparation to do yet."

Nora smiled. *This man is too good to be true*, she reasoned. *That has to be what's wrong with him. No one is this good!*

When Nora reached for her bill, Rick's hand pinned the slip to the table. "Please, let me. It's not often that I get to take such a good-looking woman to dinner," he said with a boyish grin.

She was unprepared for the sudden compliment and her cheeks began to brighten with a blush. Nervously, she twisted a strand of her shoulder-length hair.

Rick even insisted on leaving the tip, and by the time they reached Nora's car back at the *Tribune*, she was trying to figure out how a casual afternoon of work ended up feeling like a first date with a very appealing man. Embarrassed by her jumbled feelings, Nora hurriedly told Rick good-bye.

Suddenly a smile came to her lips. What would Carmen say when Nora told her that she had dinner with "the man of many qualities"? *Make that very good qualities*, Nora decided.

Chapter 3

Nora regretted picking Thursday evening to do a major trip to the grocery store. She had started the day very early in order to make her appointment with the third shelter on her list. The shelter's manager was a volunteer and needed to meet with Nora and Rick at eight A.M., before her regular job at Nation's Bank started at nine. By the time Nora left the office that afternoon, her head was aching and she looked forward to a relaxing evening at home.

When the last bag of groceries had been packed into her trunk, she drove straight home. At first she didn't recognize the vehicle in her drive, but as she got closer she realized that it was Rick's green pickup truck. She saw Chris in front of the house holding onto what appeared to be the top of a very large Christmas tree. She couldn't see the front door because the base of the tree was extremely wide, its branches fanning out in all directions.

As soon as she had parked her car, she ran over to Chris. "Where did this thing come from? It's huge!"

Chris smiled as he struggled to hold the weight on his end. "Your friend brought it. Isn't it the best tree you have ever seen?"

Nora looked toward the door where she could barely see Rick's face through the tangle of evergreen branches. "You caught me," he said with a sheepish grin.

"How did you even know where I lived?"

"In case you didn't know, you're in the phone book! Let's just say I couldn't pass up the opportunity to deliver some holiday cheer."

"But. . ." Nora was flattered that he would even think of her, though she had dumped enough of her recent sorrows on him. "How will you ever fit that into the house?"

"We're still working on that, but we have a plan."

"Men always do," Carmen said, smiling, as she came around the side of the house. "They have already been working on it for nearly half an hour."

"Then we shouldn't get in their way," Nora said as she backed away from the door. "We'll just take the groceries in through the back door."

It was another half hour before Rick and Chris managed to get the tree through the door, anchor it in the tree stand, and squeeze it into the front corner of the small living room. Branches extended out into the room and draped over the arm of the couch. The top pointed at an odd angle toward the front window instead of the ceiling.

"I hope you have enough decorations to cover this tree," Rick said as he stood back to admire his choice.

"Will you help us string the lights?" Chris asked.

Rick looked at Nora first, then said, "Sure, I'll get the high spots."

"Maybe we can even string some popcorn—"

But Carmen interrupted her son. "That will take a long time."

"Not if we all work together," Rick assured her.

Nora couldn't stop smiling. Their enthusiasm was certainly contagious.

"First, let's eat these tacos Nora helped me make," Carmen said as she pointed them all toward the kitchen table. She then asked Rick to say the blessing and Nora enjoyed the sincere quality of his prayer.

"Nora," Chris said as the food was being passed, "did you know that Rick was my football coach four years ago?"

"I didn't even know you played football," Nora replied, raising an eyebrow in question toward Rick.

"He was the smallest guy on the team, but we couldn't have asked for a faster runner," Rick said in all honesty. "I'm glad to hear that you're into soccer now, Chris."

Chris proceeded to fill Rick in on all the details of his team's winning season. Nora found herself trying to picture Rick corralling a bunch of elementary age boys into a football lineup. Watching his attentive manner toward Chris, she was sure he would be good at it.

The little scar on his chin caught Nora's attention when Rick wiped salsa from his mouth. As Nora stared, she saw his lips curve up into a smile. Rick had caught her inspection of him and his eyes danced with what appeared to be suppressed laughter. Nora felt a blush rush to her cheeks and she turned her focus back to her food.

If she wasn't careful, she would end up making a fool of herself. Just because Rick was a man didn't mean he was *the* man, the man Nora had dreamed would sweep her off her feet. *That man*, Nora assured herself sternly, *doesn't drive a pickup truck, and he certainly doesn't live in Florida.*

❧

Nora couldn't recall the last time she had had this much fun decorating a Christmas tree. They sang every carol they knew and used every ornament from Carmen's collection. Rick stayed until all the popcorn was strung, the last icicle was placed, the star was secured to the sagging top branch, and the lights were plugged in. They all stood back to enjoy the effect the tree had on the darkened living room.

"It's awesome," Chris said.

"How can we repay your kindness, Rick?" Carmen asked.

"That wonderful dinner was all the payment I could need," Rick assured her.

As Rick prepared to go, Nora walked with him to his truck.

"I hate to think that my poor attitude about being stuck in Florida for Christmas made you think you had to go to all this trouble," Nora said.

"What are friends for?"

She smiled, speechless. She liked the idea of having this man as her friend.

"Good night," he said softly.

"Good night." She stood in the front yard long after the taillights of his truck had disappeared beyond the orange grove. As a cool, moisture-laden breeze started blowing across the lake, Nora closed her eyes and began to pray.

Thank You, Lord, for this wonderful evening. I am so sorry that I have been neglecting my time with You. I know that if I am ever to be truly at peace this Christmas, I must put You first. Please give me the courage to face each tomorrow. . .even if I have to do it alone.

Chapter 4

T he final shelter on Nora's list was to be toured on Saturday. It had rained most of the night and the morning dawned overcast. Nora would much rather have rolled over in bed and gone back to sleep. Instead, she lagged in bed too long and had to rush in order to be ready by ten.

Nora had agreed to let Rick pick her up at home, and she heard his voice in the kitchen as soon as she opened her bedroom door. Walking down the hall she could see Rick sitting down at the table with Carmen. Nora noticed that his hair was still wet, but she stopped short when she heard her name mentioned.

"Thanks so much for lending Nora a hand on this assignment," Carmen was saying. "Truthfully, I've been worried about her lately. She doesn't seem to enjoy her work anymore, and we couldn't even get her excited about Christmas."

"It's natural that she would not be looking forward to her first Christmas without family," Nora heard Rick say.

"Being near her family and memories seems to mean so much to Nora."

"Maybe we don't realize how much we have until it

is taken away," Rick reasoned. "I decided to do what I could to cheer her up."

"The Christmas tree was a nice touch. I am sure. . ."

Nora didn't wait to hear anymore. She turned and retreated to her bedroom, shutting the door harder than she had intended.

As she leaned with her back to the door, Rick's words kept repeating themselves in her mind. "I decided to do what I could. . ." *So, I am just another project to him,* she burned with humiliation, *something to fill his time. He just doesn't know when to stop. I don't need him to cheer me up. My attitude is my own problem.*

Nora looked at the clock. They had only fifteen minutes before they were to meet across town with the director of the Second Hope Shelter. Nora rubbed at her eyes that were burning with unshed tears. She pulled herself away from the door and straightened her blazer.

This time Nora made sure she created more noise as she left her bedroom and entered the kitchen. Both Carmen and Rick beamed bright smiles her way as she hurriedly poured a glass of juice and sliced an apple.

"I'm sorry I'm running behind this morning," Nora said, her words icy even to her own ears. "You really didn't have to bother to come along today, Rick. I could handle this one on my own. Besides, you have enough shots from county services that should be good enough for the paper."

Rick and Carmen exchanged confused looks but Rick spoke as if nothing were wrong. "I am hoping to get some pictures with more people in them, and maybe this place will also have more Christmas decorations."

Nora didn't know how to avoid having Rick along for the day without being rude so she followed him out to his truck. She sulked in the passenger's seat, and the few questions Rick dared to ask, she answered with a minimum of words.

The Second Hope Shelter was located in some run-down buildings near the main part of town. Nothing on the outside made the place feel inviting and Nora hesitated to enter when Rick held the door open for her. The entry, though, was brightly lit, and a small artificial Christmas tree welcomed visitors. A heavyset, bearded man came toward them from a doorway at the end of a long hall.

"You must be Miss Daniels. Welcome. I'm Jim Woods, Big Jim to those who know me," he said, his voice resounding through the corridor.

"I'm sorry we're late," Nora said. "This is my photographer, Rick Thompson."

"Good to know you," Big Jim said with a firm handshake for each of them. He directed them across the entryway toward double doors. "Let's start with a look at the dining hall."

Nora and Rick spent the next two hours with Big Jim. He detailed the free meals program available to anyone who came in off the streets, while exulting in the pantry program that provided free groceries to all families meeting a limited income requirement. He praised the shelter's support for disabled senior citizens, their day-care facility, their home for battered wives and children, and their many support groups that met throughout the week. Nora kept her tape recorder running. She couldn't hope to write fast enough to keep up with Big Jim's enthusiastic presentation.

Rick took pictures of the entryway with the little Christmas tree in front of a loaded bulletin board. His camera captured two volunteers in the kitchen who were sorting a new shipment of canned goods. And when Big Jim introduced Nora to a mother and her toddler who were benefiting from shelter in the home for battered wives, Rick turned his camera on Nora.

Before the tour was through, Nora knew she had more than enough information to include in her article. Big Jim invited them both back for the shelter's Christmas Day party, and he wouldn't take no for an answer. Nora promised to return, but she didn't intend to bring her photographer this time.

Once again, Nora was quiet as Rick drove her home.

"I was thinking about doing some Christmas shopping this afternoon," Rick said. "I was wondering if you would like to come along?"

"No, thanks," Nora said. "I have other plans." *Plans to sit around feeling sorry for myself*, she thought ruefully.

As they pulled into Nora's drive, Rick turned to her. "There's a youth Christmas party I have to chaperon tonight," he began, trying hard to sound casual. "Would you like to come—free pizza included?" His smile was shaky as he searched her face for a reaction.

"No, I really can't," Nora said as she stepped out of the truck. "Thanks for driving today," she added as she hurried to her front door and inside.

Carmen and Chris were not home and Nora walked into the kitchen. She deposited her purse on the table. The window above the table offered a clear view of the front yard and driveway. Nora froze.

Rick hadn't left yet, as she had supposed. He still sat behind the wheel staring straight ahead. Nora shrank back into the shadows of the kitchen. She hoped he wasn't going to come to the door and demand an explanation for the way she had behaved all morning.

He has every right to think I am a complete idiot, Nora decided, *but I have every right to be upset.* She crossed her arms over her chest and then a flood of tears seemed to come from nowhere. Through the blur she watched as Rick slowly backed out of her drive and disappeared down the street. Her whole body ached from the strain of holding her emotions in check all morning. She hurried down the hall to her room and sank into the comfort of her bed.

Nora woke well into the afternoon and hid her face in her tear-stained pillow. Carmen and Chris were still not home. Chris would be spending the weekend with his paternal grandparents and Nora seemed to remember Carmen mentioning wanting to do some Christmas shopping.

How can I blame Rick for just trying to be nice? She choked back a fresh flow of tears. *He can't help it if he is just too good.*

As Nora rolled over and reached for her Bible, an old bookmark fell to the floor. She picked it up and read the gold lettering for the first time in a long while, the words of Proverbs 3, verses 5 and 6:

Trust in the Lord with all thine heart;
and lean not unto thine own understanding.
In all thy ways acknowledge him,
and he shall direct thy paths.

Nora realized that it wasn't for her to question why things in life didn't turn out as she would like them to, but rather for her to trust God to lead her in the right direction. She hadn't been trusting. Instead, she had been worrying about how she was going to fix her own life. . .and she couldn't. Only God could get her through the hard times and sustain her through the good.

She spent the next hour in much-needed prayer, and when she got out of bed she had a strong purpose. Her spirits continued to revive as she showered and started the day again.

By six she was feeling like a new woman. She put on a pair of navy slacks with her favorite cream and mauve sweater. The ends of her blond hair curled softly around her round face and a light touch of makeup hid any trace of her tears.

Chapter 5

N ora drove into the church parking lot as teenagers were still arriving. A space was empty beside Rick's truck and she pulled her compact car into it. *I can't believe I'm here, Lord. If only I didn't act like such a fool this morning*, she thought suddenly.

It took her a while to get up the courage to leave her car and make her way to the fellowship hall at the rear of the church. Loud Christmas music led her to the door of the long room. A kitchen connected to one end of the hall, while the other end served as a miniature basketball court. Kids were everywhere in between, talking in groups, shooting basketballs, playing table games, and loading up paper plates from a smorgasbord of junk food.

Nora stood in the doorway scanning the sea of faces for Rick. She noticed more than a handful of adults scattered throughout the room but Rick was nowhere to be found.

"Are you lost?" a deep voice said from behind her.

She whirled to face Rick. His arms were loaded down with boxes of pizza, and a pizza delivery man followed him with an even bigger load. Her gaze traveled up to Rick's face. He was smiling but his eyes were clouded by a troubled expression.

"I. . .uh. . ."

"Come have some pizza," Rick offered.

Nora stepped aside to let the men enter as a roar of "PIZZA!" filled the large room. She automatically helped arrange the many boxes on a long table and, when grace had been said, she turned to find Rick at her elbow.

"Would you like to fix a plate?" he asked.

"No, thanks, I'm not hungry."

"Then can I talk to you a moment?"

She nodded, took a deep breath, and followed him out of the room. He led her down a long hall and into the nursery. He offered her one of the four rocking chairs and sat down near her.

What should she say to make him understand how sorry she was for her poor attitude, to thank him for his sincere attempt to make her feel better, and relieve him of any duty he felt toward her? She opened her mouth to speak but he was first to get a word out.

"I am really glad you decided to come tonight. I needed to talk with you and tell you that I am very sorry. . . ."

Nora's mouth fell open. What did he have to apologize for?

"I could tell this morning that you were really needing some time to yourself but all week I kept inviting myself into your activities," Rick explained. "Sometimes I try so hard to be helpful that I end up making a nuisance of myself."

Nora's carefully chosen words disappeared. He thought he was to blame for her behavior.

"Lately, God has been dealing with me," Rick continued. "I guess I have been trying to build my own road to God by filling every waking hour with activities that I thought would please Him." Rick shrugged and Nora smiled knowingly. "I have started to run out of energy and He has been working on me. I can see now, after much introspection, that I have been looking to God as my boss instead of my Father."

Nora could relate. It was easy to give hand service to God but much harder to trust Him completely with one's heart and soul. She could see now why Rick appeared to be too good—he was covering up his real struggles and he had perfected the art of looking the perfect Christian.

"Rick, I really do appreciate your help on my article and I have enjoyed being with you. The Christmas tree was a wonderful gift, and—" She searched for the right words. "But I am the one who needs to be apologizing. I have been so focused on my own pity party that I haven't been able to see two feet in front of me." She reached over to touch his arm. "You have gone out of your way to cheer me up and I didn't have the grace to thank you. I just let myself think that the only reason you wanted to spend time with me was because you felt sorry for me." She looked at him, hoping he would say she was wrong.

"I admit, it started out something like that," Rick said, not looking at her. "I couldn't stand to see you depressed about Christmas and your job. I selfishly thought I could brighten your holiday and bring a smile to your face."

"It worked, sort of. . . ." she said, smiling. "I mean, I started to look on the bright side and renew my conversations with God. Until this morning. . ." She hated to admit that she overheard his conversation with Carmen. "I heard you tell Carmen this morning that you were just doing what you could to cheer me up, and I didn't want someone interfering—"

"And I was," Rick interrupted, now looking her full in the face. "Nora, can we start again? Can we go back to where we were enjoying spending time together and start from there?"

"I would like that," she said softly. "Want to go Christmas shopping?"

He laughed. "How about Monday evening?"

"Rick! Rick!" came a frantic call echoing through the hallway.

Rick jumped up and ran to the door. Nora moved to the edge of her chair, not knowing if she should follow. She was rather embarrassed to have kept Rick in a private conversation when he was there to chaperon mischief-prone teenagers. In the end she couldn't keep herself from following.

A crowd had gathered in the kitchen. Brad Cunningham, the youth pastor, was bailing water out of an overflowing sink but water already covered the floor.

Another chaperon was explaining the situation. "I was just rinsing some scraps down the disposal. I turned my back a moment to help one of the girls. . .I am so sorry. I left the water running, but I assumed it was going down the drain."

"Well, it is definitely clogged," Rick said, peering through the sinkful of murky water.

Nora found a mop and started sopping up water from the floor. By the time most of the floor was dried, Rick and Brad had managed to free the clog and get water flowing through the drain again.

"Was anyone missing a dishcloth?" Rick asked, holding up a mangled piece of cloth.

No one would claim responsibility and soon attention was diverted to a group game that was getting started in the main room.

Two teen girls had planted themselves on either side of Nora. They asked her many questions, curious as to why they had never seen her around before. They complimented her hair and clothes and begged her to join them in the game. Nora couldn't refuse and soon found herself in the middle of a chaotic round of "Upset the Fruit Basket."

Rick, his shirt still showing water spots, watched from outside the circle of chairs. As soon as another game was started, though, some of the youth wouldn't rest until they managed to get Rick right into the thick of things.

Nora spent the rest of the evening surrounded by energetic teenagers. She would catch glimpses of Rick across the room involved in one activity or another. Once as he dribbled the basketball effortlessly up the little court, ending with a perfectly executed layup, she found herself staring at his well-muscled arms. She hastily looked away, hoping no one caught her staring.

When almost everyone was finally convinced to sit down for closing devotions, Nora found that even a couple of the teenage guys had pulled their chairs up close to her group. While the girls showered her with questions and compliments, the boys were more inclined to tease her.

"Who'dja come with?" one freckled boy asked her.

"No one," Nora said and smiled sweetly.

"I mean, who invited you?"

"I didn't realize this was an invitation-only occasion," Nora shot back, cautious about opening herself up to more wisecracks.

"Yep," the boy continued, leaning back on two legs of his chair, his arms crossed in front of him, and a smug smile planted on his young face. "I gotta see your invitation or you're outta here."

"She's with me," Rick's voice came from behind Nora, warming her from head to toe.

"Oh, yeah," the boy said, seizing on this new bit of information. "She your date?"

Rick seemed at a momentary loss for words. Nora didn't want to look at him but she didn't know where else to look without encountering curious young eyes.

"Someone has to protect her from you, Chuck," Rick finally said. He gripped the boy's shoulders, forcing all the legs of the chair back on the floor. "Now I want to see these chairs in a nice row facing Pastor Brad," he said forcefully but also with a playful tone.

After the fellowship hall had been cleaned and most

of the kids had left, Rick walked Nora to her car.

"Did I tell you that I am very glad you decided to come tonight?" he asked.

Nora smiled. "I had a good time."

"You were great with those kids."

"They sure keep a person on her toes, but they're lots of fun."

"I can't help but like them myself," Rick said. "I am sure they would love to have you back anytime."

Nora moved to open her car door. Rick came closer to hold it open for her.

"So, are we on for Monday evening?" he asked.

"Sounds good." Nora was reluctant to leave but she didn't know what else to say. She sat behind her wheel and slowly placed the key in the ignition.

Rick seemed to feel the same way. "See you tomorrow?"

She smiled and nodded.

Rick gently closed her car door and waited until she drove out of the parking lot.

On Sunday, Nora's spirits were still soaring as she entered the Sunday school classroom with minutes to spare. This time Rick moved to sit beside her though they said little to each other. Afterward she was cornered by some of the kids she had met at the Christmas party. She didn't get a chance to speak to Rick before he had to go to the choir room.

Nora listened to each word in the sermon with renewed interest. Once again Pastor Freed became more than just a handsome man with a baritone voice but a challenger of faith and messenger of hope.

Later that afternoon Nora and Carmen sat down to wrap Christmas presents and Nora brought Carmen up to speed on all the events of Saturday.

"I don't think I have ever been more ashamed of my behavior," Nora said.

"Unfortunately," Carmen said, "sometimes it takes a fall to get us back where we need to be. Fortunately, Rick seems to be very understanding."

"Oh, he is," Nora assured her. "You know, he thought he was the one who needed to be apologizing to me. Once the misunderstandings between us were aired, we enjoyed a wonderful evening. It seems that he volunteers quite often with the youth. He is the kind of guy all the kids love to be around."

Carmen smiled. "It seems Rick Thompson has many good inner qualities, too." She tilted her head to watch for Nora's reaction.

Nora couldn't keep her face from reddening. She knew that Carmen was baiting her and she decided to change the subject to Christmas. "Will you have all of your gifts wrapped by tomorrow morning?"

"I should," Carmen answered, "but I don't have all the clothes washed that I wanted to pack."

"Feel free to put me to work," Nora offered.

"I am really sorry that we have to leave earlier than planned. Are you sure you don't want to come to Pensacola with us? We will probably spend Christmas Eve along the Gulf."

"Thanks, but if your mother isn't feeling well, she certainly doesn't need an extra guest," Nora said. "Besides, I have an article to finish."

"I'll put your gifts under the tree in case you want to open them on Christmas Day."

"I'd much rather wait until you and Chris get back. I want to enjoy your reactions when you open your gifts."

"What did you get Chris?" Carmen asked excitedly.

"I won't know until tomorrow when I go Christmas shopping with Rick."

Carmen squealed and pumped her fists. "Yes!"

Nora frowned at her friend. "I have a few things in mind, though."

"He needs a new Nintendo game. I wore out the one he got for his birthday," Carmen announced and both women burst into giggles.

Chapter 6

Monday morning Rick came to Nora's desk well before noon and placed a stack of black-and-white photographs in front of her.

"Done already?" she exclaimed as she began flipping through pictures from the four shelters they had visited together. The last picture in the pile was of herself at the Second Hope Shelter. She was leaning down to pat the head of a toddler in the home for battered wives. A pleasant smile graced her face while morning sunbeams highlighted her hair. She liked what she saw.

"You can keep that last one. I took it for you."

Nora looked up at Rick and her heart warmed several degrees. "Thanks—for everything."

"Can I take you to lunch?" Rick asked. "My treat."

"I was planning to work straight through but you just persuaded me," she said, smiling.

Later at the small coffee shop across the street they enjoyed submarine sandwiches. While Nora devoured her turkey sub, Rick entertained her with stories of his on-the-job experiences.

". . .luckily, I had remembered to take extra film with me at the last minute," Rick continued, but then his expression dimmed. "Most of the time I enjoy what I do but I don't see myself taking pictures forever."

"And what would be your idea of the perfect job?" Nora asked, intrigued.

"I have always wanted to be in the position of helping people full-time," he said sincerely, "encouraging them in their walk with Christ. I like the idea of serving God by serving others, as long as I keep the right perspective."

Their conversation on Saturday evening came back to her. "That sounds very honorable," Nora said, wishing she had a dream like his.

"I'm finishing up a correspondence course from your old college," Rick continued. "I drive up to Orlando twice a month for a seminar, and when this next semester is over in May I will have finally completed my degree."

"That's great! The college has turned out some very fine ministers and teachers. What are you studying?"

"Youth ministry."

"Oh, how wonderful—but is there any age group you are not good with?" she teased.

Rick chuckled. "Honestly, I'm not too good with little kids. I love kids, but only one or two at a time. I would be lost in a Sunday school class of elementary children. All those little bodies going in every different direction would tie me in knots. And, I'm not great with people my own age. I'm not comfortable in counseling situations or other leadership positions over young adults. Luckily, my men's devotion group is made up mainly of older men."

Nora smiled at Rick's candor. "You know Pastor Brad

is planning to move on in the next year. Will you interview to fill his place as youth minister?"

Rick shrugged. "I have to go where God leads me. I have been going my own direction too long and getting nowhere."

Suddenly she was filled with the reality that he might leave the area and their newfound friendship would end. "I only wish I knew where God wanted to use me. I feel like my life has been on hold the last two years. Since getting my college degree, I haven't had any real goals."

"You're a good writer, and newspapers need Christian reporters to represent the truth," Rick attempted to reassure her.

"I know, and I do enjoy research and writing," she said. "But I don't enjoy the pressure of the job. If I am to get anywhere in journalism, I have to hunt down big stories aggressively and get my name as a reporter recognized. I just don't have what it takes."

She raised her hand to stop Rick from saying anything. "I know I can never really be happy at the paper. I have an elusive dream," she confessed while toying with the last of her iced coffee. "I want to research special interest articles for magazines, and do it from home while raising children. Since losing my parents, a family of my own has become much more important to me. This job has just been something to fill my time and pay the bills until, well, until God shows me what else to do, I guess."

She didn't look up from her plate or she would have

seen the soft smile lighting Rick's face. "Well, no matter what tomorrow holds for our dreams, we still have a job to get back to today," he said as he rose and held her chair for her.

That evening Rick only hassled her once when she took too much time deciding on a gift for her sister-in-law, Michelle. Nora knew Michelle well and had to find the perfect gift to please the other woman's discriminating tastes.

"You're spending too much time dwelling on this decision. If Michelle is as bad as you claim," Rick reasoned, "she will just exchange anything you decide to buy for her."

Nora gave in to his logic and after she picked out a pair of earrings that she personally loved, they were able to wrap up their shopping and head home. As Rick drove out onto the highway, Nora settled back in her seat to enjoy the Christmas lights that passed by in the blackened night. She was no longer filled with anxiety when she remembered that there would be no snow for her this Christmas, and no family get-togethers.

Rick must have guessed her thoughts. "See, Christmas in the tropics isn't so bad, is it?"

"Not when you remember the true reason for the season. I think I ended up overspending, but I enjoyed every minute!" She started to hum "Hark the Herald Angels Sing" and before long Rick was joining her in a joyous rendition of "Jingle Bells."

"I didn't know you could sing," Rick said.

Nora giggled. "I was in college choir. You know, one of the people they allow to stay in just to fill a chair."

"Ah, you're much too modest," Rick insisted. "You should have joined the church choirs of the community in their production of the 'Messiah.' I couldn't fit it in this year."

"I'm not much for the classical stuff. I prefer to hide my talent—or lack of it—in the twang of good old southern gospel," Nora said. "My dad used to say. . ." But she couldn't continue.

"I bet he thought you sang like a bird," Rick said, trying to fill the void.

"I almost forgot," she mused sadly. "He used to tease me about sounding like a rooster. But then, he never claimed to have much musical—"

"Hey!" Rick interrupted her. "It looks like that car is headed in the wrong direction!"

Just then Nora spotted the car and watched as it plowed into the side of another car, sending sparks flying. "Oh, dear Lord," she prayed softly, her hands clasped under her chin.

Rick pulled to a quick stop along the road across from the still-sliding cars. "I have to see if I can help," he said as he jumped from the truck and darted across traffic to the median where the cars had come to rest.

Nora sat motionless, still stunned by the sight. Slowly she opened her door and cautiously picked her way across the highway.

Rick was pulling open the back passenger door of the car that had been broadsided. A little girl of about four was screaming frantically. Rick inspected her for injuries then unhooked her from her seat and passed her to Nora. Nora held the child tightly as she tried to soothe her sobs. Rick then crawled across the backseat and helped a boy who looked to be between seven or eight. He was complaining of a banged-up shoulder and Rick gently coaxed him to slide across the seat until he could lift him out.

Nora feared that the man in the driver's seat hadn't fared as well as the children. His head rested against his door and he appeared to be unconscious. Rick set the boy on a soft patch of grass before going to see about the man.

Nora noticed that a tractor-trailer and a passenger car had stopped. Three men were hovering around the other car and attending to two passengers. She turned toward the young boy and sat beside him while still holding the little girl.

"How are you doing?" she asked him. "My name is Nora. Can you tell me your name?"

"I'm Josh Brooks. My shoulder hurts bad," he said. "Is my dad okay?"

"My friend Rick is helping him right now," Nora assured him. "Let's check your sister. What's your name?" she said, turning her attention to the little girl who had her face buried in Nora's shoulder.

"Mer–r–" came the muffled response from under a tangle of brown curls.

"It's Merrie," her big brother supplied. "She's just four."

"And how old are you?" Nora asked, while keeping an eye on Rick as he worked over the father in the car.

"Just turned eight before we left home," Josh said with pride.

"Where do you live?"

The boy was quiet. "We used to live in North Carolina before Mama died. Now Dad says we may live in Miami."

Nora looked back to the car where she now noticed a cartop carrier. "Do you have relatives in Miami?"

"No, my uncle lives in California," Josh said with longing in his young voice. "He's going to be an actor in the movies."

It seemed no time before Nora heard sirens and a state patrol and ambulance pulled onto the scene. The children watched as their father was carefully placed on a stretcher and put into the ambulance. Nora longed for the words that would ease their worries but she didn't know what she could say. She prayed instead for God's hand on the situation.

The state trooper came over to the children and explained that he would be driving them to the hospital in his patrol car. Josh seemed to warm to the idea of riding in the fancy car but Merrie clung desperately to Nora. Rick came and tried to ease the little girl away.

"Rick," Nora said, her heart aching for the scared child. "Can't we drive them to the hospital?"

"If you wouldn't mind, ma'am," the officer said, "you could go with the children in my car."

Rick nodded. "I'll follow right behind."

Nora climbed in back of the patrol car, letting Josh ride up front with the officer. She buckled Merrie in right beside her and wrapped her arms tightly around the child.

"Where did my daddy go?" the child's tear-filled voice asked.

"They are taking him to the hospital so that doctors can check him," Nora gently explained. "We will see him soon."

The child easily accepted her words and nestled her small head against Nora's side.

Rick met them in the emergency waiting room, and the state patrol officer then went to glean information about the children's father. It wasn't long before Josh was able to interest his sister in toys at a table just for kids. The room was fairly empty except for a man sleeping in one corner and two older women sitting by the door.

"I think their dad has a concussion," Rick said softly to Nora, "and he may also have injured his left leg. Is the boy still complaining about his shoulder?"

"Not recently, but it should still be looked at," Nora said.

"I wonder if they have family that needs to be called?"

"I don't know. They are from North Carolina and. . . and, Rick, I think they may be homeless."

"What about their mother?"

"Josh said she died before they left North Carolina," Nora explained.

"It sounds like this family could use our prayers. Do you mind?"

"Now?"

"Yes, but if you would rather not. . ."

"Oh, yes, I agree. We do need to pray," Nora assured him.

After praying, Rick went to the emergency room desk where he talked with the state trooper who was preparing to leave.

"It appears that it was a very old man driving the other car," Rick said after he returned to his seat beside Nora. "He must have been confused by the multiple lanes on the highway and got going in the wrong direction. He probably panicked when he realized his mistake and steered right into the side of their car. An ambulance was arriving to transport his wife and him to a hospital just as we left the scene."

Nora and Rick halted their conversation as Merrie came over to them. "I want to see my daddy," she said while sucking on two of her fingers.

Rick pulled the child onto his knee. "It's okay, sweetheart. It will take the doctors a while to get him all fixed up. Why don't you lie down here by Nora and take a little nap?"

The child went easily to Nora. It was drawing close to eleven-thirty and the late hour was taking its toll on the little girl. Rick played game after game of tic-tac-toe with Josh as the time marched on.

A hospital representative came to them around midnight and explained that the children's father would be fine. He would need to be admitted for an overnight stay. The woman volunteered to see to it that the children were placed in temporary care.

"If it would be all right," Rick said to the woman, "we would like to stay with the children tonight. The little girl has grown very attached to Miss Daniels, and I think it wouldn't be good to separate them before the child has a chance to see her father in one piece."

"Fine then," the woman agreed. "I'll show you to a small waiting room on Mr. Brooks's floor."

"Thanks," Rick said, "and can we get someone to check this little guy's shoulder? I think he may have bruised it."

The woman immediately led Rick and Josh to an emergency examination room, then came directly back to take Nora and a sleeping Merrie to the fourth-floor waiting room. After providing them with some pillows and blankets, she left them to settle in for the night.

Chapter 7

N ora woke with a pain in her side. She had been sleeping in an upright position for too long and needed to stretch her muscles. Near her, Merrie was sound asleep on a loveseat while Josh was stretched out on the floor. Nora looked across the small room where Rick was sleeping in another chair with his feet propped up on a small table.

Easing out of her awkward position in the chair, she went to the window to look out. Another bright, sunny day was dawning on central Florida, and only two days before Christmas. She shook her head and smiled to herself. Just a few short days ago she would have let this kind of weather get her down. Now she had bags of Christmas surprises stuffed into Rick's truck, just waiting for her to wrap.

Stories below she observed the increasing traffic along Cypress Boulevard. Snowbirds, or northern retirees, were out for morning walks, children played in a day-care playground across the hospital parking lot, and transients assumed their posts near intersections, their "I'll work for food" signs clearly visible. Even the smallest of Florida's towns attracted Americans from all walks of life.

Nora turned from the window and picked her way around Josh's sleeping form and the table where Rick's feet rested until she finally reached the door. She headed for the nurses' station and asked a heavyset nurse with tight black curls where to find the nearest coffee machine.

"Are you the woman who volunteered to stay the night with those kids from the car accident?" the nurse asked.

"Yes, I'm Nora Daniels."

"I really admire you for taking the time. Those kids must have been scared."

"Anyone looking at their sad little faces would have done the same thing," Nora assured the nurse.

"Hey, listen," the nurse said, turning to a table in the corner. "This coffee is fresh and it will save you a trip downstairs."

When Nora entered the little waiting room again holding two Styrofoam cups filled with steaming coffee, Rick was up and standing by the long window. He gave her a sleep-blurred smile and took the coffee she proffered.

"How did you know what I was praying for?" Rick said and his hand suddenly reached out to cup Nora's cheek.

Nora was surprised by his gesture and her eyes shyly looked away from his gaze.

"You look as tired as I feel," Rick said, then quickly dropped his hand to his side.

Nora's gaze automatically returned to Rick's face but

she didn't know what to say. She suddenly felt confused. *Why can't I be happy just being friends with Rick and stop reading more into his actions?* she chided herself. *Lord, this is why I don't keep male friends very long. I am so afraid of being alone that I scare them away.*

Josh was stretching in his tangled blankets and Rick knelt down to tussle the boy's blond hair. "Sleep good, pal?"

"I guess," Josh said with a big yawn. "Can we go see Dad yet?"

"I was just getting ready to ask the nurse," Rick said. "Want to walk with me?"

Josh scrambled to his feet and followed Rick's broad frame out into the hallway. Rick stuck his head back around the door. "Want us to pick up some breakfast?"

Nora smiled and nodded, still lost in her prayers.

It seemed like a long while before Rick and Josh returned. When the door opened, Nora was sitting on the loveseat holding Merrie as the child struggled to wake up. Josh ran in and plopped down beside them.

"Merrie, I saw Daddy," Josh said with great excitement. "He's got a big bandage on his head to cover a huge bump. We can all go to his room soon."

Nora looked toward Rick, and he nodded. "It seems like he is recovering quite nicely," he said. He then proceeded to empty the bag he was carrying. He placed individually wrapped breakfast rolls, fresh fruit, and cartons of juice on the small table in the middle of the room. "Breakfast is served," he said with a deep bow.

Merrie craned her neck to inspect the spread, then pointed at a banana.

"Bananas are her favorite, but orange juice will make her sick," Josh said with all the wisdom of an older brother.

Nora felt comfortable in their little group. It seemed natural to look across the short space and watch as Rick teased Josh about all the food he was packing into his small body. Nora hugged Merrie to her side as the little girl slowly nibbled at her banana until the whole thing had disappeared.

When Nora's gaze returned to Rick, she flushed under his own inspection. Nervously, she pushed a thick strand of her straight hair behind her ear and waited for someone to say something.

"Merrie, want to go see Daddy now?" Josh broke the quiet as he stood and brushed crumbs from his sweatshirt. Merrie jumped up from her seat, her eyes wide with anticipation.

When the four of them entered room 433, Mr. Brooks was just pushing back his breakfast tray. He appeared to be a slender man with a balding head of blond hair.

"Come here, sweetie," Mr. Brooks said as he held his arms out to Merrie. She rushed to scramble up onto the bed and hugged her father tightly.

Josh went to sit on the other side of the bed while Rick and Nora waited in the doorway. Nora sighed, happy that the children were able to be reunited with their father and that he was going to be fine. She felt Rick clasp her hand and give it a gentle squeeze. He continued to hold her hand as if it were the natural thing to do. The heat from his hand warmed Nora, and she couldn't think of any place she would rather be.

"Miss Daniels," Mr. Brooks was saying, and Nora had to pull her attention back to the hospital bed. "Mr. Thompson explained that you have been a real friend to my little Merrie in the past hours. I want to thank you with all my being."

Rick removed his hand and indicated that Nora should sit in the bedside chair. She tucked her hand into her cardigan pocket to savor the feel of Rick's hand.

"It was my pleasure, Mr. Brooks," she answered. "Merrie's a real doll."

"Call me Tom," he said, still with an arm around each of his children. "They tell me I can probably be released this afternoon. Do either of you know where my car might be?"

"No," Rick said, "but I would be glad to check on it for you."

"I hate to impose on you," Tom said. "You have done so much already."

"Do you have family that needs to be called?" Nora asked. "Where were you headed?"

Tom shook his head. "I don't want to worry my wife's parents yet. They have a lot of physical and financial problems. My brother lives in L.A., but I'll call him later." Tom had a faraway look, and his face reddened as if he were embarrassed. "We were headed for Miami, but there is no one expecting us."

"I can't imagine that your car will be ready for a few

days," Rick said. "Can we take you someplace? Maybe a motel?"

Tom shook his head and turned away from them to look out the window. "We can't afford a place right now," he said. "You see, my wife died almost two years ago. She had a long battle with cancer, and. . ." He took a shaky breath. "There were many hospital bills. I didn't handle it very well. I was under a lot of stress at work and caring for the kids. It wasn't very long before I lost my job, and then the house."

Josh reached to pat his father's shoulder as Tom continued. "I couldn't burden Kelly's parents, so we moved to Atlanta. I had a temporary job and a tiny apartment, but it was very hard," Tom said softly, his voice cracking, "and it didn't last."

"What about your brother?" Rick said.

"I refuse to expose my children to his lifestyle," he said with new firmness.

Holding back a rush of tears, Nora said, "We'll help you find a place here, at least through the holidays."

The children captured their father's attention once again, and Rick leaned down to whisper in Nora's ear.

"I'm going to call the church and see if I can get any advice on this situation. Also, do you have the number for the Good Shepherd Mission? I was thinking about the new shelter that they just opened. Will you. . .pray?"

"Of course," she responded with all sincerity.

Nora dug in her purse and pulled out her daily planner and Rick then left with the number and she sat back to pray. Tom and the children were talking about the accident. Josh seemed to find it terribly exciting now that all the danger had passed.

❧

It was growing dark before Rick and Nora had Josh, Merrie, and a slow-moving Tom in tow and were headed for the Good Shepherd Mission. Rick had borrowed his parents' minivan and driven the Brookses to a garage where they picked up their belongings.

When they pulled into the converted strip motel, Josh asked if they had a pool.

"No," Nora said, "that was filled in a few years back."

Rick had already arranged for the key and in a short while they had the family settled in.

"I'll stop in tomorrow and see how things are going," he said.

Tom stopped Rick and Nora as they were preparing to leave. "I just wanted to thank you again. It has been a long time since anyone has. . .cared."

There were tears glistening in the older man's eyes and Nora forced herself to hold her own in check.

❧

"I can't believe that tomorrow is Christmas Eve already," Rick said as he drove Nora home more than twenty-four hours after their shopping outing had begun. "I'm going to be late for the choir's dress rehearsal tonight. You're going to be there tomorrow night, aren't you?"

"I hadn't thought about it," Nora said, "but yes, I suppose so."

"I'll watch for you."

Nora liked the sound of that.

After Rick helped her carry her packages inside, he couldn't resist commenting on his favorite purchase.

"My, that tree sure looks good!"

"Oh! I need to water it," Nora remembered.

"Where are Carmen and Chris?"

"They left yesterday for Pensacola. Carmen's mother needed her to go early and help with preparations. The entire family will be in for Christmas," Nora said.

"Do you want me to pick you up for the Christmas Eve program?" Rick asked suddenly.

"That's okay, you don't have to. I can drive myself."

Rick seemed to accept her answer but then he stopped in the doorway. "No," he said, turning back toward her, "I want to pick you up." He lifted his hand and trailed a finger down her check. Nora took an involuntary step forward and raised her gaze to meet his. As Rick leaned closer, Nora's breathing slowed in anticipation.

His lips caressed her forehead and seemed to linger imperceptibly, and then he was gone. Before he climbed into the van, he called out, "Be ready by five" over his shoulder and then started the engine and pulled away.

Nora stood motionless, still feeling the pressure of his lips on her forehead. *Don't even try to analyze the meaning of that*, she told herself. A delighted giggle bubbled out of her throat and she closed the door.

Chapter 8

N ora spent the rest of the evening wrapping gifts, and the next morning she decided that she still had to buy three very important gifts. At the local shopping center she went from store to store, searching for the perfect doll for Merrie, board game for Josh, and flannel shirt for Tom.

Passing through the fragrance section at a department store, something made Nora stop and test some colognes. One cologne for men had a nice piney scent which reminded her of Rick. She could just picture him under the weight of her Christmas tree that day she had caught him delivering it.

Then she noticed unpainted wood carvings of evergreen trees in the cologne display. Nora asked the counter attendant if she could buy one of the trees and the woman consented, seeing how the display would be changed right after Christmas. Nora tucked the cologne and a four-inch-high evergreen carving deep into her bag.

That afternoon, after catching up on her work at the office, she rushed to the post office with two large boxes to mail to her brothers.

"These won't get there for Christmas," the postmaster barked.

"I understand that," Nora said, offended by the man's attitude. "It's my fault that I didn't have them ready in time."

But when the man named the charge, Nora found that she was short on cash. "I hadn't expected that much," Nora said in surprise.

"They are heavy boxes," the postmaster defended.

"Let's go ahead and mail this one to Gary and Michelle Daniels," Nora consented. "I'll have to come back with the money for the other box."

"We close in twenty minutes," the postmaster stated.

"Well, okay, I'll mail it later," Nora said and picked up the box addressed to her oldest brother, John. She made herself turn back to the counter before leaving. "Have a very merry Christmas," she said to the postmaster with a fragile smile.

Rick arrived right at five to pick Nora up for the evening. She hurried to apply some color to her lips and find a black purse to go with her burgundy dress.

"You look great," Rick complimented when she met him at the door. He tucked her hand into the crook of his arm as he led her to his truck. Nora held a small green box against her other side and she slipped it under the seat as Rick helped her in.

Even though they were almost an hour early, the church parking lot was already filling up. Rick parked near the rear of the building.

"Will you carry my blazer?" Rick asked Nora, his arms already full of songbooks and an oversized wrapped package. Nora couldn't help but notice the crooked seams in the wrapping paper.

"Someone volunteered me to wrap the choir director's gift," Rick explained, "and it wasn't me this time." He flashed her a wide grin.

"Don't you have a bow for the top?" Nora asked.

"Uh-oh, I forgot," Rick said, staring at the bare package.

Nora reached under her seat and pulled out a sparkling green bow and handed it to him.

"Where did that come from?" Rick asked.

Nora just shrugged with a special gleam in her eye.

The hallway behind the sanctuary stage was crowded with robed choir members and the costumed cast. Rick cut a path for them to the choir room where he dumped his load. Turning to Nora, he said, "Could you hold on to my blazer during the program? I hate to leave it back here and I'll need it afterward."

Nora soon seated herself in the middle of the sanctuary with a good view of the stage. As she draped Rick's blazer over her lap, she felt an intimate connection to him, that she was watching over his things. She brushed her hand over the woolen fabric and caught a faint masculine scent.

Sighing, she turned her full attention to the

66

reenactment of the Christmas story. The actors in their bathrobe costumes and towel head dressings elicited smiles in the audience. Mary was portrayed by a teenage girl with long, glistening black hair, and the role of Joseph was performed by a tall man Nora thought she recognized as her Sunday school teacher—and the teenager's brother.

Nora watched as the couple walked across the stage toward the Bethlehem backdrop. Suddenly, she realized that the parents of Christ had been homeless travelers. They had no friends to stay with in Bethlehem and no hotel reservations. They needed immediate shelter for their son's birth, and they would continue to need a place to stay while Mary recuperated and the baby grew strong enough for the journey home.

She wished Tom Brooks and his two children had accepted Rick's invitation to the Christmas Eve program. The Brookses did not deserve their present situation. They were victims of a series of circumstances that snowballed until they could no longer control them. Nora bowed her head and said a short prayer for them and others in similar situations.

She thanked God that even though she no longer had her parents or childhood home to return to, she had family, friends, and finances to see her through. She thanked Him for sending Rick to her, a special friend whose positive attitude was helping her realize just how blessed she really was.

The service was wonderful. The praise-filled presentation by choir and cast members was followed by joyful congregational singing. When the service ended with a candlelight time of prayer, Nora knew Christ had been in their midst.

She waited for Rick off to the side of the stage, and soon he emerged from a crowd of visiting worshippers with two women following him. "The choir sounded great tonight," Nora said to him when he reached her. "You looked like you were enjoying yourself."

"Yeah, it was a great experience," Rick said as he donned his blazer. "Nora, I'd like to introduce you to my mother, Gail, and this is my baby sister, Tricia."

The younger woman rolled her eyes at Rick. "Remember, I'm a sophomore in college, Rick. I'd think you'd soon realize that I am no longer your 'baby' sister."

"You will always be 'baby' to me, Dimples." Rick squeezed Tricia's shoulders and she flashed a dimple-framed smile that had obviously won her the nickname.

"Please excuse my children," Gail Thompson said, stepping closer to Nora. "I am very glad to meet you. Rick has talked a lot about you."

Nora turned surprised eyes toward Rick. He quickly looked away but not before Nora saw the red streaks in his face. Rick hadn't shared much about his family with her but she knew from their Christmas shopping trip that he had plenty to buy for.

"We hope you will be joining our family gathering this evening," Gail said.

Nora looked toward Rick again but he seemed strangely interested in a white poinsettia.

"We will be building a fire to cozy up to and there will be a ton of food," Gail continued. "Of course you'll come."

Nora smiled helplessly. How could she refuse? "Sure . . .I mean, thank you."

Tricia rode the four blocks to the Thompson house with Rick and Nora. Nora sat quietly in the middle while Rick and Tricia talked excitedly about the evening plans. They followed the minivan full of people Nora had yet to meet into a well-lit driveway.

The Thompsons' modest home was spread out on one level. When Rick opened the door for the women, a chilly blast came from inside.

"I see Dad has the North Pole temperature set," Rick said, loud enough for all to hear. "You better build a big fire this year, Dad."

Nora hung back in the entryway as a woman came running up to Rick and planted a kiss on each of his cheeks. "You looked so good up in that choir loft," she praised.

Rick gently pushed her away from him. "I didn't see you at church. Mom said you probably wouldn't make it in time."

"Believe it or not, I was ready to leave Meridian ahead of schedule," the woman said with pride. "My home looks like a wreck but at least we're here."

Rick reached a hand back toward Nora to propel her to his side. "Nora, I'd like you to meet my sister

69

Diane, my older sister," he emphasized, "all the way from Mississippi."

Diane arched a brow in question and then she smiled warmly at Nora. "Glad you could come."

Introductions continued around the living room as Rick's father, his maternal grandmother, Diane's family of four, Rick's younger brother Brian, and Brian's wife and their baby were all presented to Nora. The sisters were sharing secret smiles that seemed to be directed toward her and Rick.

Everyone helped themselves to the festive smorgasbord Gail and her daughters had laid out on the dining room table. Nora chose to sit on the small couch near the fireplace where a blazing fire was throwing its heat into the stylish living room. Rick's sisters and sister-in-law soon joined her, and talk centered around the children's anticipation of Christmas surprises.

Diane's son could barely take time to eat. He kept hopping from one adult to another, asking when they could open presents.

"Hey now," Diane said, pinning the little boy down on the chair beside her. "You will be allowed to open one gift tonight. You know that we have to wait to open the rest in the morning."

The boy whined and Rick's father tried to compromise, saying that the children could open two gifts while the adults opened only one.

"You'll spoil the kids rotten, Dad," Diane said, laughing.

After helping to place the dishes in the dishwasher,

Nora settled back into her corner of the couch. Rick came to sit by her and his brother Brian sat on the other end of the couch, pushing Rick even closer to her until their shoulders rubbed.

Nora enjoyed the family chaos as she watched the gifts being exchanged. She was surprised when someone put a small package in her lap. The tag said it was from Rick's parents. Nora was suddenly embarrassed as she gently tugged the wrapping paper away from the gift. It was a women's devotional book in a beautiful gift package with matching bookmark and gold pen.

"Thank you," Nora said, touched by their thoughtfulness.

Rick reached over and gently squeezed her hand. His touch was warm and comforting. Nora caught the sisters' exchange of knowing looks. She slowly pulled her hand away and reached for her hot chocolate but it was hard to hide her own smile behind the mug.

"Remember the Christmas when I was twelve?" Gail asked her mother. "We got snowed in by a blizzard. We couldn't go anywhere for days, and we nearly ran out of the essentials—milk, bread, kerosene, toilet paper. . ."

Grandma chuckled and the children started asking a hundred questions about the snow.

"I always loved to walk in the snow when it came down in flakes as big as golf balls," Gail said, pulling a granddaughter onto her lap.

Diane agreed, nodding. "I love a winter morning

when the frost covers everything and sparkles in the sunshine."

The family reminisced about snowmen, sled riding, snow forts, ice skating, snow caves, skiing, and more. Nora knew such talk could make her very homesick, but she was truly comforted by this loving family who had opened their home to her.

"My mother and I. . . ," Nora began timidly, "we loved to sit by the window and watch the birds come to our feeder. We would try to name each bird." Nora smiled at her memories. "My favorites are the cardinals. Their red coloring really stands out against the snow."

Grandma was inspired to tell a story about caring for the animals during the winter months on their small Ohio farm. Nora naturally leaned closer to Rick as she listened. Soon his arm moved around her shoulder and he nudged her closer to his side.

Nora wanted to look at Rick but she didn't dare. She didn't dare look at his sisters either. Not that their expressions mattered. Nora knew that there wasn't any place she would rather be.

As the festivities wound down and the children were ushered off to bed, Rick indicated that he was ready to drive Nora home. Diane and Tricia followed them to the door.

"I guess we will be seeing a lot of you now," Tricia told Nora.

Brian and his brother-in-law laughed, but they were soon silenced by a dark look from Rick.

Nora wrinkled her brow in confusion. "I. . .I'd like that."

The sisters each hugged her and Gail insisted that she take a plate of goodies home.

Chapter 9

I'm sorry if my family made you feel uncomfortable tonight," Rick said as he waited for Nora to unlock her front door.

"What do you mean?"

It was getting late but Nora moved toward the kitchen to make some coffee.

"Well, I. . .I have never brought a woman home to meet my family," Rick sputtered as he sat down heavily at the kitchen table. Nora kept her back to him as she measured the coffee into the the coffeemaker.

"You see, I don't date much," Rick revealed to her, "in fact, hardly ever."

Nora could tell he was uncomfortable with this line of conversation and her eyes widened as she tried to grasp his meaning.

"About a year ago I had been seeing a girl on a regular basis for about three months."

Nora joined him at the table. He ran a hand through his hair and continued. "I thought she had a lot of the qualities I would want in a wife but something bothered me. Whenever I would try to talk about spiritual matters, she would change the subject. Since we couldn't talk about something that was very important to me, we grew apart." Rick finally looked at Nora. "I never invited her home. I told myself that I wouldn't bring a girl home unless I really believed she would be the one I would spend the rest of my life with."

Nora's eyes were now as big as saucers. She was speechless. *He can't mean. . .*

Rick turned his gaze back to the tabletop and chuckled. "Some of my family know my convictions and they have often accused me of being boring because of them."

Nora was having trouble understanding his words. Her heart had started a strange fluttering and her mouth was dry. She ran her tongue over her lips and looked at Rick.

He was staring at her. "Nora," he said very softly, "I would really like to get to know you better, aside from work."

Nora thought of all the time they had already spent away from work: their first dinner, decorating the tree, the youth party, lunch, shopping, the accident, and tonight. They had created special memories, memories she wouldn't trade for anything. "Yes. . . ," she said slowly. That one word came out like a squeak.

At that his hand shot across the table and covered hers. A smile brightened his face and the look of anxiety disappeared from his blue eyes.

Over cooled cups of coffee they shared quiet conversation in the suspended glow of their newly discovered emotions. Nora asked Rick when he had become a

Christian. Rick asked her more about her family. They shared their individual dreams and talked about each other's goals.

It was past two in the morning before Rick pulled himself up from the table to leave. He took her hand again and Nora walked with him to the door.

Rick turned to her. "It's funny. From the moment I took you on as my 'project,'" he teased, not unkindly, "I had a feeling I would be in danger of losing my heart."

Nora lowered her eyes, her cheeks colored with pleasure. Rick's fingers drew lazy patterns on her chin, and then his lips lowered to hers, parting hers with a hunger Nora had never known. When he pulled away, Nora's gaze followed him, wishing the moment could continue.

"Good night, dear Nora. Merry Christmas."

Nora couldn't sleep. She lay wide awake as Christmas morning dawned sunny and warm. She pushed open the window and listened to the calls of the many birds that took refuge along the shore of the lake.

She remembered the secure feeling she had sitting under the protection of Rick's arm. She recalled the warmth of his hand over hers and the taste of his lips on her own. His words replayed in her mind, "I told myself that I wouldn't bring a girl home unless I really believed she would be the one I would spend the rest of my life with."

Only a few short weeks ago Rick was a work ac-quaintance who happened to attend her church. She had welcomed his help with her article and soon found herself offended that he could possibly think her another charity case. One moment he had seemed too good to be real and the next she imagined a number of flaws that annoyed her about him. *He is definitely a bit of a slob, if his truck is any indication, but I probably wouldn't have to worry about him becoming lazy. He's nervous around groups of little kids. How will he do with kids of his own?* She flopped over onto her stomach. *He does have a strong desire to follow the Lord. Isn't that what is most important? Isn't that my desire also?*

Nora shook the fog from her head and rolled over to sit on the edge of her bed. *What would it be like to spend the rest of my life with that kind of man?* she wondered. She didn't believe Rick had ever met a stranger or turned down a chance to work for a worthy cause. Would he drive himself to burnout? *And he wants to go into full-time ministry!* Nora didn't feel called to ministry.

Then she remembered words of wisdom. *"We are each called to some form of ministry. For some it is a calling to full-time work, while for others it is in the simple actions involved in daily living, be it the friendships we make, the children we raise, the words we choose."*

Who said that? Nora tried to recall. *I think it must have been our pastor when I was in junior high. I haven't thought about that sermon for years.*

Maybe she didn't feel called to minister in the traditional sense, but she had better be sure she'd be willing to follow Rick wherever God would direct. He would be on call at all times, and she'd have to respect his calling and be willing to share him with God's people.

Nora reached for her stereo to turn on some cheery Christmas music to dispel her melancholy mood. She would need to hurry to make it to the Second Hope Shelter in time for the Christmas party.

She was dressed and having a piece of the coffee cake Carmen had left her when two minivans pulled into the drive. Rick unfolded his large frame from the first van and came bounding up to her door.

"I didn't expect to see you today," Nora said when she opened her door to his knock. She suddenly felt shy with him when she remembered his kiss and the feel of his touch.

From behind his back Rick pulled a small bouquet of red roses. "Merry Christmas!"

Nora's face glowed. "You shouldn't have!" She brought the roses to her face and sighed as she took in their sweet fragrance.

Rick tipped his head toward the vans. "I brought some of the gang."

Nora noticed Diane leaning out of the passenger window of the second van. Nora returned her enthusiastic wave.

"They'll help us liven up the shelter's party, for sure," Rick said, laughing. "I thought we could swing by the Good Shepherd Mission and pick up the Brooks family."

"That would be wonderful. I have some gifts I want to give them."

"Speaking of gifts, I found this little package in my truck this morning. Is it yours?"

Nora saw that he was holding the green package she had carried with her last night. "Oh, I. . .I had intended to give it to you." She still wasn't sure her gift was appropriate, but as Rick ripped the paper with the excitement of a child, she couldn't take it back.

"How did you know what I wear?" Rick asked, holding up the green bottle of pine-scented cologne.

"This is my favorite. Thanks." He leaned down and placed a quick peck on her cheek. Then he reached in the box and pulled out the carved evergreen. He looked at her with a question in his eyes.

"I wanted to thank you again for my Christmas tree." Nora shrugged with a smile. "I thought this one would last longer than the real thing."

"This is great," Rick said honestly. He looked at her face for a long moment as if searching for something. "We need to get going," he said quietly as he pocketed his gifts. "Thanks."

Nora hid her confusion as she placed her roses in water, then collected her purse and three brightly wrapped packages. She wanted him to kiss her again. . .but not in the doorway with his family watching. She wanted to know if he were feeling the way she did. Her heart was doing a rapid dance and her mind was a jumble of a thousand thoughts.

She was grateful that they would ride alone in his parents' van but she couldn't think of one intelligent word to say. In silence she watched him as he maneuvered across town through thin traffic.

The Brookses were watching a Christmas movie on TV when Rick and Nora arrived. The children loved their gifts. Tom was gracious, though Nora could tell that he was obviously embarrassed. Everyone then piled into the van, excited at the prospect of a party.

❧

Nora sat in the corner of the spacious dining hall at Second Hope Shelter with her notebook opened. She jotted a few notes about the events the shelter had planned for Christmas Day. She would need to go into the office and add a few lines to her article before her five o'clock deadline. She had already picked out three of Rick's pictures that she would submit for consideration.

Relaxing, Nora let her gaze roam around the room that was nearly full of people. There were many who didn't need the services provided by the shelter, volunteers of time and money who kept the program going.

Santa, having performed his duties of passing out gifts, was now enjoying a full Christmas dinner with all the trimmings. Judging from his size and white dusted beard, Nora suspected that Santa was really Big Jim in disguise.

Nora noticed that Merrie had moved away from the table where her family and the Thompsons were lingering over the remains of their dinner. She carried a game she had received from Santa as she inched toward the big man in the red suit.

Merrie reached up and tugged on Santa's arm.

"Ho, ho, ho, what can I do for you, my dear?"

Nora could barely hear Merrie's soft voice. "I'd give back my game if you could help my daddy find a job."

"Ho, ho—" Santa's voice cracked with emotion. He pulled the little girl up on his knee and pushed away the offered game. "I happen to know that the people at this wonderful place are going to do everything in their power to help your daddy find work so you can have a cozy place to live again. What you and I need to do is pray for your daddy, because God knows what each person needs most, better than any old Santa Claus." He hugged Merrie close and bowed his head to whisper a prayer with her.

Nora felt a tear fall to her notebook and she quickly wiped her eyes. If only she had a picture of this precious moment! Around the wet spot on her paper she wrote more notes. She was eager to get to the office and finish her article.

After Nora spent about an hour wrapping up her article at the *Tribune*, she went with Rick back to his parents' home and played games well into the evening. She placed a call to each of her brothers once she returned home, then fell into bed, exhausted from the holiday celebrations.

A pounding on her door late the next morning brought her running from the bathroom. She flung the door open expecting to see Rick—but instead, she got a facefull of white confetti. Bits of white paper clung to her hair, lodged in the neck of her sweater, and heaped over her bare feet.

Rick and Tricia stood on Nora's porch bent over in fits of laughter. "You said you wanted snow for Christmas," he said, chuckling at the look on her face.

"It's a little late, but. . ." Nora calmly brushed the confetti from her clothes, touched by their act of mischief. "This wasn't exactly what I had in mind, but thanks anyway."

"Have you seen today's paper?" Rick asked. "The front-page story is a real winner."

"And the pictures are sure to win a prize," Tricia added.

Nora's face brightened and she looked across her porch for the paper. Not seeing it, she looked back to Rick. His expression told her he was hiding something.

"Do you have my paper?" she asked, holding out her hand.

"Would I keep you from reading your article?" he asked with exaggerated surprise.

"Of course," Tricia agreed, laughing.

Rick handed Nora a section of the paper. She scanned the sports section and looked back at him in frustration.

"The rest, please. . .please," she resorted to begging.

"Oh, all right. What's all the fuss about? You'd think a big reporter like you would be used to seeing her byline on the front page."

Nora grabbed the front section from him and quickly reviewed her article which took up a large portion of the bottom of the *Tribune*'s first page. One of

Rick's pictures featuring shelter volunteers was indeed attention–grabbing. The article continued three pages into the paper where two more of Rick's pictures had been used.

"They used all the pictures I submitted," Nora said, amazed.

"You represented me well," Rick thanked her. "You didn't tell me, though, about the little girl who prayed with Santa Claus."

"Yes," Tricia chimed in, "that was the best part."

Nora smiled. "It was Merrie Brooks, and it had to have been the sweetest thing I have ever witnessed."

She invited them inside and, while pouring large glasses of orange juice, she related the scene she had witnessed at the Second Hope Shelter's Christmas party.

"Money and time are wonderful contributions, but prayer is something that anyone can donate," Rick observed.

"And prayer is what is needed most." Nora sighed, looking over her article again.

Chapter 10

New Year's Eve dawned with the promise of rain, and a cold, damp wind cut through Nora as she rushed from her car to the house with a bag of last-minute groceries. Rick had not made definite plans with her but she assumed they would spend the evening together.

For the last two weeks they had spent a part of each day with one another and Nora looked forward to every minute they shared. She knew she was falling in love. She didn't know when it started—maybe at the youth Christmas party—but she knew that he could very easily be the one she wanted to spend the rest of her life with, God willing.

"Did you happen to get more milk?" Carmen greeted as Nora pushed the door closed against the force of the wind.

"No, I checked and we have nearly a gallon that will last us a couple of days," Nora said.

"Uh, I'll pick some more up when I'm out later." Carmen appeared distracted.

"Well, okay. I thought I'd put together a snack mix for munching on later."

"Oh, good. Make a big batch," Carmen said.

"Carmen, did you invite someone over?"

Her roommate muttered something unintelligible and quickly left the room. Nora didn't know what to make of her mysterious mood, but she figured Carmen didn't want to talk about her plans. She wished Rick would call.

Passing Carmen's bedroom on the way to her own, she saw her stripping sheets from her double bed.

"You might want to throw your sheets in the wash with mine," Carmen called to her, as Chris marched between them with the vacuum sweeper.

"Sure," Nora replied. "When did you decide today was cleaning day?" She shook her head in confusion. Carmen was often the one who procrastinated about housekeeping.

"Oh, well, you know there are people who have a tradition of starting each new year with a clean and well-organized home." Carmen shrugged and smiled at Nora. "I thought I'd try it."

"I guess I could help."

"No, no, go on and fix your snack mix."

Nora was starting to hope that Rick would suggest that they go out for the evening.

When he called around four, he told her he had made seven o'clock dinner reservations at a popular Orlando restaurant. She could have been sore that he waited so long to set up the date, but she chose to dwell on the prospect of a wonderful evening. It would take them nearly an hour for the drive north so Nora hurried to clean up the kitchen and decide what to wear.

She pulled a fancy ice blue dress from the back of

her closet, one that perfectly matched the color of her eyes. When she was setting up the ironing board, Carmen came rushing into her room.

"Where do you think you're going?" Carmen asked, her breath coming in short gasps.

"Rick and I are having dinner in Orlando."

"You didn't tell me."

"He just called."

"But. . .but. . ." Carmen frantically looked around the room. "What time is it?"

"About four-thirty. Why? What's wrong?"

"Oh-oh-oh—" Carmen stuttered as she ran from the room.

The iron was already hot and Nora went ahead with pressing her dress. This would be her first "romantic" date with Rick and she was excited. Even though Carmen had been acting out of character all afternoon, Nora didn't want anything to spoil her evening. She reasoned that if it were something terribly important, Carmen would get around to telling her eventually.

Then Chris stopped in front of her opened door. "Goin' out, I see."

"Yes, Rick is picking me up for dinner."

"What time?"

"By six."

"Oh. . ." Chris paused as he leaned casually against the doorjamb. "By the way, what's Rick's last name?"

"Thompson. Why?" When Nora looked up from her ironing, Chris was gone. She walked out into the hallway. She could hear voices in the kitchen but she decided to go back to her task.

After showering, polishing, curling, and dressing, Nora felt she was ready for the evening. She wanted to look her very best. The new year seemed to hold great promise and she wanted this night to be a special memory.

The house had been very quiet while Nora dressed. As she walked from room to room, she admired how Carmen managed to make everything sparkle in such a short time. No one was in the living room so Nora moved on to the kitchen.

Cookies were cooling in neat rows on the counter and the Crock-Pot was plugged in beside the stove. Nora lifted the lid and smelled the sweet and sour meatballs bubbling inside.

She looked out the kitchen window toward the drive. Rick hadn't arrived yet, but she noticed Carmen and Chris tossing a baseball back and forth in the yard. Nora chose to stay in the kitchen to wait for Rick. From the table she would have a good view of the street.

A lone security lamp illuminated their part of the street. It stood as a guard where the orange grove met their yard. Darkness was deepening in the neighborhood and the light flickered on, shining down on their drive.

Just then a vehicle came down the street and turned into their driveway. Nora rose from the table, expecting it to be Rick, but under the beam of the security light she didn't recognize the large van. She watched as Chris went running off the porch, jumping in obvious excitement. A large man climbed out of the driver's side and talked to Chris, then a woman and four children came around from the other side. As the light shone down on the man's head of curly blond hair, recognition dawned on Nora. She raced through the living room and out onto the porch where Carmen was welcoming their guests.

"Hey, Sis, you didn't have to dress up for me!" the man shouted as Nora rushed into his outstretched arms.

"John. . .you didn't tell me. . .you were coming. . .to Florida," Nora struggled to say as she was squeezed against his massive chest.

"Surprise!" his family echoed while they moved in to receive their hugs.

"You wouldn't believe how hard it was to keep your secret," Chris said, talking a mile a minute. "She almost left on a date, and. . ." Chris continued for anyone who would listen, but John turned on Nora.

"Date! My little sister isn't old enough to date!"

Nora swatted at her brother. "Come inside before the whole neighborhood hears you."

As the raucous group filled up the living room, Nora exclaimed over how much her nephew and three nieces had grown. The oldest girl was now level with Nora's shoulder.

"We left Ohio Monday morning. Work couldn't do without its best foreman over the weekend," John said. "We laid over in South Carolina last night, but from Jacksonville to here seemed to take forever. And the kids were sure disappointed to see that you don't live by the beach."

"Hey, this is farm country," Nora said, chuckling. "The

beaches are about two hours both east and west but we still have sand everywhere."

Time passed so quickly Nora had forgotten about Rick until there was a knock at the front door. She wiggled her way to be the first to reach the doorknob. He stood under the porch lights in a crisp suit with his tie draped around his neck.

"Oh, I am so sorry," Nora said, not taking into account that he was the one late to arrive. "If we leave now, we may still make it."

"You have company," he said softly.

"Oh, yes, you have to meet—" She then realized that there would be no romantic New Year's Eve date, and Rick knew it.

"Chris called me and shared the surprise," Rick said. "I told him I would do my best to help and delay our departure."

"Thank you," Nora said with double meaning. She took his hand and led him into the living room for introductions. She gave a sigh of relief when John refrained from any more smart remarks and genuinely seemed to like Rick.

Nora was glad for the extra food when Carmen announced that it was time to eat. She praised Carmen's success in cleaning the house while preparing a wealth of food. She was also glad when she remembered that her Christmas gifts for John's family were still boxed and waiting to go back to the post office. John's family also had gifts for Nora, and it was Christmas all over again.

John had a special gift for Nora. "This is something

Aunt Midge had borrowed from Mom not long before
. . .you know. It was a favorite among the heirlooms
passed down from Great-grandma Mercer," John said,
handing a wrapped box to Nora.

Nora eagerly ripped the paper away. Inside the box
was a delicate, handblown, handpainted vase. "Oh, I
remember this. It sat at the back of Mom's china cabinet. She said it was very old and probably pretty valuable." Nora was thrilled to have this reminder of her
mother. It was the perfect gift.

"I thought you'd like to have it," John said, and, having been too serious for too long, he launched into a joke
while downing more of Carmen's food.

It was nine o'clock before the excitement seemed to
settle in the house. Nora hadn't taken time to change
out of her dress but she had long since kicked her heels
off into a corner.

She went into the kitchen to make a pot of coffee
and Rick followed her.

"Pretty crazy evening," he said as he leaned against
the counter.

"Not exactly how we planned it," she responded,
shy about showing him just how much she had wanted
a romantic evening with him. "When did you say Chris
told you about the surprise?"

"I'm not sure, but it really wasn't that long after I
had hung up with you."

"Now I know—he wanted to know your last name
so he could look you up in the phone book."

Rick moved closer to Nora and the sizzling

coffeemaker. "Do you think we could escape to the backyard for a few minutes?"

"Maybe," she said, enjoying his nearness. His breath warmed her cheek and she slipped away from his reach. "I need to get my shoes."

When she sneaked back to the kitchen for their rendezvous, she noticed Rick had a blanket in one hand. They closed the door softly behind them. In the darkened backyard, Rick spread the blanket over the wooden picnic table bench and they sat close together. He draped his arm across her shoulders and pulled her closer to him. The wind had died down but the night air was chilly and damp.

"I found out today that Tom Brooks has a job offer," Rick said.

"Oh, where?"

"Our church is in need of a full-time janitor now that activities are scheduled there every night of the week. It won't be much, but it's a good place to start."

"That's wonderful," Nora said. "Merrie's prayer is being answered."

They sat in silence for a while, admiring the stars, then Rick said, "Now I'm glad I didn't spend a week planning this evening."

"Just how long did you plan this evening?"

"It was on my mind since the moment I woke this morning. It is New Year's Eve—a time to look ahead—and I wanted it to be very special for us."

"Me, too." Nora sighed and rested her head against his shoulder.

"The stars will have to take the place of the candle-light I was hoping to have."

"They are still special."

Rick moved so he could look at her. "There's something I need to tell you."

She looked at him, curious but silent.

"Things just came together and I'm going to start a new job in May," Rick said.

"Does it involve your youth ministry degree?" Nora didn't know what to say, but she knew this man was committed to serving the Lord.

"Sort of. I've accepted the position of manager at a Christian camp in Ohio. I'll be in charge of oversee-ing the grounds and I'll also work with a committee to organize activities. When the committee doesn't have an event planned, I'll be responsible for renting out the grounds to various groups. It will be a heavy load, but it will also offer me the opportunity to work in both direct and indirect ministry."

"It sounds very interesting," she said numbly. *Only it means you will be moving. What about our future? Lord, do You mean to take him from me?* She looked toward the stars seeking His answer.

Rick continued, obviously excited. "I'm going to be able to work with both youth and adults. Sometimes I will plan and carry out retreats where I can use my ministry skills—"

"When do you leave?" she interrupted, her anxiety showing.

"By the end of May. But Nora, there's something else,

something more important than the job," Rick said, as he gently pulled her chin to face him.

Her gaze flew to his face.

"I want to cherish you forever," he breathed as he held her face between his strong hands, kissing leisurely her forehead, the tip of her nose, and then her lips.

She pulled away after a moment. "What do you mean?"

Rick took a small box from his pocket. It was wrapped in white foil with a sprig of evergreen for a bow. He reached for her hand and placed the box in her palm. "I want this to be yours, Nora."

Nora stared at the box for a long time before opening it. *Dear Lord, can this be real? This has been my dream, but Lord, Rick is so good, too good for me.*

Inside the box a diamond solitaire winked at her in the starlight. Rick took the ring out and got down on one knee.

"Nora, will you be my wife?" he asked softly. "I know we really haven't had a long. . .courtship, but. . ."

She felt the tears coming and with a sob in her throat she said, "Yes, oh, yes." Feeling utterly contented, she realized her most dreaded holiday had become the one she would treasure forever. She threw her arms around his neck and kissed him spontaneously.

He hugged her to him. "God has been so good to me this Christmas," he breathed in her ear. And this time when he kissed her, an endless, warm, passionate kiss, a night bird called from a nearby tree.

"Uh, Nora. . .I have to get up," Rick said suddenly. "I

think some fire ants have found my ankle." He jumped to his feet, stomping and shaking the offending ants from his leg.

Nora's tears turned to giggles at the sight. "Let's get you in and doctor those bites," she finally managed to say.

"Your ring," Rick said, and looked surprised to see it still in his hand. He limped over to her and took her left hand. "I promise to love you always," he said, as he placed the ring on her finger.

"I love you, Rick," she answered simply and he gathered her again in his arms.

They tried to enter the house quietly through the back door but John and Chris were in the kitchen, hungry again.

"There you lovebirds are," John bellowed. "We thought you deserted us."

John was ready to tease but Rick was all seriousness. "John, I'm really glad you and your family could come for a visit. I hope we get to know each other well—like family," he said, extending his hand.

"Like family? Do you have designs on my sister?"

Nora pushed her left hand between them. "Yes, he does," she said, beaming.

John's tone changed instantly. "Do you love him, Nora?"

"With all my heart."

The serious moment gone, John gave a whoop and locked Nora in another one of his bear hugs. The kitchen was soon full of people congratulating the couple.

By midnight everyone had gathered in the living room in front of the television, waiting for the ball to drop in Times Square, the official start of a new year. Rick's bandaged foot was propped up on a stool and Nora sat tucked in by his side on the couch, her cheeks rosy with excitement.

And when the new year began, Rick smiled knowingly at Nora and kissed her, the promise of their future whispered in one word. . .evergreen.

Rebecca Germany

Rebecca is the senior editor of fiction at Barbour Publishing, and *Evergreen* was her first published work. She has always loved inspirational romances because they are wonderful tools for sharing the gospel message. Rebecca lives on a small farm in rural, eastern Ohio. She is actively involved in her church and enjoys keeping up with numerous family members.

Search for the Star

Mary Hawkins

Chapter 1

Jean Drew rolled her stiff shoulders and then moved her head from side to side. It had been a long day's drive from Sydney and she was tired even though she had stopped for a good break in Toowoomba. The rolling hills around that "Garden City of the Darling Downs" were well behind her now and the road ahead across the black soil plains was straight to the horizon.

But it wasn't only her physical condition—and the last rays of the setting sun in her eyes—that made Jean ease her foot on the accelerator, she acknowledged with a deep sigh. Ever since saying farewell to the director of nursing, her mind had been in a state of turmoil.

Jean remembered her colleague's parting words with some alarm. Miss Fisher had looked at her sadly and said, almost crossly, "Instead of just long-service leave I suppose soon I'll be saying good-bye permanently to the best nurse educator this hospital's ever had."

Then, smiling at her confusion, she had added, "The last few weeks you've been so excited about this newly discovered niece of yours. Since she's your only living relative, I just thought you'd be wanting to live closer to her one day."

Jean's immediate reaction had been denial, but the

thought had been growing in her mind. Was this God's prompting? Did He want her to move to Queensland to be nearer to Hilda?

Although her nursing colleagues would never believe it, Sister Jean Drew was feeling shy and a trifle nervous at seeing Hilda again. What would be expected from the bride's only relative these next few weeks leading up to Hilda's wedding, not to mention Christmas?

"I shouldn't have let her talk me into coming to stay for so many weeks before her wedding, especially over Christmas," she muttered out loud, and then her lips twisted wryly. There had been no way she could say no, even though she had known she would have to endure the bittersweetness of the Christmas season as well.

Thus, she had delayed making a decision, and only a couple of weeks ago had confronted the director of nursing and requested some of her long-service leave off over the Christmas and New Year summer holidays. Now, remembering the surprised look on Miss Fisher's face, Jean scowled.

"Why, Jean, for years you've always insisted on working Christmas Day," the director said sharply. "I do wish you'd given me more notice. You know these next few weeks leading up to Christmas are the busiest in the hospital year and I've already drafted out the rosters. As usual, the surgeons have also scheduled full theaters to tidy up their waiting lists before the holiday period."

It had been the surprise, and then the disapproval, that made Jean realize just how many Christmases she had spent working to be taken so much for granted. For so many years she had really hated Christmas, happy to stay busy on the wards until all the madness was over.

Even the last few Christmases, when she had been able for the first time to worship as never before and thank God for the birth of Jesus, she still automatically filled the day with work to try and dull the ache of being alone. Despite invitations from her new friends at church, her pride had made her reluctant to take advantage and intrude on their family get-togethers.

So, despite the director's displeasure at the short notice, Jean had stuck to her request for eight weeks' leave. But these last few days, as she had prepared to be away, all her dislike, no, her dread, of the whole Christmas period had welled up inside.

This would be the first time she had seen Hilda, as well as her old friend Marian Stevens and her son Jim and his wife Gail since their brief, wonderful reunion last year. At that time Hilda's fiancé, Reverend Rance Telford, had informed them that the birth mother Hilda had been trying so hard to find was none other than Jean's younger sister who had died several years ago.

As her next-door neighbor, Jean had always liked Hilda and felt sorry for her being the only child of older parents. Now, although she hated to admit it, Jean was feeling just the tiniest bit scared at her new status. Hilda had always called her "Aunt Jean," and that was now exactly who she was.

During this long day's drive, Jean had been forced to acknowledge that she was at a crossroads. These last few weeks she had found her job in the large Sydney hospital less satisfying than ever before. She had snapped at a couple of students doing their clinical experience, and then felt ashamed that she had slipped back to her old cranky self, spoiling her Christian witness.

Now Jean was seriously considering the possibility of getting a job closer to Hilda and the Stevenses, but there were few nursing jobs available anywhere at the moment. She certainly didn't think she could live out here in the country, but if there were nothing in Too-woomba, Brisbane was much closer than Sydney.

"Lord, if only You'd speak out loud and clear some-times and tell a body what You want her to do!" she muttered out loud, and then pulled a face at herself.

She knew the answer to that. He did guide, but He also expected her to live by faith, not sight—or hearing!

To try and distract herself, Jean studied the passing countryside more closely. She had traveled this road many times but rarely at this season of the year when most of the golden wheat paddocks lining each side of the road had already been harvested. There was an occasional harvester still working in the distance and several large, grain-filled trucks had rumbled past her on their way to the railway silos.

In the distance she saw a large black car pulled well over to the side of the road. Jean had turned off the main highway some miles back and knew that vehicles along this stretch were not plentiful. But long ago on other visits she had learned that out here, so many miles from anywhere, you always stopped to see if anyone needed help.

Still, even in the country these days, a woman by herself had to be careful. Reluctantly, she slowed down as a male figure opened the driver's door, stood up, and imperiously signaled her to stop. She peered at him as she slowly cruised past and then frowned.

Despite the shining black sedan, she didn't like the look of him one bit. He appeared decidedly scruffy with more than one day's growth of bread. Tall and dark haired, he was wearing jeans and an unbuttoned shirt, which he was at least making some attempt to rectify as she took her time parking the car.

She left the motor running and watched him warily as he approached her. His face was drawn and there were dark circles around his eyes. But there was something familiar about that relieved smile, those thick black eyebrows that almost met, those eyes. . .

She thought she must be dreaming. She closed her eyes tightly for a moment and when she opened them. . . Jonathan. It was Jonathan Howard.

But, she thought suddenly, *he just couldn't be, not after all these years and certainly not right out here on the black soil plains of the Darling Downs in Queensland, at least a thousand kilometers from Sydney.*

The last time she had seen him had been in her office in St. Kilda, a bustling Sydney hospital. He had shaken her hand, formally wished her all the best for her wedding the following week, and then turned and walked out of her life without a word.

The last time she had been able to find out anything

about him had been a couple of years ago when she had heard he wasn't even in Australia but was using his surgeon's skills in some little-known locale in Africa.

At closer inspection the years had not been kind to him. His unruly dark hair, which was considerably longer than it used to be, curling down to his shoulders, had even more gray than her own, her silver streaks carefully hidden. His face was more heavily lined than she would have expected.

He leaned down to peer at her through the car window and she caught her breath as his smile widened. It was that same crooked, gleaming smile that had once played havoc with her senses. She only realized she was gaping at him when his smile faltered and a slightly puzzled look crossed his face.

"I'm sorry to stop you, but I wonder if you have a mobile phone or if you could give me a lift," he said rather casually.

His deep, crisp voice stopped abruptly as a frown crossed his face and he looked a little closer at her. She held her breath, waiting for him to recognize her, then a flood of disappointment swept through her when he said, "Look, you're not afraid of me, are you?"

Afraid? Oh yes, she had been afraid once, not of him, but of how he had made her feel, what he had made her confront, what he had. . .

She came to her senses when he took a step back from the car and said impatiently, "For goodness sake, I assure you I'm genuinely stuck out here and only need a lift to the nearest phone."

Jean quickly turned off the motor and scrambled out on slightly shaky legs. "Afraid? Of course I'm not afraid."

Her voice was unnaturally high-pitched and she swallowed convulsively. She was acting like one of her silly first-year nursing students. How stupid could a woman her age get, being thrown into confusion by a doctor she had once worked with all those years ago! *And he's married,* she reminded herself.

She managed to smile at him and say in her usual efficient tone, "I'm sorry, Dr. Howard, of course I'm not afraid. I just couldn't believe my eyes it was you."

Chapter 2

Surprise but not recognition filled his face as he studied her carefully.

Jean was dismayed at the sadness that swept through her because he obviously did not remember her. But then, she had always known that to him, despite being the most senior nurse, she was simply one of the operating theater's staff, even though they had developed a friendly working relationship and even socialized at hospital parties.

She straightened. "You don't remember me, but I was in charge of the theater at—"

"Jean. . .Jean Drew!"

Absolute amazement transformed his features and then he smiled warmly. "Why, Sister Jean Drew, of course I remember you. Or as the new nursing etiquette requires, should it be Miss Drew, RN? Afraid I still call registered nurses 'Sister' even in hospitals! How absolutely amazing to meet you on this lonely country road. Are you going to come to my rescue again after all these years?"

Jean's smile turned into a delighted chuckle. So he did remember her after all. As they stared at each other, she suddenly realized he was still holding her hand between his strong capable ones and she quickly pulled away.

"Oh, I don't think you ever really needed much rescuing, Jonathan."

He chuckled. "Oh, yes, I did, especially that time I slept through my alarm and arrived thirty minutes late for old Fergy's first op on his list. My very first week, too!"

She put her hands on her hips in mock indignation. "Now really, Dr. Howard, could I help it if that operating theater autoclave took thirty minutes longer to sterilize Dr. Ferguson's special instruments than anticipated?"

This time he threw back his head and laughed loudly. A lump suddenly lodged in her throat. She realized that the years may have aged him, but his unkempt appearance in no way detracted from that masculine charisma that was part and parcel of such a capable, compassionate man. His mere presence had so often reassured and comforted patients and staff alike.

Jean remembered a little sadly that this was how he had laughed during that first year as Dr. Ferguson's surgical registrar. Later, when he had taken over as chief surgeon, that laugh was heard less and less often and then disappeared altogether. Those last few weeks she had worked with him even his smile had lost its sparkle and had seldom reached those wonderfully expressive eyes that were now filled with delight as he looked at her.

"And what on earth is that old dragon of a theater nurse doing driving by herself so many miles from Sydney?"

"And what is that eminent surgeon doing with a broken-down car, a Mercedes, if I'm not mistaken, parked

107

on the side of a minor country road in the middle of the Darling Downs?" she countered with a tilt of her chin.

"He's going to a wedding."

Something clutched at her heart. "A wedding?" she managed faintly.

"Well, not today, but in a few weeks' time, after Christmas, in fact. A young friend of mine is taking the plunge."

Jean's heart steadied as he continued. "More accurately, I'm escaping for a holiday. I need some R & R in the quiet countryside," he said as he pulled a face. "But it's a little too quiet this evening. I've been stuck here for well over an hour and had almost given up and started walking, only I haven't a clue where I am or how far it is to the nearest farmhouse."

After an uncomfortable pause, she could not wait any longer to find out. "That wedding you're going to wouldn't by any chance be on New Year's Day, would it?"

It was his turn to look surprised as he nodded.

"And it wouldn't just happen to be Reverend Rance Telford and Hilda Garrett's, would it?"

Again he nodded, and then a rather strange expression crossed his face. "And by some weird chance you wouldn't happen to be the 'Aunt Jean' Rance so fondly wrote about?"

It was her turn to nod helplessly and then they simultaneously burst out laughing.

He recovered first, and with his eyes still twinkling said, "Well, Aunt Jean Dr—" He stopped and then added swiftly, "Oh, I'm sorry, that was your maiden name. I don't think I ever did know the name of the man you left the hospital to marry."

Jean froze. Obviously, the hospital grapevine hadn't done its job, but then he probably hadn't given her another thought. *And why should he have?* she acknowledged fairly. Despite the closeness that had sprung up between them, they had shared only a working relationship, at least from his point of view.

After too long a pause which had him raising those incredibly thick and straight eyebrows, she said, "It's still Drew."

At her quiet tone all trace of amusement disappeared and something besides surprise flashed across his face, but he didn't speak. At last she said reluctantly, "I changed my mind and didn't get married after all."

Now why on earth did she tell him that instead of what nearly everyone else believed was the truth?

He was silent for another moment, and then he said softly, "I'm sorry, Jean, I never did hear that. At. . .at that time I was going through some bad stuff in my own personal life."

Bad stuff? Jean frowned. What did he mean? Could that have been why he had seemed so distracted, so quiet and reserved those last couple of weeks? Embarrassed, she had thought that somehow, despite all her efforts, he had realized how she felt about him, feelings she had only just discovered herself.

Not for the first time did Jean acknowledge she had made a mistake cutting herself off so thoroughly from the staff at St. Kilda. With all that had happened, it had seemed the easiest option at the time. But she had still felt very lonely and had often wondered over the years what she would have done if she had not phoned her old friend Marian Stevens.

She turned and looked toward his car. "Your wife couldn't come with you, Jonathan?"

When she turned back to him she was startled by the change in his face. He had quickly donned that professional mask she had seen so many medical personnel put in place when dealing with distraught patients or relatives.

He opened his mouth, and then apparently changed his mind and merely shook his head. "Perhaps it would be a good idea if we postponed this conversation to some future time," he said abruptly. "Now, I don't suppose you're staying with Hilda Garrett, too?"

She stared at him for a brief moment and then looked away. Inexplicably, she felt hurt at the sudden coldness in his voice. After all, there was absolutely no reason in the world why she should be upset that he so obviously did not want to talk about his wife.

Then she realized what he had said and turned back. "You're staying with Hilda?"

He nodded and said in that same expressionless voice, "Yes, Rance told me she insisted."

He hesitated for a moment and then sighed. "I only arrived back a couple of days ago from a pretty heavy operating schedule overseas to discover my house had not only suffered severe damage in a bad storm but been burgled as well. Apparently when Hilda found out from Rance she insisted I come here while the repairs are being made. He wanted me to stay with him but he's moved out of the Toowoomba manse and is living with his mother and stepfather until he commences at his new church in Brisbane."

Jean studied his face for a moment, noting again the dark circles of weariness under his eyes. Why on earth had he traveled all the way from Sydney when surely he should be nearer to supervise the house repairs? And what about his wife; did she accompany him overseas? Why wasn't she with him now?

It is none of my business, she scolded herself silently.

Jean forced herself to say crisply, "Actually, you nearly made it. The Garretts' farm is not that far from here." She smiled at the face he pulled. "We'd better get moving as it's already much later than I told Hilda to expect me."

When Jonathan's oversized body was at last sitting beside Jean, the inside of her car seemed very small. She straightened, feeling irritated with herself for letting this man affect her so much, and for suddenly wishing fervently they were hours away from the farm.

"Your car is a Mercedes, isn't it?" she asked brightly. "Congratulations, Jonathan, you've obviously done very well."

He snorted and she glanced quickly at him and away again.

"Yes, it is a Mercedes, but it is not my car," he said sharply. "If it had been, it wouldn't have run out of petrol. A friend lent it to me. Mine was in the garage the tree fell on during the storm."

"Oh, dear, your car was damaged, too?"

"Yes," he told her just as curtly. "Half the roof of the house was crushed as well. Although my neighbors called the emergency services to put tarpaulins on, the rain had already poured in and now it's unlivable until the builders have finished."

That raised many more questions concerning the whereabouts of his wife, but Jean merely grinned across at him. "Oh, and after escaping that bedlam the borrowed car ran out of petrol, did it?"

There was a long pause and then he drawled, "Yeah."

The word was accompanied by a low chuckle and Jean relaxed at her success in lightening the atmosphere between them. "And the car of eminent surgeon Jonathan Howard wouldn't dare run out of petrol, would it?"

She heard the smile in his voice as he said in a false posh accent, "Most decidedly, Sister Drew." And then he explained in his normal deep tone, "I did know the tank wasn't full, but I think the gauge may not be registering properly. Whatever, I underestimated how many kilometers to the liter it used up."

"But surely you had some idea by the time you'd driven all this way, didn't you? And what about your wife; has she gone to friends also?"

He was silent for a long moment and she glanced swiftly at him in the now rapidly descending dusk to find that he was watching her with a considering look on his face.

"Jean," he said so quietly she found herself tensing in response. "As I never heard about your wedding, obviously you never heard that my wife died not long after you left St. Kilda. I've been based in Brisbane for some years."

Chapter 3

The car swerved slightly as the shock hit Jean.
All those years ago, at the last moment, she had canceled her wedding to a decent man and broken his heart because of Dr. Jonathan Howard. All those years ago, she had hated and despised herself for being stupid enough to fall in love with a happily married man. All those years ago, she had cut herself off from mutual friends and workmates because it hurt too much even hearing his name mentioned.

And all these measures had achieved was to help her become a hard, bitter, lonely woman. It had taken her years to heal, and that healing had only begun when she discovered it was possible to have a personal relationship with Jesus Christ and she yielded her life to Him.

Now, ten years too late, she had just heard Jonathan say he was free after all. If she had only stayed around. . . .

Then she realized how horrible and utterly selfish that sounded. To become "free," this man had suffered an incalculable loss.

The old pain and guilt clenched its fist inside her again and she reached out desperately to God. The pain eased and after a moment she breathed a fervent prayer, asking forgiveness for such a petty, selfish thought, and a plea for the right words.

Jonathan was still watching her when she at last turned her head. She hoped he would not notice her tear-filled eyes as she said steadily, "I'm so very sorry, Johnny, I know you loved your wife very much. You're right, I didn't know. I've lost track of most of those we worked with at St. Kilda."

A strange look flashed across his face. "You're the only person who's ever called me that."

Tears threatened to choke her and she looked away. She had forgotten that once, to ease a tense moment in the operating theater, she had flippantly called him Johnny. That had been before she realized her liking for the surgeon was changing to something deeper.

"I. . .I'm sorry."

"Oh, no, don't be sorry," he said quickly. "I like it."

He was silent for a long moment before he said, "Yes, I'm afraid I've gotten out of touch, too. I ended up leaving St. Kilda not that long after you did."

His voice was just a little too casual, but Jean took note that he had not even acknowledged her reference to his wife. "I did hear something about you working in Africa. Is that where you've just come from?" she asked, perhaps too quickly.

He gave a deep sigh and stirred restlessly. "I actually flew into Sydney a couple of days ago, visited the mission headquarters for a debriefing, and then flew to Brisbane to find my house in an incredible mess," he said wearily. "I've been camping there in one relatively undamaged room sorting out what's been stolen for the police and arranging for the repairs to be done.

"Unfortunately, all the reliable builders recommended to me are busy on other jobs and can't start for another couple of weeks or even more. It was good to lock the door behind me and escape at last. I haven't even had electricity in the house."

"No wonder you look so. . .so. . . ." She bit her lip, and with considerable relief heard him give a low laugh.

"So disreputable, or should it be old and worn?" he finished for her.

She threw him a grin to find that he had turned and was watching her. "Well, definitely very tired."

Too tired for the man to even bother about his appearance, she suddenly realized.

His steady regard unnerved her and, annoyed with herself, she added crisply, "So, you have been working with a missionary society in Africa. I did wonder about that since I knew you had been a very committed Christian."

He was silent again for a moment but this time she sensed his surprise. She glanced at him with a slight smile to find he was looking at her now with considerable speculation. However, he made no comment but instead started to tell her where he had been working and some of the primitive operating conditions at the makeshift hospital near a refugee camp.

She found herself fascinated with his quiet narrative, realizing as he talked that he was exhausted and traumatized by what he had seen, and had tried to repair, of the horrors done to human bodies by war. She threw in a few questions that kept him talking in more detail about some of his patients until at last she slowed the car and turned onto the track leading to the Garrett farmhouse.

"Well, almost there," she said with a sigh. "I do hope we'll get a chance to talk some more about your work while we're here. It's fascinating."

"And yours, too, Jean." There was considerable contriteness in his voice. "I haven't even given you a chance to tell me about the surgeons you're keeping in control these days."

She laughed. "I've found that student nurses are much easier to terrorize any day than egotistical doctors in operating theaters."

"Student nurses?"

"After. . .after I left St. Kilda I became a tutor sister." She then added quickly, "When the nurses' training changed from the hospital to the university degree, I became a nurse educator supervising nurses doing clinical experience." She pulled a face. "Like you, after all the years of being called Sister Drew, sometimes it still seems strange to be called 'Miss' on duty. I also organize any hospital in-service training, assess the newest graduates on their practical abilities, and relieve on the wards to keep my hand in."

"It would be interesting to hear what you think about the two training methods," he said in a thoughtful voice.

"Well, that's a real hobby horse of mine," she said a shade ruefully. "You'll probably find it hard to stop me once I get going, so it's just as well we've arrived."

"Aunt Jean!"

Jean glowed as she saw the vibrant young woman racing toward the car. Hilda hardly gave her a chance to get out before she was hugging and kissing her.

She had always been fond of this girl but now added love flooded Jean's heart and she tried to stop her eyes from filling with tears. "There, there, girl, do give me a chance to—"

"Oh, I'm sorry, I didn't realize you weren't alone!" Hilda was staring at the tall figure who had alighted from the car and was watching them both with a rather bemused smile.

Before Jean could introduce him, Hilda gave a delighted laugh. "Aunt Jean, don't tell me you've taken me up on my offer of bringing the man in your life with you and at last introducing me to him!"

Jean felt her face flood with heat. To her utter embarrassment, Jonathan was staring at her with his eyes full of amusement and some other expression she couldn't quite make out under the dim outdoor lights.

Before she could gather her wits, he said easily, "Sorry, Hilda, mistaken identity. I'm Jonathan Howard."

Now it was Hilda's turn to blush. "Dr. Howard! Oh, I'm. . .I'm sorry. Rance had hoped to be here to greet you but he couldn't get away, some urgent hospital visit or something. He was very disappointed."

"I found Dr. Howard stranded on the highway," Jean

explained quickly. "He needs someone to take him back to his car with some petrol. What about we phone Jim Stevens and then see about unpacking this car?"

Hilda gave her another quick hug, whispered a fervent "Sorry," and then chanted cheekily, "Yes, Sister Drew, of course, Sister Drew, but no, Sister Drew, I'll soon fill up a can and drive him back myself! Jim's had a hectic day getting the last of the crop in."

Jean smiled at her affectionately and pretended to cuff her ear. Then she felt embarrassed all over again when she encountered the wondering smile on Jonathan's face as they went inside.

"Looks like the old battle axe has been tamed at last," he whispered, laughing softly in her ear.

Old dragon and now old battle axe! Jean stared at his back indignantly as he swung past her with her bag he had insisted on carrying. Then she grinned a little wryly. She probably had been all of those things once, but he had a lot to learn about the changes in her life these last few years.

Hilda insisted the car would be quite safe until they had eaten the meal she had prepared. "In fact, I'm sure it would be okay until morning," she said, smiling shyly at Jonathan.

"If it were my car, I wouldn't hesitate, but seeing it's not. . ." He shrugged.

"I'm so sorry about your house, Dr. Howard. Rance told me it was that bad windstorm that hit Brisbane about three weeks ago," Hilda said sympathetically. "But I'm really pleased at the chance to get to know such a good friend of my fiancé."

When Jean saw Jonathan's pleased look, she felt even more proud of her warmhearted niece. After unloading the car and stowing the luggage in their rooms, they rejoined Hilda, and Jean gave in to her curiosity and asked one of the many questions she needed answering.

"How do you happen to know Rance, Jonathan?"

She was immediately rewarded by his brilliant smile. "I met him soon after he started coming to the church in Sydney I was attending. He had not been a Christian for long and still had to sort out some problems from his past. At that time I badly needed his enthusiasm and excitement in his newfound faith in Christ."

He shrugged, and Jean saw that shadow of pain cross his face again. "We just clicked. He's a wonderful young man and sharing with him at that particular time in my own life helped me very much as well. Later he became one of my most reliable prayer supporters when my trips overseas started."

He had answered one question but Jean's thirst for knowledge had barely been quenched.

Although there was no further opportunity that evening for him to satisfy her curiosity, Hilda told her more the next morning while they shared an early cup of coffee.

"Rance was absolutely thrilled that Dr. Howard would be home and able to be at our wedding. Apparently, he helped Rance tremendously to get away from the crowd he had been running around with before he became a Christian."

She pulled a face. "From what he's told me, my Rance

was a wild lad then, into drugs and goodness knows what else. He still doesn't like to talk about it much. Dr. Howard took him through basic Bible studies about his new faith and was always there for him as he sorted out his life.

"He was very supportive, including financially, when Rance was in theological college studying for the ministry. At the time he was having problems with his own son, and I believe he got Rance to talk to him."

"His son?"

Hilda nodded. "I think he's in America at the moment."

Jean toyed with her cup, trying to remember if he had ever mentioned a son. Perhaps all those years ago she had just tuned out painful reminders of his unavailability.

"And what about Rance's son?" Jean said to change the subject. "How's young Nathan doing?"

Hilda's face softened. "Getting more and more excited about Christmas and the wedding—in that order too, the poor little scrap. This first Christmas with Rance is showing us again how much he's missed out on."

Jean already knew about the woman Rance had been living with before his commitment to Christ. He had completely cut himself off from her when he was battling the temptation of going back to his old lifestyle. But she had been unable to break her drug addiction and had only this last year, just before she succumbed to AIDS, contacted him to tell him they had a son from those wild days. He had been devastated at the news, but now Nathan was his joy and delight as well as a typical bundle of nine-year-old mischief.

"That old life Rance experienced is one of the reasons why he's had so much success ministering to others caught up in similar lifestyles," Jean said softly. "God has been working all things in his life out 'for good.'"

Hilda beamed at her proudly. Her love for Rance glowed from her, and Jean could not help contrasting this contented woman with the distraught girl of the past year.

"Oh, Hildie, I'm so glad you're my very own flesh and blood," Jean burst out in a choked voice. "You're such a great woman. My sister would have been so proud of you."

Hilda was across the room in a flash.

After a couple of hugs and a few tears, Jean pushed her away. "Gracious me, you've turned me into as big a crybaby as yourself!"

Hilda merely kissed her again and smiled mistily. "I don't know what I would have done without you this year. Your own faith and certainty of God's goodness and love has helped me more than you'll ever know."

She looked over Jean's shoulder and said with mild confusion, "Oh, Dr. Howard, I didn't realize you were up yet."

Jean took her time turning around and wishing him good morning, hoping all traces of her tears had gone.

He looked at her keenly as he advanced into the room. "Good morning, Jean." He hesitated, and then added softly, "Forgive me for overhearing what Hilda just said, but have you become a Christian since St. Kilda days, Jean?"

"Yes," she said as softly. "Putting my trust in Christ has transformed my life."

She felt the warmth radiate through her at the wonder and the joy she had known these last few years because of the most important decision she had ever made, and saw its reflection in the smile that filled his face.

"I'm glad," he said simply.

"You should be," she said, smiling a little shyly at him. "I've longed to tell you for years the impact your own faith in Christ had on my life."

His eyes widened.

"Oh, I always knew that you prayed for and even sometimes with your patients. Some of them told me," she added hastily. "Most who mentioned it were so astonished that you bothered. It's not that you ever said much, but. . ."

She stopped. How could she tell him about the time she had burst into the staff room to find him reading the Bible? After he had gone she had picked up the book he had left on the table and been taken aback to find out what it was.

That particular day had been one of turmoil. It had only dawned on her earlier that morning that her affection for the handsome Dr. Howard was much, much deeper than a woman with a wedding dress already hanging in her cupboard should have.

Desperately seeking answers, after her shift that day she had searched until she found her own old Bible, which had not been opened for years, and started to read.

"Do you pray for your patients now, Aunt Jean?"

Jonathan was delightfully disheveled although his jaw was now revealed in all its square strength. He looked wonderful and Jean quickly turned away, feeling the warmth in her cheeks increase as she focused on Hilda and then nodded.

"Of course, and I even pray for a pesky niece, too," she said teasingly, keeping her eyes averted from the tall figure who was pulling out a chair and sitting at the table beside her.

"Knowing you, you've been praying for me ages before we even knew we were related."

"I. . .I hope you'll pray for me, too, Jean."

Jean risked turning to face him and caught his piercing glance. There was that touch of pain in his eyes again before he looked away.

"I've been finding hanging onto faith in a loving God very difficult these last few weeks," he admitted candidly.

There was no way Jean could tell him how often and how much she had prayed about and for him these last few years, so she just nodded. "Of course I will, Johnny," she said softly.

Warmth tinged her cheeks as he smiled gently, and she realized she had used her special name for him once again.

Chapter 4

Jonathan was quiet while he ate the breakfast Hilda prepared. As Hilda chattered away about the plans for the wedding and all the things she wanted Jean to help her with, Jean exchanged a couple of little smiles with him in mutual amusement at the excitement of the bride-to-be.

After he had finished he pushed his chair back and stood up, interrupting Hilda in full flight. "I wonder if you'd mind if I commandeered Jean for a little while, Hilda?"

Although he had phrased his request politely, his was the tone of the autocratic surgeon who thought he only had to crook his little finger and susceptible young nurses would rush to do his bidding. *Well,* Jean thought to herself, *I'm neither young nor susceptible any longer.*

Staring up at him indignantly, she saw the slight twitch at the corner of his mouth and knew he was laughing at her. She was sure of it when he added blandly, "We have ten years of catching up to do, and she's going for a walk with me down to the sheds."

As they started across the yard, Jean began to chuckle.

She heard the answering amusement in his voice

as he said mockingly, "For a moment there I thought Sister Drew was going to make sure I never got above meself agin!"

She laughed outright. "Was I really that bad?"

"Most definitely! Many times over the years when I've started to fling orders around, I'd remember a certain lady with her hands on her hips reminding me coldly that the nurses took their orders from her, not some cocky young surgeon still wet behind the ears!"

"I never said any such thing."

"Perhaps not, but your flashing blue eyes said it all for you."

"So what brought it on this time? Thought I needed rescuing, did you?"

"Well, your beautiful blue eyes did start to rather glaze over when she started talking about the clothes they are planning for young Nathan to wear. Besides, I wanted to see what you'd do," he added impishly.

Warmth flooded through Jean. She couldn't really remember the last time she had felt so protected and cared for. Her personality was such that she was the one who sorted things out for others.

She laughed with delight. "Well, that did come rather quickly on top of what was happening to get a dress for Beth Smith, her matron of honor."

"Beth Smith?"

"She's the daughter of my friend Marian Stevens and was Hilda's neighbor until her own marriage."

"Oh, is that Arthur Canley-Smith's wife? Rance wrote to me about his accident and the way he's now getting the use of his legs back." His voice deepened. "He was so delighted and encouraged when Arthur committed his life to Christ publicly—and right after he had preached his first sermon in his new church in Brisbane."

Jean beamed. "That was a glorious day. We'd all been praying so much for Beth and Arthur."

Jonathan smiled gently back at her, and then said quietly, "I can't begin to tell you how thrilled I am about your faith in Christ and to hear you talking so naturally about prayer, Jean."

"It's strange, I'm usually much more reserved," Jean heard herself saying thoughtfully, and then added quickly, "but then you were always very easy to talk to, Jonathan."

"Yes, we did enjoy some good talks, didn't we, Jean?" There was a strange note in his voice, but then he said, "Hilda seems a fine Christian as well as a delightful young woman. She seems to be coping with the traumas of this last year very well."

"Yes," Jean agreed, hesitating. "How much has Rance told you about what happened, Jonathan? Did he mention Jim Stevens and Gail?"

"He told me that after her mother had died, Hilda had mistaken her friendship with Jim for the love of her life. She was devastated when she found out he had fallen in love with Gail Brandon."

"Did he tell you about Hilda's father's death?"

He nodded. "It was a tough time for both of them, especially so soon after her mother had died. Rance was trying to come to grips with finding out about Nathan as well as trying to help Hilda through the double grief of losing her father and then finding out about her adoption."

"And it all led back to my sister," Jean said softly.

"Rance has sung your praises almost as much as he's raved about the beautiful woman he's going to marry. I still can't believe that the Aunt Jean he referred to is my very own Jean Drew from years ago."

His very own. . .

A great longing filled Jean. She looked swiftly up at him. There was such a teasing, tender light in his face that Jean's eyes blurred and she stumbled on a deep rut in the black soil.

He reached out and grasped her arm to steady her. "Oops, can't let the bride's aunt break a leg before the big day."

Jean managed to smile back up at him. "Well, she'd be in the hands of the best surgeon she ever worked with if she needed surgery."

He smiled gently back at her but a shadow briefly touched his face before he looked away.

They walked on silently and somehow Jean found her hand remained clasped firmly in his strong one.

They inspected the huge tractor and other pieces of equipment in a large shed. Jim was still using the huge harvester on the Stevens property after finishing the harvest here first.

"The arrangement for Jim to share-farm this place with Hilda should work out very well," Jonathan said thoughtfully. "It is a shame the Garretts didn't have a son to carry on the place."

Then Jean said a little hesitantly, "Jonathan, Hilda said your son's in the USA. I've been trying to remember if you mentioned him years ago."

The hand in hers tensed and he was silent so long she looked up at him inquiringly, wondering whether he resented her wanting to know about him.

"I probably forgot to mention Robert." His tone was tinged with sarcasm and bitterness.

Jean pulled her hand away. "I'm sorry, I shouldn't have—" She took a couple of hasty steps away from him but his quiet "Jean" stopped her.

She turned reluctantly toward him. He was standing with his hands tucked into the back pockets of his old well-washed jeans. His shoulders were hunched forward and he suddenly kicked hard at a clump of dirt.

"From several things you've said yesterday, Jean, I gather that you think me some kind of wonderful person. The truth is, ten years ago I may have been a good surgeon, but I was a miserable failure as a father and a husband."

She stared blankly at him, not knowing how to respond to the raw pain and self-condemnation in his face.

"As you know, the study and training it takes to become a doctor is very demanding. Sandra and I met when I was a second-year med student and she was a second-year nurse. We married as soon as she finished her training."

He stopped and Jean's heart ached as she saw him become lost in memories. At last she prompted gently,

"You were both so young."

He gave a bitter laugh and started to walk slowly again toward the shade of a couple of old gum trees. Jean caught up with him and boldly slipped her hand around his elbow. His own came to rest on it.

"We were both twenty-one, old enough perhaps in years, but now I know she was a lot more mature than I. During all those years of study at university I drifted away from a close relationship with Christ and became incredibly selfish about my own career. Not long before her death, when I was working with you, in fact, I realized how weak my faith had become."

"Surely she would have understood your dedication to your job?"

"She was wonderful."

Jean wasn't sure if her need to know about him included hearing just how wonderful his wife had been!

But she remained silent, and after a moment he said, "She rarely complained, except when she felt I was neglecting Robert too much. Even then I would try and not miss out on his special days, but there were few I ever managed to share with them. It took me years to build a relationship with Robert after she died."

"How old was he then?"

"Sixteen, and believe me, he didn't hold back one word of what he thought of his father."

Jean thought of the hurting teenagers over the years she had tried to comfort when someone close to them had died. So many of them had erupted into rage as well as bewildered grief.

"But surely by now he must know—"

"He knows his father spent so much time on his precious patients he wasn't home when his family needed him!" he exploded. "Even when Sandra had been begging me to drive her to visit her mother in Newcastle I didn't have time." His voice choked on the old pain and guilt.

"Jonathan. . ."

It was as though he hadn't heard her as he continued in a low, tortured voice. "Her mother had cancer and had been told she should have another course of chemotherapy which she was refusing. Sandra wanted me to talk to her. I had two full days in theater and booked the next day to drive her to Newcastle, but then just as we were ready to leave there was that inevitable call from the hospital. It was one of the rare times Sandra became really angry with me and said she'd go by herself, as usual. She went for an early morning swim. If I'd been there. . ."

He paused to take a deep breath. "The few times I did go with her we enjoyed that time of the day with the surf to ourselves. No one knows what happened. She disappeared and her body was washed up two days later."

This time it was Jonathan who peeled her suddenly clenched hand from him and strode furiously away.

His face had been filled with such pain, she let him go without protesting. Her heart lifted him up in prayer as she watched him stop and lean against the gnarled trunk of a tree and stare out across the bleached wheat stubble.

She felt stunned. When they had seen each other almost every day she had thought he was one man who had it all together, his career, marriage, and especially his faith and relationship with God coexisting harmoniously.

She longed to follow him but he obviously needed to be alone, perhaps even to pray alone. Reluctantly, she returned to the house.

She was helping Hilda make out lists of things still to be done for Christmas as well as the wedding when she at last heard his steps on the veranda. When he appeared just before lunch it was obvious he had managed to get some sleep.

He still looked bleary-eyed and rumpled as he said, "Sorry if I'm late. Afraid I fell asleep."

His voice was husky with sleep, and Jean busied herself pouring out a cup of tea so she did not have to look at him.

"Please don't ever feel you've got to apologize," Hilda said gently. "Rance warned me you would need lots of sleep and time to recuperate after Africa. I want you to feel free to come and go as you please."

Jean looked up swiftly to find his eyes on her as he sat down at the table. "As far as I'm concerned, there's certainly no need to apologize either," she added. Her eyes were steady on his until she saw a smile creep into them.

"Thank you" was all that he said, but she knew he understood she hadn't meant being late for a meal.

In the following days Jean found that Jonathan Howard crept into her prayers constantly, both during her set-aside morning prayer time as well as throughout the day. To her increasing disappointment, however, she didn't see as much of him alone as she would have liked. She was busy with Hilda and he seemed content to spend most of his time sleeping, reading, or going for long, solitary walks.

She sensed that he was still trying to cope with his experiences in Africa, even before coming home to a damaged house. Almost fearfully, she also hoped his talking about his wife and son had not added too much to the stress he was under.

Rance phoned and expressed his disappointment at not being able to get out to the farm for another couple of days because Nathan had the flu. When he did arrive at last early one morning, it thrilled Jean to see the delight in both men's faces as they shook hands and then hugged each other boisterously.

Then they had wandered off and spent hours in deep conversation. Jonathan reentered the house with a lighter step and his old laugh rang out several times that evening as he joined her in teasing Rance and Hilda. Suddenly Jean remembered Elijah the prophet. He, too, had needed physical rest and God's ministry to him after a battle with evil.

She was considerably relieved and yet somehow felt rebuffed and saddened that it had been Rance who had been able to help him. It was only as she was standing at her bedroom window staring out across the moonlit paddocks that she acknowledged to herself that her old feelings for Jonathan were returning and could become stronger than before.

"You stupid, stupid woman," she scolded herself out loud. "He still doesn't show in any way that he likes you any more than he ever did. Besides, you're over forty years old!"

That didn't stop the ache in her heart but it did drive her to her Bible and to prayer.

God had been teaching her many lessons the last few years. That night, when she eventually turned her light off, she immediately fell asleep. Peace had again filled her heart. She still didn't have any direct guidance, but one thing she did know: A loving heavenly Father was in control and He was still weaving the pattern for her life as she loved and trusted Him. Her pattern may not include Jonathan Howard, but God's grace would be sufficient.

Chapter 5

J ean had mixed feelings that Hilda had waited to buy her dress and veil until her aunt could go with her. While she was thrilled, at the same time it emphasized their relationship and her own new responsibilities to this delightful young woman.

She was relieved to find out that Hilda had done some initial looking, including a trip to some big bridal-wear shops in Brisbane. But as she had said with considerable frustration to Jean that first evening, she had ended up with too many ideas and too many choices, "and it wasn't fun at all since Gail and Aunt Marian were too busy with the harvest to come with me."

While Jonathan watched silently, Hilda had then hugged Jean again with that sparkle of excitement that reminded Jean so much of her sister. How she wished her sister could have lived to know her beautiful daughter!

"Oh, I'm just so pleased you're here to come shopping with me before the Christmas rush," Hilda said, her eyes brimming with tears.

The day after Rance's visit they set off for their first shopping excursion. Jonathan had laughed quietly behind Hilda's back as he assured them he would quite enjoy a day by himself.

But despite her initial reluctance, as Hilda tugged her excitedly from one shop to another, Jean began to enjoy herself immensely. For the first time in well over twenty years Jean felt she had someone who belonged just to her, and she felt part of a real family.

When she realized Hilda would soon belong to a husband as well, she felt a momentary tug of self-pity which she dismissed angrily. After all, there was no way she would ever want Hilda to know the loneliness she had experienced.

As Jean discussed animatedly their successful shopping expedition that evening over tea, she saw Jonathan's eyes twinkling understandingly at her. He had been a little distant since he had told her about his wife and she felt a sudden flood of happiness. She grinned happily back at him and then saw the smile in his eyes suddenly disappear.

Hastily she looked away. Hilda was looking at them both and then slowly smiled at Jonathan. Jean looked quickly back at him. His eyes were on his food but she saw the slight smile on his lips.

She took in little of Hilda's excited discourse the rest of the meal. Feeling rebuffed again, she wasn't at all prepared later for his comment when the two of them were clearing the kitchen for Hilda. "And now, what about me?"

Jean looked up and stared at him blankly. A wave of relief swept through her when she saw he was smiling. She smiled back at him and asked crisply, "What about you, Dr. Howard?"

"It's my turn now, don't you think?"

"Your turn for what?"

"For spending some time with you, and for you to help me with my shopping, of course."

His eyes were twinkling and she laughed outright. "Is this that same decisive, extremely competent Jonathan Howard I used to know who kept the whole theater staff on their toes? I doubt if you needed help to buy things even when you were a small boy!"

"But I hate shopping, especially for clothes and especially Christmas presents for people I don't even know."

Christmas presents!

Jean's smile faltered. How could she have forgotten about them! In the past she had sent out a few cards, only buying small gifts for some of the staff she would work with on Christmas Day.

Even since becoming a Christian she'd had to battle these feelings each year, that Christmas was a time to remind her how alone she was in the world. But this year she had Hilda to buy for, and now there was Jonathan. She exhaled slowly.

Jonathan was watching her with a slight frown. "I take it you are going with Rance and Hilda to his mother and stepfather's place for Christmas dinner?"

Jean nodded. "You're going, too?"

Somehow she felt immensely relieved. As much as she'd wanted to spend Christmas with Hilda, she had been diffident about intruding on Rance's family.

"With Robert still away, and with my house situation,

137

I couldn't very well say no." He hesitated, and then said slowly, "Besides being the celebration of our Savior's birth, I've discovered Christmas can be the loneliest time of the year and a day I've sometimes wished would disappear from the calendar."

"Oh, you feel like that, too?"

He nodded grimly and then his face gradually relaxed into a thoughtful smile. "But somehow, this year seems different."

To her secret astonishment, in the days that followed Jean found he was right. This year was very different. She found herself enjoying writing down a list of all the people she would be spending Christmas and Boxing Day with, staring with tingling delight and amazement at the name of Jonathan Howard at the top of the list.

But their shopping excursion was soon put on hold. Before either had a chance to mention their plans to Hilda, she had started on a massive cleaning of the cupboards. They found her staring with considerable dismay at the contents of a large cupboard in the store-room attached to the laundry.

She turned and they saw the pain of old memories in her face. "I thought Dad had sorted out all of Mum's things, but it looks as though he just tossed a lot of them in here," she said with a catch in her voice.

Jean looked at Jonathan helplessly and he smiled understandingly at her. There was no way Jean could leave Hilda to do this heartrending task by herself.

Before they knew it, several days slipped by. Not only had the storeroom yielded up treasures and trash that needed dumping, but they found numerous other tasks that had to be done in the sheds. An easy comradeship developed between the three of them that Jean treasured. Jonathan automatically helped and fitted in as though they had known him all their lives.

Then at last Hilda insisted their shopping expedition could wait no longer. At the large shopping center in Toowoomba Jean found herself caught up in the excitement of the atmosphere of the brightly decorated shops and the bustling Christmas crowds.

For a while she and Jonathan wandered around watching an animated display of cartoon characters that enchanted groups of wide-eyed children. Another scene showed a typical snow-covered pine forest with many varieties of animals peeping out at them.

Despite the air-conditioning Jean wiped at the perspiration on her face. "Wouldn't mind a bit of real snow right now!"

"I never know why we always have so many displays at Christmas with Northern Hemisphere snow scenes," Jonathan growled. "Look, they've even got pots of red and white poinsettias for sale when ours always flower in July. And I don't see even one wombat, koala, or kangaroo."

Jean tried to hide a smile as she had often thought the same. But she chided him gently, "I once spent Christmas in England and it was a really beautiful white Christmas. It was a lot prettier than a dusty, Aussie outback scene that most people seem to think so typifies us." She gave a chuckle and pointed. "But you're wrong; this time someone else must agree with you."

"You know, I've been realizing more and more since I've been going on these trips overseas, that we Aussies don't really have any specifically Australian traditions at Christmas," Jonathan said thoughtfully, and even a little regretfully. "I am often asked what they are, but when I try to explain I realize I'm describing traditions that are not peculiar to us but the same as found in America and England—ah, that's more like it!"

Another display showed Santa's sleigh being pulled by several large kangaroos across a typical outback scene of red dirt and sparse vegetation.

"Hmm, somehow it looks all wrong," Jean said with her head tilted to one side. "Give me reindeer any day."

They moved on and both stopped before a rough bark and timber construction that sheltered a beautiful, natural nativity scene.

"Now, that's something we all have in common," Jonathan whispered.

Jean couldn't speak. She stared at baby Jesus in His mother's arms. Along with Joseph and Mary, there were animals, and the shepherds and wise men looking to where a single bright beam of light shone from the star down onto the baby Jesus. The brightness of that light cast all except Jesus into shadows.

Jonathan reached out his hand and Jean felt her fingers curl around his. They stood very still for several long moments and then looked at each other. Jonathan's eyes were suspiciously bright and Jean smiled gently at him through her own wet lashes as he squeezed her hand.

There was no need for words. Both had worshiped and paid homage to the real reason for Christmas.

Together they chose gifts for Hilda, Rance, and the entire Stevens clan before tackling the difficult task of buying small gifts for Rance's family neither had ever met. It took them some time to buy just the right gift for Jonathan's son, Robert. Jean was surprised at how hesitant and unsure the usually decisive doctor became and she wondered again about Jonathan's relationship with his twenty-something son.

She found her heart aching for both of them when he said wistfully, "I do wish he could come home for Christmas."

But at last a book about Australian birds and a good dress shirt were purchased. As they left the last shop Jean said triumphantly, "Now there's just Nathan. What do nine-year-old boys like these days, Jonathan?"

He grinned and a look of anticipation spread over his face. "I really don't know, but it's going to be fun finding out!"

And it was. They spent more time in the sprawling toy shop than any other, and Jean was sure they had played with every conceivable variation of truck, car, superhero, and computer game before Jonathan at last made his choices.

She was still laughing as they unloaded their purchases into his car. "I hope Rance and Hilda will appreciate the piercing siren on that fire truck."

"From what I've seen of your loving niece, she'll be too thrilled at watching that boy enjoying himself. Rance told me he had a pretty deprived life until he found out about him."

Jean nodded. "It's absolutely incredible the difference in him now, but he's lost a lot of his childhood."

"Well, these should help make up just a little."

"More than just a little," she exclaimed and then laughed. "What if everyone else has the same idea of buying several gifts for him? I know Rance has already bought him heaps of stuff and will probably spoil him rotten this Christmas, too."

"Well, kids make Christmas extra special and I haven't had kids in my Christmas for far too long."

Jean silently agreed. She had made it a point of visiting the children's ward each Christmas, but the pale-faced children not even allowed home at that time of the year had only increased her heartache.

"It'll be great fun watching him opening them all and besides, a bit of spoiling won't hurt him his first Christmas with his dad," Jonathan said softly as he looked at his watch. "My goodness, no wonder I'm hungry, it's almost afternoon teatime and we've yet to have lunch. I'm so sorry, Jean, I've been neglecting you."

"Neglecting me? After that huge chocolate muffin and ice cream you insisted I try for morning tea?"

He laughed back at her. "And which I helped you eat, don't forget. Now, where will it be, fast food or plain old fish and chips in the park?" he added teasingly.

She shuddered. "It's far too hot to go to the park."

After considering for a moment, she looked at him. "You told me you've never been to Toowoomba before, so I know just the right place."

Jonathan agreed heartily as they ate in the quiet, elegant restaurant perched at the top of the mountain range overlooking the beautiful Lockyer valley.

"You know, you haven't told me what made you commit your life to Christ, Jean," Jonathan said as they waited for their main course to be served. "I can't get over the difference in you. You're. . .you're so full of the sheer joy of living compared to the woman I remember."

Jean stared out of the window for a moment, wondering how much she should tell him. At last she looked back at him and said softly, "My life was in an absolute mess, and it was actually you who made me turn to the Bible for answers, my friend."

She smiled gently as confusion and then delighted surprise filled his bright eyes. She took a deep breath and continued quickly before her courage failed.

"As I got to know and. . .and like you, I realized there was something about you that was very different from other men. Remember that time one of the theater staff discovered he had an inoperable tumor? You had such compassion for him and spent so much time visiting him in the ward."

He dismissed that with an impatient gesture. "Plenty of other people do those kinds of things, Jean, not only believers."

"Yes, I know, but once I visited him just after you had

left. As it turned out, it was only a few days before he died, but at the time I couldn't get over the peace he had despite knowing he was terminally ill. I found myself blurting out something about it and he told me that you had led him to a personal relationship with God. Faith in Jesus Christ had taken away his fear of death and dying.

"One day," she continued quickly before he could comment, "in fact the same day I finished at the hospital, I happened to see the Bible you'd left behind in the staff room. But I was looking for pat answers and I discovered there was so much I didn't understand about what I read that I ended up with even more questions. Then my. . .my situation suddenly became worse and at last, in sheer desperation, I rang Marian Stevens. We'd been friends since our teens, but she had become too religious for me after she got married. We hadn't seen each other for years."

Jean paused, a smile lighting her face. "You know what that woman did after I blurted out to her on the phone some of my questions about God?"

"She wasn't happy to answer them only on the phone but flew down to Sydney to meet you," Jonathan said promptly, a tender look on his face that shook Jean to her depths.

She stared at him speechlessly and he added with a smile, "I asked Hilda if she knew when you became a Christian and she wasn't sure, just that Marian had gone racing off all the way to Sydney and later you had accepted Christ as your personal Lord and Savior."

"Well, er, yes," Jean said weakly, feeling secretly thrilled that he had been interested enough to want to know about her.

There had been more to it than that. She was thankful Marian had kept her secret, and for a moment she wondered if she dared tell him. Then the waiter brought their meals and the moment was gone.

Jonathan seemed thoughtful but she was glad that he did not return to the subject. Instead, he started chatting away about the upcoming wedding and Christmas celebrations.

"So, are you going to brave Boxing Day with the Stevens clan, Jonathan?" she asked as they lingered over a final cup of coffee. "Every year they go to the river for a bush picnic. We eat leftover Christmas ham, turkey, cake, and lamingtons, and of course watermelon for a hot day."

"Wouldn't miss it for the world," he said cheerfully.

The absolute delight that filled her was disturbing. She was falling deeper and deeper under this man's spell and something inside her warned caution. This man still had the power to hurt her too much. Besides, she had been learning to seek out what God wanted in her life, and so far she didn't know His will on this relationship.

Later that night she escaped to her room with an anxious, wondering heart. "Jean Drew, get a grip on yourself!" she scolded as she stared into the mirror. "The man's already caused you enough grief. Face reality, you're too old now for all this falling in love nonsense!"

But she knew that wasn't necessarily true. When she was with Jonathan she felt so much younger than her forty-plus years. And was there any age when a woman was too old to fall deeply in love with an attractive, dynamic man?

Had she ever stopped loving Jonathan Howard?

Chapter 6

It was a long night for Jean. Part of it she spent in prayer and seeking help from scripture. Once again she fervently wished that God could tell her directly what He wanted of her in this situation. At last she fell into a restless sleep, and then awakened with little heart or energy for Hilda's task of the day.

"I do hope you don't mind, Jonathan," Hilda was saying when Jean arrived late for breakfast. She turned and greeted Jean quietly and then turned back to the two large boxes on the kitchen table. "Mum and Dad always liked the house to look festive for Christmas and New Years," she added wistfully.

Jean caught Jonathan's eyes and recognized instantly the warning in them. It was unnecessary. She, too, had seen the moist brightness in her niece's eyes.

"More things to sort through, Hilda?" she asked gently.

"Well, kind of, but I'm not sure I'll be wanting to toss any of these out before the removalist takes my things to the manse in Brisbane." As she spoke, she reached into the box and pulled out a bundle of shining tinsel streamers. "Mum always made a big thing of putting up decorations each year. She said if we did it for our own parties we should do the very best we can to celebrate our Lord's birth."

"It's been quite a few years since I bothered with more than just a wreath on my front door," Jonathan mused and then turned toward Jean. There was a distinct glint in his eyes as he said challengingly, "Well, Sister Drew, are you going to help us put up some Christmas decorations?"

How could she maintain that protective shield around her heart, which she had decided last night was her only defense against this man's impact on her senses, when he looked at her this way?

Jonathan's face was filled with boyish enthusiasm as he climbed the stepladder again to adjust the red, green, and white streamers they had just erected in the lounge room.

"How's that, Hilda?" he called down in his deep voice that always pulled on some inner chord of Jean's being.

"Perfect!"

As he flashed his radiant smile at her niece, Jean knew her resistance to him had once again plummeted to a low ebb. Perfect indeed! Only she didn't mean the hanging bells and the paper and foil decorations!

As she watched him, she realized how different he was from the worn-out, dispirited man who had first arrived at the farm. Perhaps Rance had known how much he would need the peace and quiet here.

Jean's dilemma of the night before slowly faded into the background as the morning progressed. Doing this simple family activity seemed so normal and natural with Jonathan. She could not remember the last time she'd had so much fun, or felt as young as Hilda.

It seemed as if every childish decoration that Hilda had ever made and dragged home from school must have been kept by her parents. What could have been a tearful time full of memories was circumvented by the antics of Jonathan. Jean felt helpless as her admiration for him continued to grow.

Constantly teasing Hilda and herself, he suggested strange places like the bathroom to put some of the more outrageous decorations until everything in the boxes had been used and the house was transformed.

He even held a crude, cut out picture, which they decided was supposed to be mistletoe, over Hilda and gave her a smacking kiss, saying with mock fear, "Seeing as we don't have any of the real thing and as long as you don't tell on me to Rance." Then he had turned toward Jean with a special gleam in his eyes, but she had beaten a hasty retreat. She merely scowled at him a little later as he muttered, "Chicken!" when Hilda's attention was elsewhere.

All morning Jean had found it difficult to drag her eyes away from Jonathan's animated face. Never before had anyone—except this same incredible man—had this impact on her.

Oh, God, I'm already in deep trouble here, she prayed silently several times, and she wondered helplessly what she could do short of packing her bags and removing herself from his vicinity. Hilda needed her, so that was out of the question. But then, she hadn't seen the man for ten years and that had done nothing to stop this quick return of her feelings toward him.

"Well, I think that must be the last of them." There was definite regret in Jonathan's voice as he climbed down from the stepladder and wiped his face with a crumpled linen handkerchief. "Phew, just as well, it's getting very hot. I could certainly do with a drink."

"One coming up." Jean was glad of the excuse to disappear into the kitchen, but as she carried a tray of glasses and ice-cold soft drinks back to the lounge room a few minutes later, she nearly tripped over the unwieldy coil of colored lights Jonathan was trying to unravel.

Hilda was looking doubtfully at him. "I don't think we need to do anything outside this year. After. . .after the wedding there won't be anyone here until Beth and Arthur move in."

She hid her face as she bent over the cable and Jonathan looked swiftly at her and then up at Jean inquiringly.

"Oh, Hilda, but aren't you still planning your yearly barbecue for Christmas Eve this year? Besides, don't stop him now," she managed to say with a teasing laugh, "I'm dying to see Dr. Howard clambering around under the eaves among the spiders and cobwebs. If only old Dr. Ferguson could see you now," she added for good measure as they exchanged smiles of relief and Hilda gave a rather shaky laugh.

Although it was obvious that Hilda loved Rance very much, it was also obvious what an upheaval it was for her to move from her old home. And suddenly Jean was fiercely glad Jonathan was here with her to share that knowledge, and to help make it as easy as possible for this niece she was learning to love more each day.

Not only did they end up stringing the lights around the outside of the house, there was also enough to loop around the lower branches of the old gum tree that gave shade on the hottest day to the back patio where Bob Garrett had built the outdoor barbecue. They had found a couple of long ladders for this task and had almost finished the tree when they heard the phone ring. Hilda dropped her end of the lights and raced to answer it.

Jean hesitated for a moment and then she reluctantly climbed up the ladder to help Jonathan. She had always hated heights and a few moments later thankfully started back down the ladder. She was congratulating herself on not doing anything foolish when her foot slipped.

She gave a startled yelp. The ladder tilted alarmingly and she started to fall. Suddenly strong arms grabbed her and the next thing she knew she went sprawling on top of Jonathan.

Winded, she lay still for a moment and then realized how tightly his arms were holding her. For one delicious moment she wished with all her heart she could stay wrapped and protected by them, but then he moved and she quickly started to push herself away.

"Th–thank you," she gasped and tried to scramble to her feet.

At that moment one large hand reached up and settled firmly on the nape of her neck. He tugged gently and she lost her balance and fell against him once more. Long fingers caressed her face as he drew her head down.

151

With a quickening heartbeat she stared into his dark, passion-filled eyes. The low moan that welled up in her throat was muffled as firm lips possessed hers. Then, suddenly, she was clinging to him and something deep inside her sprang to life.

Jean wasn't sure who pulled away first, but she realized he had moved and her head was being cradled against his shoulder as their breathing gradually returned to normal. Then it hit her what had happened and frantically she pulled away from him and scrambled to her feet.

"Jonathan, Aunt Marian wants to speak to you, too!" Hilda called from an open window.

He stood up slowly and they stared at each other. So many times in the days that followed she wished Hilda had not interrupted them just then. Perhaps he would have said something that would have explained the startled, arrested look on his face as he looked at her.

When he had disappeared inside the house, she stood for a moment with her hand touching her quivering lips.

"Aunt Jean, you'll never guess what's happened."

She turned and stared blindly at Hilda for a moment and then realized she was saying something about Beth and her husband.

"What did you say, Hilda?"

Her niece looked at her closely. "Anything wrong, Aunt Jean?"

"No, no, I'm sorry. You were saying something about Beth and Arthur." Even to her own ears her voice sounded strange and she turned away and reached down to pick up the ladder.

"Aunt Marian just rang to say that they've been given a fortnight's notice to get out of the house they were renting in Brisbane."

Jean swung around. Hilda nodded at her and added, "She's absolutely furious. Fancy giving a young family such short notice with Christmas so close! They rang Aunt Marian to ask if they could move in with her until after the wedding, but I told her that's ridiculous. I told her they should move straight here where they were going to anyway at the end of January when Art starts working for Jim."

Hilda took a deep breath and looked worried. "So, Aunt Marian's inviting Jonathan to stay over there for the rest of his stay. I do hope he doesn't mind."

Jean longed to cry out, "No, he can't go! Not when I haven't seen enough of him yet after all these years. Not when I've just realized how much I love him."

The thought almost stunned her as much as his kiss. She swallowed rapidly, trying to think rationally as well as find her voice.

"He won't mind," she managed simply at last, her voice sounding husky. Then before her courage faded she cleared her throat and said, "Hilda, this house only has four bedrooms."

She paused, hoping her niece would not be upset at her suggestion. "Don't you think it would make things much easier for all of you if I moved over to Marian's too? Her house is so much bigger. It's only five minutes away and we could still spend the days here together getting everything organized for Christmas as well as the wedding and the removal of your things to Brisbane."

Hilda's face dropped, and Jean added quickly, "There is no way I'll move until the day they are due to arrive. You won't have to spend another night here alone," she said understandingly and saw the relief on the young woman's face.

Jean could not read Jonathan's expression when he joined them and told them it was all arranged that he was to move to the Stevens home when the other family moved in.

Then her heart leaped when he added casually, "I hope you two don't mind, but I suggested to Mrs. Stevens that it might be a good idea if Jean came, too. It will save the brother and sister from having to share a room. From what you've both told me, their two youngsters have had enough unsettled months this last year or so, especially since Art's accident, and the sooner they get settled the better."

It was all said in the crisp, authoritative voice that Jean had heard many times and she relaxed. For years she'd always had to be the strong one, the organizer, the one others relied on and drew strength from. Here was someone who so naturally could shoulder her burdens as well as his own on his broad shoulders.

Then suddenly she knew she was wrong. From things he had said the last few weeks, she knew that he had learned not to shoulder his own burdens. He leaned very heavily on his Lord, handing everything over to Him.

Those first two days he had been exhausted and it had been only a passing moment of discouragement.

There was no doubt about Hilda's disappointment but she was very philosophical about it all. "At least with Art being able to walk again we don't have to worry about building those ramps for his wheelchair before they move here." Then her face lit up. "And there will be kids here for Christmas!"

"Mmm, then there's something we haven't finished yet." Jonathan's eyes twinkled at Jean's apparent discomfiture. "We haven't finished with the decorations yet."

She glared at him for a moment and then looked at Hilda who returned her glance with a slightly puzzled look before she turned back to Jonathan. "But we've put up so many already I don't think there's much room left," she said with a slight laugh.

He just smiled at Hilda and cocked one of those incredibly thick eyebrows.

Light dawned on Jean just as Hilda exclaimed, "A Christmas tree! The kids will want a tree!"

"I don't know about kids," Jean said wistfully, "but I haven't even erected an artificial one in years."

"Neither have I," agreed Jonathan.

Hilda looked from one to the other and Jean could see that for the first time she had begun to appreciate how different their Christmases had been from her own family-filled ones.

"Right," Hilda said briskly. "We won't get one until a couple of days before Christmas. With this heat they dry out and drop too much by Christmas despite the bucket of water we stand them in. But the job of getting it is the responsibility of you two while I finish clearing out the rooms. I have a horrible feeling the next few days are going to fly by with all that has to be crammed into them!"

But that wasn't the last of the phone calls that disrupted their program.

"The builder's going to be able to start work before Christmas after all and he wants me to come and finish choosing paint colors and carpets," Jonathan told them that evening after hanging up the phone. "It's a bit earlier than I'd wanted," he muttered as he stretched out in the lounge chair.

Jean stared at him, wondering if she'd heard him correctly. Under his scowl those thick eyebrows actually met in the middle. Then the incredible thought came to her: *He wants to spend even more time with me.*

He looked up so suddenly he caught her staring at him and she hurriedly looked away, something she had been doing a lot of since that kiss.

"Hilda, would you mind terribly if I steal Jean for another day?"

His voice was a little gruff and Jean's eyes swung back to him, her own widening.

Hilda looked from one to the other, something she also seemed to have been doing quite a bit that day. Her eyes started to twinkle.

"Well, as long as it's no more than a day, I think I can spare her. Remember, you promised to get the tree, and Jean was going with me for that last fitting of my dress. I want to have everything ready for the wedding so I can just concentrate on packing most of my things to make room for Beth's," she added with a beaming smile at him.

"Hey, just a moment," Jean protested. "What happened to asking if I wanted to go with you?" She was so confused by the rush of feelings a few minutes ago that she wasn't at all sure it would be wise being with him for a whole day.

Then as he smiled at her and said softly, "I really do need your help, Jean," all her resistance crumbled as she knew it always would with this man.

Later, traveling down the highway to Brisbane, she knew spending more time with him would make it even more heartbreaking if once again they had to say good-bye.

Chapter 7

J ean liked Jonathan's house immediately. It was set
on a couple of acres on the southern outskirts of
Brisbane, not too far from the glorious beaches of
the Gold Coast. Although the remains of the tree had
been removed, the tarpaulin still covered the damaged
roof.

While they avoided the bedroom where the ceiling
had fallen in, several other rooms were also in disarray
from the storm. Because the tree had come down in the
very center of the house, only the kitchen and laundry
had escaped relatively unscathed. However, Jean could
tell the rooms had been decorated with a quiet elegance
that would be very restful after a day dealing with sick
and injured patients.

I could live very happily in this house, she found
herself thinking wistfully, and then felt her cheeks burn
as she hurried after Jonathan.

The stench of mildew and rotting wool made Jean
wrinkle her nose. "Phew, I see what you mean about
new carpets."

"And new curtains," Jonathan added grimly. "By the
time I got home they had all gone moldy as well. That's

what happens in a subtropical place like Brisbane. I managed to toss the curtains out but the carpet had to wait. When I eventually got here there were still pools of water on them that had been there for days. I mopped the water off as much as I could. I suspect we'll need more hot days to dry the floor after they are taken out."

While they waited for the builder to keep his appointment, they looked over the carpet, fabric, and wallpaper samples Jonathan had already acquired. Jean knew that Jonathan had made good money over the years but she was impressed that he was not even considering more lavish, expensive replacements. Then again, she mused, from what he had told her about his stints overseas, she was sure his own money had financed the majority of those projects.

The builder arrived on time and was so brisk and competent that when he did leave, Jonathan looked at his watch with satisfaction. "Great, as I hoped we have most of the afternoon to ourselves. After we find some lunch, how would you like to take me to meet Beth and her husband and kids?"

Jean stared at him and then slowly smiled. "You were planning this all along, weren't you?" she accused.

He grinned back. "I just thought if I were in their shoes I'd feel pretty bad about guests having to move out so they can move in. If they meet me I'm sure they'll feel better about it all."

And once again, Jean realized later, this amazing man was proved right. It was obvious as soon as they met Arthur that he was not only annoyed about having to move so soon, but very embarrassed when introduced to Jonathan.

Jonathan cut across Arthur's apologies immediately. "It's I who am imposing on your family, and I'm only too happy to move a few kilometers or so as long as Jean comes with me. We haven't seen each other for ten years and we still have a lot of catching up to do."

Jean felt her cheeks catch fire as Arthur stared at her. She was absolutely speechless as she gaped at Jonathan, who was looking at her blandly, a fact that did not escape Arthur.

Arthur grinned wickedly at her. "I'm very glad to hear that," he said, and then took pity on her and changed the subject by asking Jonathan about his friendship with the "Rev," as he called Rance.

Jean stood up quickly and muttered something about seeing how the kids were and escaped to the backyard where Jacqueline and Robbie were playing with their collie puppy.

As the children bubbled over with excitement about moving back to the farm life they loved, Beth said something about their packing that set Jean thinking.

"No problem," Jean said cheerfully, noticing Jonathan had joined them. "The children have started their summer holidays, haven't they?" When Beth nodded, she asked hurriedly, "Would you like to have us take them back so you could concentrate on packing and moving?"

Jean glanced at Jonathan as she spoke and saw surprise flash into his face. She looked quickly back at

Beth who was shaking her head.

"That would be lovely to get them out of our hair, Aunt Jean. But Mum said she was coming down to help us and I don't like leaving them with Jim and Gail when they are still finishing off getting the crop to the railway terminal."

"Oh, I'm sure Jean and I could handle a couple of kids for a few days until you arrive, don't you, Jean?" Jonathan's voice held a smile in it, but his eyes were watching her with a challenging glint. "I happen to know Hilda is all for the idea. I've already asked her."

Jean was lost for words. Then a warm feeling swept over her. They thought alike about so many things and she enjoyed this forceful man taking control.

It was a rush to pack as much as they could cram into the car for the children, have tea, and set off before it became too late. The collie dog, Bonnie, was also established between the two children on the backseat. Although at the start of the trip the children's tongues wagged furiously with excitement, they had traveled not even halfway when all noise and movement ceased in the back of the car.

"All asleep at last?" Jonathan murmured after Jean had twisted around and surveyed the sleeping children.

"Yes, thank goodness," Jean said with heartfelt relief.

He smiled at her and she relaxed in a pleasant haze of weariness. After a comfortable silence she said softly, "You're very good with the children, Jonathan."

"So are you, Jean. It's a shame—"

He stopped abruptly and it took her a moment to realize what he had been going to say. It was a shame she had never had children of her own. Suddenly she longed fiercely for at least one child she could have watched develop and grow. Now her childbearing years were slipping away so very quickly.

It was almost as though he could read her mind when he murmured, "It's wonderful how medical science has made it possible for older women to safely have children."

Emotion clogged her throat for a moment. "I'm not sure if having older parents is really the best for a child."

"It worked okay for Hilda, didn't it? Rance told me her parents were in their forties when they adopted her. Besides, it apparently didn't worry God how old Abraham and Sarah were when He gave Isaac to them, did it?"

"And what about you, Jonathan, would you like another child at your age?"

Jean had blurted out the words before she could stop herself. There was a long silence and the easy atmosphere between them was gone. She was annoyed with herself for not passing his comment off lightly.

"I do know one thing. I'd very much like a chance to make up for the mistakes I made with Robert." He stopped abruptly and then added, "It would entirely depend on who the mother was."

She felt him turn and look at her. Suddenly she could hardly breathe. She didn't dare move.

"If she were committed to doing God's will and that

is what His will was," he continued in the same soft murmur, "then the answer would have to be yes."

Somehow she plucked up the courage to turn and look at him then. He darted a quick glance at her before returning his attention to the road.

"How does a person find out what God's will is for something so important, Jonathan?" she whispered desperately.

After a long pause she saw his shoulders move in a shrug. "I believe God shows each of His children His will in ways that are right for that individual. What is right for me may not be right for you. You have to find His way for you, Jean," he added gently.

Nothing more was said that night, but in the busy days that followed his words haunted her. She was sure he had been trying to say more to her than had been on the surface. Was he actually thinking it was possible for them to have a relationship?

Dare she even wonder if he were thinking of marriage, even perhaps of having a child together?

Her prayers and heart-searching intensified. For many years now she had put all thoughts of marriage behind her. Even if Jonathan were growing to love her, could a marriage between them work?

Above all, what was God's will for them, and how and when would she find out?

Chapter 8

S uddenly it was Christmas Eve. To the children's delight, a beautifully decorated pine tree filled a corner of the lounge room. Jonathan and Jean had enlisted their help to choose just the right one and then to decorate it. A tenderness, and a deepening sense of intimacy, had developed between the couple as they had helped the children, and some days Jean had found herself drifting along in an unbelieving haze.

Hilda's wedding dress was safely hanging in her bedroom and all her things had been moved to Brisbane except what she needed for the next week. Jonathan and Jean had moved without any fuss to Marian Stevens's house the day the removalist had arrived with the Canley-Smiths' belongings.

"Well, the house is still in a mess, but no one seems too worried about it at all," Jonathan had commented with considerable amusement as he drove the short distance back to the Stevens home late that evening after spending all day helping the family to unpack and settle in.

Jean had just smiled wearily at him, closed her eyes, and been almost asleep when he finally stopped the car. There had been more important things to do than unpack everything and keep the place tidy. The Christmas shopping was all done. Food that could be stored in the freezer had been prepared for the barbecue on Christmas Eve and the picnic on Boxing Day.

The women were thankful that Rance and Beth's mothers had been adamant that, with all the upheaval, Christmas Day was their sole responsibility this year.

When she awoke on Christmas Eve morning, the first thing Jean remembered was the tender amusement in Jonathan's voice as he had helped her from the car and led her straight to her room. A tender, gentle wisp of a kiss had brushed her mouth as he left her at her door.

She lay there for a few minutes listening to the warbling of a couple of magpies in the pepperina trees near her bedroom window. Her sleep had been deep and peaceful. The last few days had been too busy to spend much time considering her future, but she knew that the tension and awareness between herself and Jonathan had increased.

She knew that Jonathan felt it, too. Sometimes when they had brushed against each other or caught each other's eye, there was an expression of heat in his that caused her to turn away in considerable confusion.

As they had waved them good-bye last night, Beth and Hilda had laughingly told them they were sacked. Both of them were now officially guests again and would be treated as such.

Suddenly Jean remembered Jonathan had said something about driving to Dalby this morning to see the charming country town. Looking her straight in the eye, he had said, "We'll have a chance then for a serious talk."

She had been too tired to realize what he might mean, but suddenly a sense of excited anticipation sent Jean flying from bed and into the shower. She dressed carefully, smoothing on light makeup. As she studied herself in the mirror, she wished for a fleeting moment that she still wore the blush of youth instead of the lines the years had brought.

God can restore the years the locust has eaten.

The thought flashed into her mind and for a moment her hands tightened on the top of the dressing table.

"Oh, God, are You still doing that for us both?" she prayed out loud. The peace that suddenly swept through her was an answer.

There was a knock on her door and she moved slowly to answer it, wishing suddenly she had more time to open the scriptures and find that passage about the locust and the wasted years. Jonathan was standing with his shoulders hunched and his hands thrust into his pockets.

He was dressed as she had seen him so many times when she had first met him. His dark business suit fitted him perfectly and he looked every inch the successful surgeon.

For a moment they stared at each other, and then her heart took a nosedive at the expression on his face.

"Jean, I'm so sorry, but our trip to Dalby is off."

She was astonished at the depth of her disappointment and couldn't speak.

"I had a phone call a little while ago from my partner's wife. He was supposed to be operating today—a mastectomy for cancer." His words were clipped, expressionless. "He's had an accident, fractured his leg, and is in traction. The operation can't be delayed. There may not be a theater available again for another two weeks. Other surgeons he's tried are either fully booked or already away for the holiday break."

His face suddenly looked so bleak that her hand reached out and closed on his arm. His hand touched hers and then their fingers clung together.

"That's fine, Jonathan, of course you have to go," she said quickly.

"Jean," he stopped and cleared his throat, "you do realize I don't have any choice, don't you?"

She looked at him with surprise, feeling offended. "Goodness, Jonathan, I'm a nurse, aren't I? Surely if anyone could understand about a doctor's interrupted private life, I do," she said teasingly, and was then amazed at the relief that flooded his pale face with color.

His hand tightened on hers and suddenly she was in his arms, his lips plundering hers with something that felt almost like desperation. Then he wrenched himself away and looked at her. His face was transformed, his eyes suspiciously bright.

"Jean."

That one word, her name spoken so tenderly, so full of love. . . . And then he was gone.

When she had regained control of herself enough to venture out of her room, Marian met her with the message that Jonathan expected to be home in time for the barbecue.

"He was terribly upset after he got off the phone," her friend teased her. "And I'm sure it wasn't just because his holiday was interrupted. Do I hear wedding bells for you two?"

"Marian!"

Her friend was unperturbed by her shocked face. "I wasn't born yesterday, Jean Drew. It's been obvious to all of us how much you like each other. Why, you can hardly bear to let each other out of sight! Besides, he looks at you in a way there's no mistaking. If you ask me, you're perfect for each other."

Before Jean could recover her senses enough to answer, Marian had whisked herself out of the room. For a long moment Jean stared after her, and then a smile spread across her face and she laughed out loud.

When she next saw Marian she was relieved that she refrained from further comment. The day dragged by, and when it came time to drive over to the barbecue, Jean tried to hide her disappointment that Jonathan had not arrived.

"Never mind, I'm sure he'll get back as soon as he can," Marian said comfortingly, and Jean felt herself blush that her concern was so obvious.

Under the colored lights, which enlivened the outdoor setting, as the smell of cooking meat and frying onions permeated the air, Jean made a real effort to join in the laughter and conversation. When headlights on the track to the house signalled a new arrival, it was Jean who hurried to meet the tall dark figure who alighted from the car.

"You're just in time," she called out. "We've saved a juicy steak just for you."

Then the man moved into the light and a voice with a faint North American accent said, "And that will make me very welcome. I've been starving for a good Aussie steak ever since I left home."

He was in his midtwenties, but it was the familiar slant of his jaw, the dark eyebrows that almost met above his strong nose, and the teasing hazel eyes that made Jean gasp in amazement, and her face light up with delight.

"Robert? Robert Howard? Oh, I'm so thrilled you're here. Jonathan will be absolutely delighted!"

The young man relaxed. "So my father is here. I haven't let him know I was coming. Only made up my mind at the last moment that I was tired of battling the snow and icy winds and only a good dose of a hot Christmas Day could cure it. And. . .and I had this need to see my dad."

As he looked so eagerly around, Jean hated to disappoint him. "I'm sorry, he had an emergency this morning and had to go to Brisbane, but we're expecting him back this evening."

His face fell and he gave a rueful laugh. "Oh, well, it's nice to know some things don't change. Dad always has these emergencies and I suppose I'd better get used to them myself. At my mature age I've decided I'm going to see if I can get into medical school myself."

"I know that will make your father very, very happy," she said quietly. "And I know also how much he was missing you this Christmas."

He looked at her keenly for a moment and then followed her as she proceeded to introduce him to everyone.

To her deep disappointment, Jonathan never showed up by the time they dispersed for the night, but Robert did not seem surprised in the slightest.

"Probably found he had to be on hand for post-op care," Robert said with a resigned shrug that told Jean only too well how many times over the years this must have happened. Despite Jonathan's self-condemnation, Robert realized the necessity for putting another person's life before his family.

And if by any wonderful chance you do become a surgeon's wife, you'll have to accept it as a fact of life, too, my girl, she told herself grimly. She already missed him so much that even a few hours spent with him would be worth more than all day with someone else.

At Marian Stevens's insistence, Robert camped on a foldout bed in the lounge room. When they met in the dining room Christmas morning, he was as disappointed as Jean that his father had still not arrived. Their "Happy Christmas" greetings were a little forced, but fortunately having a hurried breakfast and getting ready for the Christmas service left them little time to dwell on his absence.

All through the service Jean expected Jonathan to slip into the vacant seat beside her. Rance's sermon was as inspiring as always, but Jean still felt a depth of loneliness she had not known. She sadly acknowledged that if Jonathan Howard were to disappear from her life again, her faith in God's sufficiency would be put to the test as never before.

After the service Beth and her family returned with Marian and Jim and Gail Stevens, while Rance and his son accompanied Jean and Robert back to Hilda's place for quick refreshments—and to exchange presents—before setting out for Christmas dinner with his parents. Apparently, Nathan had already opened some of his gifts from his grandparents before the service, and his eyes glistened with excitement when he saw the pile of gaily wrapped gifts beneath the huge Christmas tree.

"Are. . .are any of them for me?" he faltered as he looked at Hilda.

"Why," teased a wide-eyed Hilda, "didn't Santa Claus find you at your grandparents'?"

"Don't tease the young man, Hilda," Jean scolded mockingly. "Of course some are for you, but I was just wondering if we should wait for Dr. Howard."

Robert then cocked his head as if he heard something. "That's probably him now," he said, striding rapidly from the room.

The repeated sound of a car horn sent Jean leading the eager rush outside, but she stopped suddenly and watched as Jonathan saw his son. The wonder and joy in his pale, exhausted face moved her to tears.

"Robert?"

"Happy Christmas, Dad!"

His son gave a choked sound and then the two men were hugging each other. Jonathan pulled back after a moment and then looked around. His searching eyes found Jean and a wary, anxious expression filled his face.

Jean feasted her eyes on him and of their own volition her feet moved her toward him. It seemed the most natural thing in the world for him to pull her into his arms.

She ignored the surprise on the faces of those watching and clasped him tightly.

"I'm so sorry, Jean."

She frowned for a moment and then realized he was apologizing to her for not getting back when he had said. Even more, for having to leave at all when they had not had their "talk."

"There's nothing to be sorry for, my dear," she said simply. "Is your patient all right?"

Relief lit up his tired, black-circled eyes for a moment. "She wasn't for most of the night. The surgery had to be far more extensive then we thought and I had to explain her ongoing care to her when she was completely recovered from the anesthetic, and then later to her husband," he added sadly.

Jean moved closer to him. Without him saying anymore she knew that the woman's future prospects were not good and silently offered him her support and encouragement. Jonathan's eyes softened, acknowledging his appreciation.

Then he turned back to his son who was watching

them keenly. "You've met Jean, Robert? Did she explain that we worked together years ago?"

Jean had enjoyed a long talk with Robert at the barbecue. They smiled at each other and she felt the heat flood her face as he said mischievously, "Oh, yes, she explained that and much more. She's one very special lady, Dad."

Someone cleared their throat and they swung around to see Hilda beaming at them. "I hate to break this up, but I'm not sure Rance can hold Nathan back much longer from ripping into all those exciting parcels you two spent so long buying and wrapping."

Jean had already been enjoying her Christmas in a way she never had before, but suddenly with Jonathan by her side she felt as though God could not have blessed her more.

She was wrong.

Nathan had almost finished with his "loot," as Robert laughingly called his presents, when Jonathan rather impatiently handed Jean a beautifully wrapped box. She eagerly ripped the paper off and lifted out a crystal star. Held up carefully to the light, it sparkled and gleamed.

Speechless, she looked at Jonathan.

"It reminded me of that star over the nativity scene at the shopping center," he murmured. "I've thought about that a lot."

So had Jean, but she waited for him to put it into words.

"The. . .the star showed the wise men where God wanted them to go, what He wanted them to do. It led them to Jesus," he finished simply.

There was silence. Even Nathan stilled and looked from one serious adult face to another. Then Jonathan stood up. "If I remember correctly, Hilda, a certain tin shed is still out near your garage?" he asked.

Hilda looked startled and Rance gave a short bark of laughter.

"I told you about that, did I?" His eyes were dancing, but he said solemnly, "Yes, it's still there. I recommend it to you, Jonathan, for what you obviously have in mind. I'm just glad we are not in the middle of a thunderstorm this time! And please, don't worry about being late for dinner. I know Mother will understand. Just one thing—I won't be working again until after my own honeymoon!"

Jean had not taken her eyes from Jonathan, but at that last statement she looked at Rance, wondering what on earth he was talking about. Suddenly she remembered that as a minister Rance performed wedding ceremonies. A tide of warmth swept through her.

When Jonathan looked back at her with his face full of unconcealed love, she knew that Rance had told his old friend about the time he had proposed to Hilda in the old tin shed during a thunderstorm.

She tilted her chin and tried for her best old dragon stare. "Well, what are you waiting for then, Dr. Howard?"

He stared at her, an answering gleam entering his eyes. "Just for this, Sister Drew," he retorted in his most arrogant surgeon voice.

He took a couple of steps closer to where he had

flung his suit coat. Impatiently she watched him remove a small gift. Then she felt his hand grasp hers firmly and pull her toward the door.

With dawning hope she realized what a box that size might contain as he raced her past a grinning, startled Robert and across the yard to that old tin shed.

There he stopped and swung her around toward him. "Jean, I've been really seeking God's guidance for what He wants me to do about loving you like I do."

He paused, and she said with a laugh in her voice, "Did He suggest to you that perhaps you should tell me what you told Him?"

"I didn't want to say anything because I knew you, too, were still trying to find out His will about a relationship between us."

She reached up and ran a hand lovingly down his cheek where he had not even stopped to shave. "Johnny, you must have been busy this past twenty-four hours to not even take the time to shave," she said irrelevantly.

The hesitancy disappeared entirely from his face and he reached up to take her hand in his. He didn't say anything, just held it tightly in both of his and waited. The blaze of love in his face said it all.

There was so much she wanted to tell him but somehow she knew that he already knew it, or most of it.

Perhaps he didn't know yet that her breaking off her engagement and wedding to Mark had been the hardest thing she had ever done. Perhaps he didn't know that she had found out only the day before the date that had been set for their wedding, that Mark had not canceled it. Instead, he had pleaded with her one more time. He had been very upset at her gentle refusal, and on his way home his car had run off the road and into a tree. She would always wonder if his accident had been deliberate.

Perhaps he did know there would be times when she, too, might resent the demands his profession would make on him.

Perhaps he knew that she would want to travel with him and share the challenges in Africa as his nurse.

They were both mature in age but also in their faith in Christ. These were all things they could talk about some other time and then leave safely in a loving Father's hands.

But she suspected he already knew about the star.

Otherwise, why would he have given her the crystal one that would hold pride of place in any home they made together in the years to come?

So there was no misunderstanding, she put it into words anyway. "I've asked God constantly about loving you; I've sought His will earnestly and knocked loudly."

The star was still clutched in her hand. Very carefully she put it in a place where a stream of sunlight touched it with a brilliance that made it seem alive.

His hands grasped hers again even tighter and the light in his eyes, the love and understanding, made her swallow before she could continue.

"He opened His Word to me, He answered me, and I found His will. Like the wise men who followed the star, He led me to Jesus, the Babe of Bethlehem, but also the very Prince of Peace."

His arms wrapped around her and Jean knew that her years of loneliness were gone forever.

"I love you," he whispered at last, and the peace wrapped around them both, holding them safely in His will.

Mary Hawkins

A resident of New South Wales, Australia (outside Sydney), Mary and her husband have three grown children. Her first inspirational novel, *Search for Tomorrow*, was voted the second most favorite contemporary romance by Heartsong Presents' readers. Mary has written four inspirational romances for Heartsong Presents.

The Christmas Wreath

Veda Boyd Jones

Dedication

For Aunt Punch, who has a special friendship with every person she knows.

Chapter 1

Jennifer Faucett knew she'd be the first one there. She'd planned it that way. She needed time alone in the house before her two brothers arrived. After all, she was the oldest and had been the closest to Grandma. And now that Grandma was gone, who better to open the house in Mulberry for the first time since the funeral?

It looked the same, this place she loved best—the two-story white house on the corner with the front porch that wrapped around two sides. She parked in front of the house in the space that Grandma had used whenever she didn't want to fool with parking in the detached garage. Up the walk, five steps to the porch, and then that big front door with the beveled glass window.

With key in hand, Jennifer walked slowly to the door. *Dear God,* she prayed silently, *please give me courage to do this.* The lock turned easily, and she found herself stepping back in time as she crossed the threshold, back to past Christmas family reunions in the small Arkansas town and her own annual weeklong summer visits with Grandma, back to a time filled with long, lazy days and laughter and love.

The house was cold, not freezing cold, but it had

that furnace-turned-way-down feel. A closed-up smell assailed her nostrils, and she sneezed as she turned up the thermostat.

After Grandma had died of a sudden heart attack last August, the Faucett grandchildren had agreed that they would not act in haste, but would close up the house for a few months before deciding what to do with her things. Jennifer had arranged the Christmas reunion at Grandma's. That was their tradition. And Jennifer wanted it—just like old times.

Grandma's will, written soon after Jennifer's mother had died, specified that her estate be split equally among her three grandchildren. Once they went through the place, choosing who would take what furniture, Jennifer supposed they would sell the house and divide the proceeds. But before that she'd have this last Christmas in this wonderful home.

She pulled her cell phone out of her purse and dialed Sarah McFarland, who lived down the block and across the street; Sarah had been keeping an eye on the place for them.

"I wasn't expecting you until late this afternoon," Sarah said. "I was going to go over and turn up the heat, and Beth planned on coming into town this afternoon to help me get beds made up and such."

"I would love the company," Jennifer said. She and Sarah's daughter had become best summer friends on her annual visits. They'd played dolls together when they were young and double-dated when they were older, Beth always persuading her current boyfriend to find a date for Jennifer.

"Be over in a jif," Sarah said and hung up.

Jennifer turned the thermostat even higher, then walked through the house, opening windows as she went. Open windows this time of year weren't energy efficient, but the place needed a few minutes of fresh air. She surveyed the living room. They'd left the house in good shape after the funeral last August. A quick vacuuming and dusting would give the place a lived-in feeling again.

She flicked the light on in the kitchen. This had been the center of Grandma's world. Before her brothers arrived, Jennifer would have it looking and smelling like old times, with Christmas cookies cooling on a rack, waiting to be decorated. She made a mental note to buy that refrigerator cookie dough instead of all the ingredients for sugar cookies.

The refrigerator door stood open. Jennifer glanced at the empty interior before she shut the door and plugged it in. The familiar low hum and then the sound of water running into the ice maker made the house seem more alive already.

"Yoo-hoo! Anybody home?" Jennifer had never known Sarah to knock on that front door before, so there was no reason to expect her to now. Jennifer smiled and hurried to hug Grandma's neighbor.

"You're just as pretty as ever," Sarah said. "I still can't figure out why you're not married like Beth."

"Just haven't found the right man," Jennifer said. They'd had this same conversation for years. Beth had married right out of high school, and Jennifer was still happily single at the old-maid age of twenty-eight.

"Well, Johnny has some friends," Sarah said with a smile. "Beth can fix you up with one of them, just like old times."

"Just like old times," Jennifer echoed. "You said Beth was coming to town this afternoon?"

"I left her a note that I was here, but she'll pull in here as soon as she sees that red car. Yours?"

"No. A rental. I flew into Fayetteville. The drive seemed too long, and I could get good connections. Only had a half-hour layover in Memphis." She didn't add that she didn't own a car. She worked in downtown Chicago and lived within walking distance of the financial planning office. With parking spaces at a premium, and the el-train available for transportation, a car was unnecessary.

"You shouldn't be driving alone that far anyway," Sarah said. "Well, let's get this place in tiptop shape. Shall we start upstairs?"

In a systematic way they charged from one room to the next, vacuuming, dusting, shutting windows, and making the beds.

They'd just finished the living room when Beth knocked on the door and then opened it. She plopped a sack in a chair and threw herself at her friend. "Jen," she squealed. "I knew you'd get here early."

Jennifer hugged Beth, then gently pushed her away and looked her up and down. "You never change—except for that twenty-pound weight gain from time to time.

How are you feeling?"

Beth patted her seven-month midsection. "This one's a kicker. Must be a boy."

Her mother smiled. "Hi, honey. I wasn't expecting you until after lunch."

"I brought lunch." Beth picked up the sack. "Subs and a two-liter of soda. Just like old times."

"Well, we haven't finished the house yet," Sarah said, all business. "Lunch will have to wait another twenty minutes." She installed Beth in the kitchen, she took the dining room, and Jennifer scurried into the den, the place she loved best.

Long ago the den had been Grandpa's haven, then Grandma had turned it into more of a library, with bookshelves installed in every available spot. Jennifer had cut out paper dolls at that old oak desk and sought the warmth of the big chair near the fireplace on cold December days as a place to read and dream.

This would be her center during the two days before her brothers arrived. She could sort through Grandma's things in front of the fireplace. Make lists at the desk. Put up the Christmas tree in front of the bay window. Get a grip on life without Grandma, her anchor. She shook off the touch of melancholy and tackled the room.

A few minutes later the threesome assembled in the kitchen, and Sarah announced she was going home. "Enjoy lunch, girls," she said and waved off Jennifer's thanks.

Beth placed two foot-long subs on the kitchen table. "This is hard for you, isn't it? Coming back."

"Yes, it's hard," Jennifer said. She couldn't begin to explain to Beth, who had a husband and children, a mother and father, how hard it was to be the oldest member of a family. She hadn't even labeled all her ambivalent feelings for herself. That's what she hoped this last trip home would do for her. Get her life in some sense of order. She got glasses from the cupboard and held them up to the light filtering through the window.

"Look clean," she said, then opened the freezer. "No ice yet, though. Is the soda cold?"

"No," Beth answered. "I'll run down to Mom's and get some."

"Stay put. I'll see if Ruth has some extra ice. It's closer, and I haven't said hello yet."

"Ruth's gone," Beth said. "After she broke her hip, she moved in with her daughter. Mike Shannon's living there now."

"Mikie lives here?"

"He might not like you calling him Mikie," Beth said. "How long has it been since you saw him?"

"I don't know. I guess not since high school. Our visits to our grandmas didn't coincide after that. Well, I'll see if he has ice. Be right back."

Jennifer didn't bother with a coat as she grabbed a bowl and slipped out the back door. She walked next door to Mikie's house, thinking that it seemed odd to have Ruth not living there. After a moment's hesitation, she veered off the beaten path to the back door, deciding to use the front door instead. Ruth had always stayed in the back of the house, near the kitchen, but Jennifer doubted that was Mikie's main area. She punched the doorbell.

"Mikie," she called. She heard footsteps, then a moment later the door swung open.

"Mikie?" She remembered him as a skinny guy who wore glasses and wasn't much taller than her own five-foot-six. This man wore a heavy-knit sweater that hugged his broad chest, and he was at least six feet tall. No glasses hid the brown eyes that Jennifer remembered as being kind and thoughtful. The eyes were the same, but they were the only thing about this man that she recognized.

"Jennifer? Come in. Sarah mentioned that you'd be here over the holidays." He stepped back and motioned her inside.

"I came to borrow ice." Jennifer held up the bowl and followed him inside. "You've changed." She wondered why her voice sounded so breathless, as though she'd been running.

"So have you," he said and studied her with frank male admiration. "Amazing what a decade or so can do for a person," he added.

Jennifer stifled the urge to fluff her hair. "I guess it has been a few years," she said. "I remember you as the boy who taught me how to ride a bike." She felt as if she were babbling, but something about this Mikie was unsettling. She could see why Beth had remarked that he might not like her old name for him. They walked through the living room toward the kitchen.

"You've kept all of Ruth's furniture," she remarked.

"Yes, Grandma is staying at my folks right now, but she wants to return home. She knows I'm keeping the place up for her, so it gives her hope."

"And will she return?"

"Not a good chance," he said. "As she would say, she's mending poorly."

Jennifer nodded. She could imagine Ruth saying those words. "Well, it's nice that you could keep the house open for her." She paused by the dining room table and picked up a hardback book. "Oh, I'm reading this, too. I bought the paperback at the airport. He's a good mystery writer."

Mike grinned and his kind eyes twinkled. "Thanks."

"Thanks?" Jennifer looked at the cover. *Rafe's Charm* by Mike Perry. She turned the book over, and there staring out from the back cover was none other than Mikie Shannon. She looked at Mikie, then back at the picture of the author. "You're Mike Perry?"

"When I'm writing mystery I am. I write westerns as Shannon Barnes."

"Wow! Mikie Shannon, an author. Who would have guessed? Wait—I thought you were a history teacher."

"I was until last year, when I quit my day job to write full time."

"Do you go on book tours and talk shows?"

"Only one book tour. Sitting at a card table at the entrance to a bookstore isn't my idea of having a good time. It's like running a garage sale. People won't look you in the eye. And no talk shows."

Jennifer nodded because she didn't know what else to say. Mikie was full of surprises, and that's just how she felt—surprised. The words stunned and bemused were also accurate descriptions for her current mental state.

"Grandma must have known. I wonder why she didn't tell me."

He shrugged. "She always told me writing was personal. You wanted ice?" He walked on to the kitchen, and Jennifer put the book down and followed him.

"Yes. Beth is waiting for me at Grandma's house. The boys won't be coming for a couple of days, then we're going to sort out Grandma's belongings."

Mikie cracked ice trays and filled the bowl. "Then you're alone for a while? If you don't have plans for dinner, why don't you come over later and we'll have a bite and catch up on old times?"

"Good." To her horror, her voice cracked on the word, and she tried again. "That sounds good."

"Six?"

"Perfect." Jennifer opened the back door. "I'll see you at six."

She hurried back to Grandma's house. "Why didn't you tell me?" she called before she was even inside the back door.

"Tell you what?" Beth asked, as if she didn't know. She had a cat-ate-the-canary look.

"He's. . .he's changed," Jennifer said. The first words

that had come to mind were "gorgeous" and "handsome,"
but those thoughts made her seem shallow, as if she were
judging a book by its cover. Or by its back cover. That
thought made her laugh out loud.

Chapter 2

Beth left around three, and Jennifer headed to the grocery store. Luttman's on Main Street had been there ever since she could remember. During her summer visits as a child, she'd walked to Luttman's each day and picked up groceries for Grandma. And each time Jennifer picked up a loaf of bread or a few slices of lunch meat, she would say "Put it on the bill," and Mr. Luttman would write it on a pad. At the end of each month, Grandma would go in and settle up.

That procedure had changed a few years back, and the store had become modernized, too. Now it carried video rentals, and the frozen food section had tripled, but the hardwood floors and the overhead ceiling fans remained the same, keeping the small-town atmosphere.

Jennifer pushed a cart to the refrigerator case to get cookie dough, then decided against it and steered to the aisle that held baking supplies. Any groceries she had left over after her ten-day stay, she'd give to Mikie. Or Mike, rather. She needed to start thinking of him differently, because his nickname no longer fit him. Maybe it would be easier to think of him as Michael.

After Jennifer had carried in groceries and empty boxes for packing Grandma's things, she started a fire in the fireplace in the den, then made sugar cookie dough and stuck it in the refrigerator to chill. Next she made a batch of brownies to take over to Mikie's. . . Michael's.

The delicious aroma of baking chocolate spread through the house and lightened Jennifer's heart as she searched through the downstairs storage room for Christmas decorations. It didn't take long to locate the boxes because each one was clearly marked, some in Grandma's handwriting, and some in Jennifer's bold block letters from two decades earlier.

The Christmas tree was contained in three boxes. Grandma never could get the branches back into the original box. Once they'd discovered that her brother Kenneth was allergic to pine trees, Grandma had invested in an artificial one, but she wanted one that was extra full. "It may be fake, but it won't look like it," she'd said. She'd bought pine scent that wouldn't make Kenneth sick, to bring the smell of evergreen into the house. And the Christmas wreath on the front door was always real. Jennifer planned on making one the next day.

She carried box after box to the den. When Kenneth and Cody arrived, they'd be surprised to see the tree twinkling in the bay window, just as when Grandma was alive. Jennifer took a deep breath to stifle a sob.

This coming home was harder than she'd expected. She thought she had already dealt with the grief of Grandma's loss. But didn't doctors say the holiday season was especially hard after the loss of a loved one? And if ever anyone was loved, Grandma was.

Jennifer put Christmas music on the stereo while she assembled the tree. She wasn't going to turn maudlin at the Yuletide season. It was one of her favorite times of the year, and she knew Grandma would be looking down from heaven and shaking her finger at her if she didn't enjoy it.

By the time she had the eight-foot tree together, it was nearly six. She quickly freshened her makeup, put the brownies on a plate, and scurried next door. She blamed her hurry for her rapid pulse as she stood on the back porch and knocked.

A five o'clock shadow on Mikie's cheeks gave him a roguish look, and when he smiled, his white teeth gleamed against the dark whiskers. As he ushered her into the kitchen, Jennifer glanced at him sideways, hardly able to believe he was the same person she used to know.

"Yum, smells good," Jennifer said.

"My specialty," Mikie said. "Chicken potpie—from the freezer. I did make the salad myself. Are those some of your world-famous brownies? For me?"

"My specialty. Remember all those times we ate brownies on Grandma's front porch?"

"How could I forget? I even remember the bitter taste the time you forgot to put in the sugar."

"You're not supposed to remember the bad stuff, only the good."

He laughed and pulled out a kitchen chair for her. "I need the bad stuff. I put your bitter brownies in a mystery novel. I had a villainess appear to be a terrible cook.

In the first chapter her boyfriend manages to choke down her horrible desserts. But by the second chapter, she'd put poison in the brownies, and he was so used to eating foul-tasting food, that he thought she'd forgotten the sugar again. Turns out she was actually a gourmet cook, but she'd set him up." He shrugged. "Hey, the novel reads better than this sounds, but I got the idea from your bitter brownies."

"Glad I could help."

He carried water glasses to the table and then pulled two chicken potpies from the oven and turned them over on their plates.

"I hope you like ranch dressing. It's all I have," he said as he set it and a large salad in the center of the table, then took a seat.

After they filled their plates, Jennifer asked, "When did you start writing? That really surprises me."

"It shouldn't. Your grandma was the one who showed me how much fun writing could be."

"Grandma?"

"Didn't she ever tell you about her journals?"

Jennifer shook her head.

He looked into space for a moment as if in thought. "It must have been the summer before my senior year. I didn't want to leave my friends in Little Rock and come visit my grandparents in the first place, and I was probably acting like a jerk. My summer job had ended, and it was the last week before school started."

"I came early that year," Jennifer said. "I remember missing you because the summer before you'd driven that old Ford up here, and we took it everywhere."

"Well, that fateful summer I moped around until your grandma gave me a journal. It was a spiral notebook, and she made me sit on the front porch and record everything I saw and heard and felt and smelled."

"She made you?"

"She asked me to. Same thing. Jessie Faucett could make anyone do anything she wanted, merely by asking. Your grandma was a powerful woman in a soft-spoken way."

Jennifer nodded her agreement. "So you wrote about this poky little neighborhood in Mulberry, Arkansas, where you didn't want to be."

"At first. Then she told me to make up a background on a person who had a lot of enemies. I showed her the profile, and she made a big X over the page. 'Somebody killed him,' she said. 'You're the detective. Find out who did it.' So I did."

"And that was the beginning of your career."

"Not exactly. I turned to westerns, because I was interested in history, but that was the birth of Sam Morgan, the detective in all my mysteries. I wrote that whole week, and every day Jessie would read what I'd written and tell me what she liked about it, and then she'd shoot holes in it. I've never sold that story, but I'd like to revise it now and set it up in correct form and all. It's still in that journal in my awful handwriting."

"Would you leave the story set in Mulberry?"

"I don't know. Publishers like big-city settings because so many people are city people these days—and they like to read about their city or a life like they lead."

"Which is why you use New York in your mysteries?"

He nodded. "But it might be time for a change. What if Sam Morgan comes to Mulberry to visit someone? An elderly aunt, perhaps."

Over their dinner they plotted together, and by the time Jennifer said she'd better be heading back home, they'd created a framework for a new mystery.

"You're a good writing partner," Michael said as they walked the short distance to Grandma's back door.

"All I said over and over was 'Why would he do that?' You did all the work yourself."

"Maybe. But you're a good listener. Just like your grandma. I used to call her up and tell her my plots, then she'd point out logic problems, just like she did that first summer. I miss her."

"Me, too," Jennifer said with a catch in her voice, and she felt her heart get that heavy feeling again.

Michael put a comforting arm around her. "Jessie would have a fit if she thought we were carrying on over her loss instead of celebrating the season." But Jennifer thought she heard a catch in his voice, too.

She leaned against him and could have stayed that way forever. His cologne smelled musky, and she felt safe and secure with his arm around her. The loneliness that had haunted her today disappeared, and in its place was a warm feeling like summer sunshine.

She shook her head and pushed away a little. What was she thinking? This was Mikie, her old summer pal.

"Big plans for tomorrow?" Michael asked.

"Uh-huh." She tried to think of what they were, but her mind was having trouble focusing. "Decorate the tree. . .bake cookies. . .make the wreath."

"Need help?"

She looked up at him. "I'd love help. I want the house all ready when the boys come home. Just like old times."

"I'll come over tomorrow morning." When he stepped away from her, she felt as if a winter chill had returned.

"Around ten?" she asked.

"See you then," he answered and whistled as he walked back to his house.

Too keyed up to go to bed, Jennifer wandered into the den to check the fireplace. She switched on a lamp and wandered from bookshelf to bookshelf until she found his books—seven Mike Perry mysteries and five Shannon Barnes westerns. She'd always figured her grandmother liked the authors. Now she knew there was more to it than that. She pulled the first one off the shelf and read the dedication.

"To Jessie, who believed in me."

Why hadn't Grandma mentioned her neighbor's grandson becoming a writer? And why hadn't she told Jennifer about the journals?

Jennifer glanced around the room and was drawn to the low cabinets on the far wall. There behind wooden doors were rows of notebooks, most spiral-bound. Were these the journals Michael had mentioned?

She picked the last one. "1996" was written on the front. She flipped through it and skimmed a notation written in red ink. "CW has finally made it! What a day!" Who was CW? She slipped the notebook back in place and took out the one next to it. "1995." So every notebook was a different year.

She'd seen one on Grandma's desk last August, but she'd been too occupied with grief to read it. Yes, there it was, just as if Grandma had left it there with plans to write in it again. Jennifer put it in its rightful place on the shelf.

Let's see. The summer that Michael had been a senior, she had been a freshman. 1984. She flipped through the notebooks until she found that year.

It started on January first. Sometimes a week went by without an entry, and sometimes there were daily entries. Michael had said he'd visited Mulberry right before school started. She flipped to August and found his name.

"August 19. Someday Mike Shannon will be an author. He's always had an eye for detail and he can read people's emotions. Today I gave him a notebook and had him create a setting and a story. I suggested a mystery because he has a logical side and could line up clues. He worked for hours on the plot and when he showed me his first few pages, his eyes twinkled with excitement. I told Orey that Mike was a born storyteller, but he said not to fill the boy's head with nonsense. Orey's never had a use for my little poems. He said they were silly verses. I should never have shown them to him. And I won't tell anyone about Mike's talent. That will be for him to share. Then he can choose to tell those who will appreciate the work that goes into his stories."

Ah, so that was why Grandma hadn't mentioned Michael's books. But once in print, why wouldn't she have? . . . Jennifer let that thought go. Grandma was gone, and she had no way of reading her mind, except by reading her journals.

"August 21. Ruth and I canned 14 quarts of tomatoes today. I enjoy putting up Orey's garden. Mostly I enjoy opening up a jar of vegetables in the dead of winter. It's a real taste of last summer's hot days and sunshine, and reminds me that spring will come again.

"Mike's still writing. We talked today about how famous he will be someday if he practices his writing, and I told him that he might want to use a pseudonym. I shared with him my experience with my poems, and he asked to see them. I told him someday I'll let him read them, but for now they are just for me."

Grandma had never told Jennifer that she was a poet. Where would she have hidden the poems—and had she ever shown them to Michael? Grandpa Orey must have really wounded Grandma's feelings for her to hide her talent from everyone.

Jennifer quickly looked through the bookcase. Two long rows were journals, but there wasn't a sign of a collection of poetry. Of course, she wasn't sure what she was looking for. The poems could have been on scrap paper and left here and there, but more likely

Grandma would have put them all together. Maybe in a three-ring binder? Maybe in a box?

This vacation of sorts was to close up Grandma's house. Surely in the nine remaining days she'd be at the house, Jennifer could find the poems. It would be her quest. And if the poems were good, and somehow she knew they would be, she'd find a way to get them published. It was one last thing she could do for Grandma.

Chapter 3

The next morning, Jennifer changed the battery in her cell phone and slipped the extra one in the charger. She'd given this number to her brothers and to her boss, and she needed to keep it working. Beside, she needed to check stock quotes and see if any of her clients had buy or sell orders.

After hooking her laptop computer's modem to the phone, she pulled up her file list and noted activity since she'd left the office Wednesday evening. She probably should have checked yesterday, but Michael Shannon had pushed Wall Street dealings right out of her mind.

She was still working at the big desk in the den when Michael came over.

"I'll be done in two shakes," she said. "Help yourself to some coffee."

She forced herself to finish one transaction and set up the last one, even though she would have rather just looked at him.

"Jessie told me you worked for a big financial firm." Michael set his coffee cup down and looked over her shoulder. "Do you like it?"

"I love it. I feel good when I help people set up their

future financial security." She typed in a few more figures, watched the sale register, and signed off. "Can you take the day off from writing?"

"Anytime I want, as long as I meet my deadlines. But I've already put in several hours this morning."

"What time do you get up?"

"Five. Run a couple of miles, eat my Wheaties, then sit down at the computer by six. I'm best in the morning, and it frees up my day. What's first on your agenda?"

"This morning let's decorate the tree and bake the cookies. This afternoon we'll ice them and then make the wreath. Good plan?"

"Good plan."

Jennifer rolled out the dough and Michael cut out trees, Santas, reindeer, stars, and wreaths. They worked together easily, and Jennifer realized how easy being with him had always been. His familiar presence gave her a safe, comfortable feeling—so why, she asked herself, was her heart racing?

As soon as she'd popped the cookie sheets in the oven, Jennifer set the timer and headed back to the den. Michael followed with the timer in hand. "I remember too many burnt cookies in your past. I'll make sure we hear the ding."

Jennifer grinned at him. He remembered her as a bad cook, and she had to admit, she was. Grandma had said she didn't have the patience for it. She either rushed things on the stove, so that they burned, or she forgot things that were in the oven. That missing sugar in the brownies was a onetime error, though, for Jennifer was good with details. She thought that was why she liked financial planning.

"The box over there is full of lights. Shall we start with them?"

At first she thought the ringing of the phone was the timer, but immediately realized her mistake. It was her boss on the other end of the line.

"How are things in Cranberry?" Trevor asked.

"It's Mulberry, and they're fine." She cradled the phone between her ear and shoulder, and handed Michael one end of a string of lights.

"How long are you going to be in that little town? We miss you already. Mrs. Wedell called and wants to talk to you. She seems upset, and said no one else will do."

"I'll call her," Jennifer said. "I've already taken care of this morning's e-mail."

"I know. I saw your activity on the printout. When are you coming back?" Trevor asked again.

"The Monday after Christmas," she said. Lately Trevor had been paying her a lot of attention at the office, and although he was nice enough, she didn't want to encourage an office romance, especially with her boss. A way to let him know that suddenly occurred to her. "Trevor, do you have any Shannon Barnes westerns in your collection?"

"Every one he's written, plus every Louis L'Amour, Loren Estleman, Jory Sherman—"

"An extensive collection," Jennifer interrupted him. "Well, Shannon Barnes is here right now helping me decorate the Christmas tree."

"You're kidding."

"No, really. His name is. . ." She remembered what she'd read last night in Grandma's journal about not revealing Michael's talent and she quickly changed tact. "He's an old friend from my childhood. I'll see if I can bring you an autographed book." She raised her eyebrows at Michael and he nodded.

"That would be great, Jennifer. Just be sure you bring it back personally."

"Of course," she said, wondering how else he thought he'd get it. "Thanks for calling, and I'll give Mrs. Wedell a ring right now."

"Trouble at the office?" Michael asked.

"An elderly woman client needs to talk. This will just take a minute." She let him work on the other strings of light while she pulled up Mrs. Wedell's file, then dialed her number. Her client had just answered the phone when the timer went off. Jennifer covered the mouthpiece with her hand and whispered, "Would you?" then went back to her conversation. When she'd finished the call, she found Michael in the kitchen rolling out the next batch of cookies.

"Got the problem solved?" Michael asked.

"Yes. It's a pity how criminals prey on the elderly. I'm glad Mrs. Wedell thought to talk to me. She got a call about a very illegal pyramid investment scheme. Of course, it wasn't presented to her that way."

"Of course," he agreed.

They took three hours to decorate the tree amid trips to the kitchen to tend to the cookies. Shortly after one o'clock, they put the empty decoration boxes in the storage room and decided to fix lunch.

They carried their sandwiches to the den and admired the tree while they ate. When she'd finished, Jennifer set her plate down and walked over to the cabinet where Grandma's journals were kept. She pulled out "1984."

"You found her journals," Michael said.

"Yes, look at this," she said and pointed to the August entry.

He read the page, then looked up at her. "She always had faith in me, even then."

"Did she show you her poems? Do you know where they are?"

He shook his head. "I never saw them, although I asked her about them several times. She always put me off. 'Someday,' she'd say. And before I sold my first book, she talked to me again about a pseudonym. 'It'll protect you,' she'd said. 'If you want people to know, you can tell them. If you can't take their criticism, they'll never know it's you.' "

"And you took her advice." It was a statement, not a question.

"Yes. And she was right. I'm not as wounded by bad reviews if they're written about Mike Perry's or Shannon Barnes's work. Somehow that insulates me. Of course, when I get good reviews, I accept the work as my own," he said with a smile.

"Your picture's on the back cover. People must know who you are."

"You didn't—although of course the friends I see all

the time know. And the picture is only on the hardback mysteries. Shannon's never had his picture on a book jacket."

"So you keep the identities separate?"

"I try." He shrugged and changed the subject. "Where do you suppose she kept her poems?"

"I haven't looked, except through this cabinet, and they're not there. I intend to find them before I leave. If they're here, we'll locate them—and then I want to publish them."

He nodded. "Good idea." He handed her the journal and she replaced it.

"I want to read all these." She ran her hand along a long row of journals. "Do you think that's violating her privacy?"

"I think that would depend on what you're going to do with the information." He moved beside her. "How many are there?"

"One a year, starting in. . ." She pulled out the first one that was a collection of multisized sheets in an old binder. "1942." She did some quick math. "That would have made her twelve or thirteen." She smiled. "I guess I want to read them because I'd like to know Grandma better. I thought I knew her well, but you seem to know more about her than me, her only granddaughter."

He put a protective arm around her, just as he had the night before. "I imagine every person she knew had a different relationship with her. And each relationship was special. You knew a side of your grandma that I never knew. And I knew things she wanted only me to know. Look at the different relationships you have with Beth and me or with your boss and your brothers."

"You're right." She giggled. "I treat Cody and Kenneth differently than I do anyone else."

"Exactly." His arm tightened for a moment, then he let her go and walked over to the fireplace. "I think Jessie would want us to know the real person, put together the different parts we know, and make her a whole person."

She pointed an accusatory finger his direction. "You want to read her journals, too."

He grinned. "Yes, I do. With your permission."

"Granted. I'll start them tonight and give each one to you as soon as I finish it. Then we'll talk about them."

"Okay. What's next on our list for today?"

A voice came from the entry. "Yoo-hoo! Anybody home?"

"We're in the den, Sarah," Jennifer called.

"Well, hello, Mike. Fancy seeing you here." Sarah walked on into the den. "Beautiful tree. I know it's the same one and the same ornaments, but it looks different every year. When are your brothers due in?"

"By tomorrow evening," Jennifer said.

"I brought you some candy. Made fudge today. Jessie and I used to make it together. Her recipe, the one with walnuts."

"Here, I'll take that to the kitchen," Mike offered.

As soon as he was out of hearing range, Sarah leaned toward Jennifer. "This is a first. Mike Shannon giving up his writing time."

"He's already written a few hours today," Jennifer

explained. "He said he can write whenever he wants as long as he meets his deadlines."

"That's not what he told me. He's nice enough about it, but he has a machine answer his phone calls until he quits writing for the day around four o'clock. He said it interrupts his characters."

"Oh," Jennifer said, and Sarah cast her a knowing look. "Uh, we're headed to get supplies for the Christmas wreath," she said to change the subject. "Is it still all right to get greenery at the old Mosler place?"

"As long as you take your own ax and talk to Earl about it. He likes visitors, and he's getting up there in years."

"We'll talk to Earl," Michael said from the doorway. "Wouldn't have it any other way. Can we bring some pine back for you?"

"No, I was out there a couple of days ago, just haven't got the wreath made yet. Think I'll go do that now. Anything you need, Jennifer? You doing all right?"

"I'm okay." Jennifer exchanged a look with Michael. "Sarah, did Grandma ever show you her. . .journals?" She wanted to ask about the poems, but she had thought better of it.

"Can't say that she did. You mean like a diary?"

"Like that, yes."

Sarah shook her head. "No, I never knew her to write a diary. Did she?"

"Yes. She once showed Michael."

"That shouldn't surprise me. Nothing about Jessie should surprise me. She was a different woman to every

208

friend she had. But she was always a good friend."

Jennifer nodded. Michael had said the same thing.

"I'll be going. If you need anything, come on over," Sarah said, "but I reckon Mike's closer. Being next door and all," she added. She gave Jennifer a wink behind Michael's back, and Jennifer flushed.

After she left, Michael and Jennifer got supplies for cutting pine boughs. Michael insisted they take his car, and he drove the three miles out of town to Earl Mosler's place. The piney woods behind his house had been the source of Christmas trees for residents of Mulberry for as long as Jennifer could remember.

The old man recognized Jennifer immediately. "You're the spitting image of Jessie at your age. I was sweet on her myself back then. Of course, half the town was. I miss her."

"We all do," Michael said.

"She told me you're a stocks and bonds gal," Earl said to Jennifer. "I've got Wal-Mart stock. Most of us around here do since old Sam Walton was from these parts. Should I sell or hold on to it?"

"Keep it. Wal-Mart's an undervalued stock right now, but I predict it will hit forty again by summer."

"Thanks, I'll do that. You planning on setting up an office here?" he asked.

"Oh, no. My work's in Chicago," Jennifer said. She swung the ax in her hand. "You want to come back with us?"

Earl declined to accompany them to the woods. "My knees just aren't what they used to be for walking, but you go ahead and cut anything you need." He waved them off.

"What about a tree for you? For Ruth's house?" Jennifer asked Michael once they were in the woods. "This little one is perfect."

"That little one is a good six feet tall. Trees look smaller when they're in the ground." He stood beside it, and she had to agree it was his height.

"Sure is pretty, though," Jennifer coaxed. "Ruth used to put it in front of the picture window, so anyone going by on the street could see it. I'll bet we could find the decorations."

"Probably," he said in a noncommittal voice.

"Oh, Michael, she'd be so pleased if you put it up. I'll help you." She hadn't put up a real tree in a long time. It would be like grabbing a piece of her childhood.

"But it has to come down, too," Michael protested. "And it'll be prickly."

"I'll help with that, too."

"Promise?"

"Promise."

He playfully dropped a quick kiss on her lips. "A promise sealed with a kiss can't be broken." They looked into each other's eyes for a long moment, then Michael blinked and stepped back. "You sure we want this tree?" he asked in an odd voice.

She nodded. She was so dazed by that simple gesture, that soft kiss, that she couldn't speak.

Chapter 4

Putting up Michael's tree proved to be a longer process than Jennifer had planned. He got it in the stand, and she had him turn it this way and that until the thin side was hidden. Decorating a second tree a few hours after the first one wasn't as much fun as she'd thought it would be, but she insisted on finishing the task. She'd make the Christmas wreath tomorrow and still have it on the front door before her brothers arrived.

"I wish Grandma could see it," Michael said when they were done at last. They stood side by side admiring their handiwork.

"Ruth always liked Christmas and decorations. I remember one year she strung gold tinsel from each corner of the ceiling to the center, right here." She pointed up. "And where the glittery ropes came together she hung a big gold bell. Then she let us drape silvery icicles over the tinsel. It looked pretty gaudy, but I thought it was wonderful."

"I remember that Christmas, but I didn't know you had a hand in throwing all those icicles up there. We usually drove up on Christmas Eve and left late Christmas Day, so it was all decorated before we got here. I wish. . ." he trailed off.

"Do you think it's possible?" Jennifer knew what he was thinking. "Could Ruth travel that far? What is it, four hours?"

"About that. Dad has a big new car, and it's a luxurious ride."

"They could make a little bed for her in the backseat, and she'd probably be lulled to sleep." Jennifer was caught up in the possibilities. "It could be just for Christmas Eve and Christmas Day. You all could join us for Christmas dinner."

Michael walked over to the phone and dialed. Jennifer listened to his part of the conversation with his mother, but she couldn't tell if the suggestion met with a positive response.

"Well?" she asked when he hung up the receiver.

"She's going to talk to Dad and then with Grandma. She thinks it's possible."

He walked over to Jennifer and hugged her. "What a great Christmas present this could be. On Christmas Eve we could have the neighbors over for a bit, so she could see everyone."

"It'll be marvelous," she said and hugged him back.

When Michael bent his head and kissed her, at first it seemed only natural. But this kiss wasn't like the one in the piney woods. This wasn't a kiss between friends; this kiss was between two adults. Jennifer's heart pounded.

When the kiss ended, Michael pulled back. "Wow!"

he said, his voice fast and breathless. "That belongs in a book. Maybe I should give Sam Morgan a love interest."

Jennifer looked into his kind brown eyes and silently asked him to kiss her again. She took a deep breath. "Do you need more research?"

For an answer, Michael kissed her once again.

"I think I had better go ice cookies," Jennifer said at last. She moved away, unable to look at him. What was she doing? This was Mikie. And he lived here and she lived in Chicago. The feelings that had blazed to life between them had no future, and she didn't want to ruin an old friendship.

"What about dinner tonight?" he asked, following her to the door. "Want a bowl of canned stew?"

"I told Beth yesterday that I would call her about getting together tonight—so I'd better find out what she's planned."

"Okay. How about tomorrow night?"

"My brothers will be here." She saw the disappointment in his face, and despite her better judgment, she added, "Why don't you join us for supper?"

"Sure."

Jennifer slipped into her coat, and Michael walked her to her back door as the last rays of the sun streamed over their shoulders. "Oh, I forgot the greenery," she said.

"Where do you want it?" he asked. "Here on the back porch?"

"That's fine, but I'll help."

"No, I'll pile it here. See you tomorrow," he said.

Jennifer walked slowly into the kitchen. She put on the teakettle and phoned Beth. Out the kitchen window she could see Michael as he carried pine boughs to her back porch.

"Hi, Beth. What's on for tonight?" Jennifer listened to her friend, but she kept her gaze on Michael as he climbed his back steps. He turned and glanced at her window and waved.

"I'm sorry. What did you say?"

"Come for supper. The potatoes are almost ready to mash."

"Is it that late?" She glanced at her watch and found it was already after five.

"We eat early since the kids are in bed by seven-thirty."

"If you're sure you have enough, I'll be right there."

Icing cookies would have to wait until tomorrow. And she still hadn't looked through even one room of Grandma's belongings. Well, it was up to Kenneth and Cody to help with that, she rationalized.

A few minutes later she drove out to Beth and Johnny's home. Theirs was a cheerful farmhouse, and Jennifer could feel the love of family when she knocked and walked in.

Johnny was helping seven-year-old Ben read at the kitchen table, while Angie sat in a high chair with a piece of paper and some crayons. Beth turned from stirring gravy on the stove to greet her. National news flitted across the screen of the small TV on the counter. Beth reached over and turned it off.

"Have a seat," she offered. "The only news I want to hear is about your neighbor."

"Actually your mom was over this afternoon," Jennifer said.

"That's not the neighbor I mean and you know it. Mom told me Mike was at your house today. Last night's dinner must have gone well."

"We had a lot to catch up on."

"That's it?"

"He helped me decorate the tree this morning, and we got greenery and put up his tree this afternoon."

"The question is," Johnny inserted, "do I need to call up one of my bachelor friends or are you doing all right on your own?"

Jennifer laughed. Johnny had set her up with a parade of fellows through the years. "I'll manage on my own this time. Besides, I'm leaving a week from tomorrow, and I have tons to do before then." That thought stopped her short and she frowned. She had a plane to catch the Saturday after Christmas. Grandma's things would be sorted out by then, the house would be put on the market, and she'd have no reason to come back to Mulberry. Odd. Her life in Chicago, which had been content enough, now seemed unsatisfactory.

Surely she'd have to come back to sign papers when the house sold, she remembered. She could see Michael then—but should she? What would be the point when she would be going right back to Chicago?

"I've only talked to Mike a few times since he's come back," Beth said. Jennifer forced a smile before her

215

friend turned around from the stove. "He's always nice and socializes some with the townspeople—but not during the day when he writes."

"Which means?" Jennifer asked.

"Which means. . .God works in mysterious ways," Beth said in an all-knowing tone. "Today was a writing day, and he was at your house. Mom found that quite revealing."

"What's to reveal? He's probably taking some time off for the holidays. Even writers need a break." She hesitated. "What do you mean he socializes? With whom?" She could feel her frown was back.

Beth laughed. "Do I detect a little jealousy?"

"Don't be silly. Yesterday was the first time I'd seen him in fourteen years. He's interesting, and he's as kind as ever. Did I tell you that Michael taught me to ride a bike about twenty years ago?"

"I was there, you goose. I saw him run behind you holding that seat until you rode a few feet on your own. If I recall, it took quite a few tries until you managed without him running along beside you."

"That's right, I'd forgotten you were there." Now why had she blocked Beth out of that picture and only remembered the way Mikie had made her feel safe on that bike?

"I can ride my bike," Ben piped up.

"I'll bet you can ride everywhere," Jennifer said and focused the conversation on the little boy.

❧

When Jennifer returned to town shortly after eight

o'clock, it was with a sigh of relief. Beth hadn't let up with the innuendoes about Michael, and Jennifer really didn't know how to handle them.

And she certainly didn't know how to handle Michael's three kisses. That man was Mikie Shannon, she reminded herself. And those kisses were stolen moments of. . .happiness? Joy? No, insanity. Mulberry had always worked its magic on her, let her regroup, relax, draw strength to return to a faster-paced life. Those kisses were a part of the magic, that's all. They weren't reality.

When Michael had put a comforting arm around her, she'd felt safe, secure, and that was something lacking from her life lately. She was the oldest member of her family, and that position brought a responsibility that made her feel vulnerable and unsure of herself. She didn't need to latch onto Michael as a way out of that unsheltered feeling. She had to face life on her own.

Besides that, she told herself, *I'm leaving Mulberry very soon.*

But that didn't keep her from looking at Ruth's house and seeing a light in the room Michael used for writing. So, he was working tonight.

Although she was tired, she made a cup of tea, fed the fire, and sat in an easy chair with a stack of Grandma's journals beside her. She'd promised Michael he could read them as soon as she finished, so she wanted to get started.

She didn't put down "1956" until two in the morning. She had covered momentous times in Grandma's life, cried with her at the end of World War II when her only brother came home from Europe, and cried again when he was killed in Korea.

Grandma had written poems in high school, and a few were scattered in her journals. They were filled with the angst of a teenager trying to find her place in the world. Jennifer made a list of the poems and the journals in which they occurred.

If her journal reflected her true feelings, Grandma hadn't a clue that half the town was sweet on her, as Earl Mosler had implied. She'd met Orey Faucett at a dance in Gravette when she was seventeen, and she'd married him the following year, two weeks after she'd graduated from high school.

She'd loved being a wife and with delight had set up housekeeping with Orey. When she was twenty, she'd borne Robert, Jennifer's father. That was a joyous year, and from then on the journals were peppered with stories of how Robert had learned this and that.

Two years after Robert was born, Orey's father had died, and they had moved to the big house, this very one, to live with Orey's mother. Grandma's mother-in-law survived her husband by only five years, then Grandma had become mistress of the house in her own right. She'd loved Orey's mother, but those five years living with her mother-in-law had been difficult for Grandma, and throughout her journals were little prayers for help in giving up some of the independence she'd had and letting her mother-in-law run the household.

The journal "1956" ended with Grandma hanging

the Christmas wreath on her front door. She had written in detail about the pinecones and red winterberries she'd used on the wreath. Orey had climbed a big tree in Ruth's yard to get mistletoe, and she'd stuck a sprig of it in the wreath to represent the love in her home.

Jennifer was glad she'd hadn't made the Christmas wreath yet. She had remembered the pinecones, and picked up several in the woods, but she'd forgotten about the winterberries, and she hadn't even known about the mistletoe. There was a holly bush in the backyard. That must have been where Grandma had gotten the winterberries. And tomorrow she'd scout around until she found a tree with some mistletoe in it.

With a yawn, Jennifer carried her empty teacup to the kitchen. She glanced across to Ruth's house and saw the house ablaze with lights. What was Michael doing at this hour? When she'd returned from Beth's only the light in his writing room was on.

She could see his silhouette at the living room window, then a moment later, her cell phone rang.

"You're still up? Come see what I've done," he said in an excited voice.

"It's after two, Michael, but I'll be right there."

"Come to the front door," he said and hung up.

Jennifer shrugged into her coat and ran across the yard to Ruth's house. Michael waited on the front porch.

"Close your eyes," he said, then led her across the threshold and into the living room. "Now open them."

Jennifer squealed with delight. Gold tinsel ran from each corner of the living room to the center where a big bell hung. Silvery icicles hung over the tinsel rope.

"It's gaudy, it's flashy, and I love it," she said. "I take it Ruth is coming?"

"She'll be here Christmas Eve before noon."

Chapter 5

Jennifer awoke with the morning sun streaming in the window. It was after nine, and she had lots to do, but she stretched and smiled, and as was her custom she took a moment to thank God for the new day. Then her thoughts turned to last night.

What did his actions say about a man who stayed up late at night to decorate the house to surprise his grandmother? Thoughtful? Absolutely. Kind? No question about that. Caring? Of course. At least he cared about his grandmother, but what about Jennifer? Did he care for her as much as she was beginning to care for him?

She pushed the question away, for she had no time to dwell on what was happening between them. She didn't have an answer anyway. To get her mind off it, she whirled into action.

She dug out Grandma's decorating set and did an artistic job of icing the cookies. She liked the green wreaths the best, making red dots for winterberries and red icing for the bow. With that chore done, she hooked up her computer modem again and checked her e-mail for messages.

"How are things in Huckleberry?" Trevor had written.

"It's Mulberry," she said to the screen.

"Walton, Miggan, and McCoy called with buy requests, and I ran them through for you. Their files have been updated." She downloaded the changes so she would be on top of the situation if she needed to speak with those clients.

This working at long distance was going well, much better than she'd expected. She checked yesterday's closing price on Wal-Mart stock in case she saw Earl over the weekend, then disconnected and turned her thoughts back to Christmas.

Jennifer had seen the box labeled "wreath" in the storage room when she'd carried the decoration boxes to the den. Grandma had always used the same form, saying it was silly to throw out the whole thing when it could be reused. Jennifer carried the box and the greenery to the kitchen table. It was too cold to work on the back porch, and the kitchen would clean up easily enough.

She opened the large box and stared. The form was in there all right—and so were several packages wrapped in Christmas paper.

"Oh, Grandma," she whispered. A tear rolled down her cheek, followed by another and another.

The tag on the first package she lifted out was to Cody. The second was for her and the third for Kenneth. Each one was a small, flat box, the sort of box Grandma used to buy her handkerchiefs in, but the boxes were heavier than handkerchiefs. Jennifer gently shook the package that bore her name, but nothing rattled.

Jennifer smiled through her tears. Grandma had always Christmas shopped whenever she found something special, no matter if it was still summer. A few years ago Jennifer had been with her when she'd found a present for Cody. Grandma had said, "If I don't wrap it right away, I'll be tempted to give it to him now." So as soon as they arrived home, she'd wrapped it and put in the storage room. Jennifer hadn't known the wreath box was her place to hide gifts, but it made sense. Grandma usually made the wreath last, after she'd decorated the house. When she unpacked the wire form, she'd have the gifts right there to go under the Christmas tree.

Jennifer carried the presents to the den and placed them around the tree. "Grandma," she said softly, "even in death you remember your family."

She brushed another tear away as she walked back to the kitchen, and with a deep breath, she resumed her task. At the side of the frame was a red velvet bow. It was a little crushed on one side, but an iron could straighten that out. She poked greenery through the wire frame and artfully arranged it to form a full wreath. Now for the winterberries.

The holly bush was one that Grandma had planted decades ago, and it was heavily laden with the crimson berries. Jennifer had broken off a handful of shoots and started back for the house when Michael hailed her from his back porch.

"Good morning," she said. "I forgot to tell you last night that I've read through a stack of Grandma's journals, and in one I found how she made her Christmas wreath."

She glanced up at the huge tree in Ruth's back yard, but saw no mistletoe. "Grandpa found mistletoe in this tree, and she stuck a sprig in the wreath. I was wondering. . ."

"Why do I feel like I'll be climbing a tree before long?" he asked.

Jennifer grinned. "Have you noticed any mistletoe around? There's usually a lot in the park."

"Those old trees must be seventy feet tall. I suggest we look a little closer to home and closer to the ground. Come on." He held out his hand. She laid her winterberry shoots on the back porch, then took his hand. They walked a couple of houses south before Jennifer spied mistletoe.

"Oh, no!"

"What?"

"There's some." She pointed up.

"Well, sure enough." He grinned at her.

"But it's in Mr. Elliston's yard."

"That's more in his air space than his yard," Michael said. "You ask permission; I'll go get a ladder."

"You want me to talk to him alone?" When she was young, Jennifer had picked some roses from Mr. Elliston's yard. He'd called Grandma and complained about her stealing his flowers, and Jennifer had been forced to apologize. Of course it was wrong to take his flowers without asking, but she was only five, and she'd thought Grandma would like a bouquet for the table. Mikie had walked her over to Mr. Elliston's and waited on the sidewalk while she told the man she was sorry and gave him back his flowers.

Now Michael laughed. "You're a big girl now, Jennifer. You can do this. I'll wait for you just like I did last time."

"Of course," she said. With a quick prayer for courage, she marched to the front door. She knocked and waited, then knocked again.

"I'm coming," she heard from the other side. Finally Mr. Elliston opened the door. His gnarled hands gripped a walker for balance.

"Mr. Elliston, what happened?"

"Fell and broke my hip a few months ago. I heard you were coming back, Jennifer. You look more like Jessie every day."

"Thank you," she said. "Mike Shannon and I were wondering if we could get some mistletoe out of your tree. I'm making a wreath and. . ."

He waved her to silence. "Jessie got it out of that tree herself last year. Go ahead. Just don't fall and sue me."

"We'll be careful. Do you need some for decoration?"

"Now what would a man my age do with mistletoe?" he asked gruffly.

On impulse Jennifer said, "Bring it over to the Christmas Eve party we're having for Ruth Shannon."

"Ruthie's coming home?" His eyes lit up.

"Just for the holiday. I'll send one of my brothers to help you over there around seven. Okay?"

"I guess I could come over for a little while," he said.

Out of the corner of her eye, Jennifer saw Michael approach, carrying the ladder. She waved him on.

"Thanks, Mr. Elliston." She skipped down the steps

and held the ladder while Michael climbed up. Once he got off the ladder and into the tree branches, she stepped back so she could watch his progress.

"I'm going to drop it down," he called after he had reached a clump that clung to a branch some thirty feet in the air. "Is that enough?"

"If we had more, we could find a use for it," she hollered.

As she watched him straddle the next limb and inch out, she wished she hadn't asked for more. Holding his pocketknife in one hand and leaning forward until he was almost lying down, he cut the next clump free. Jennifer picked it up off the ground.

"That's plenty. Come on down now. Be careful."

She held her breath until he was in reach of the ladder, then she steadied it again and didn't take a deep breath until he was on the sidewalk beside her.

"Be right back," Jennifer said. She zipped up to the porch and saw Mr. Elliston peering out the window. She waved the mistletoe, then opened the door without knocking and laid some on the entry table. "Thanks. See you Christmas Eve."

She sprang back down the steps and picked up the end of the ladder. "You won't believe this, but I asked Mr. Elliston to your grandmother's party."

Michael's eyebrows shot up.

"Well, it is Christmas," Jennifer said.

"Peace on earth, goodwill toward men?" Michael said.

"I couldn't have said it better."

"I don't know, maybe the lambs lying down with the

lions is more like it," he said with a laugh. "If I remember correctly, you'd cross the street before you'd walk in front of Mr. Elliston's house."

"That was a long time ago," she said firmly. "Oh!" She dropped her end of the ladder and sprinted ahead, then launched herself at the huge man who came down Grandma's front porch steps to meet her.

"Oops!" she called over her shoulder. "Sorry about the ladder."

"It's okay." Michael leaned it against the house and walked toward them, his face tense as he watched Jennifer disappear in the big man's embrace.

"Michael, you remember Cody," she said at last.

A look of relief washed over Michael's face. "Cody! You've changed a bit since I last saw you."

"Michael. . .Mikie?" At his nod, Cody said, "You've changed a bit yourself."

"Cody was named to the All-American team this year," Jennifer said. "He's the best tackle Oklahoma State's ever had."

"My sister is a little biased," Cody said.

"Sisters should be biased," Jennifer said and hugged her brother again. "I didn't think you'd be here until late afternoon."

"I gave a fraternity brother a ride to Fort Smith and stayed the night with his folks. Got anything to eat?"

"Of course, let's go in." Jennifer opened the door, then turned back to Michael. "Oh, let me help with the ladder."

"I've got it," Michael said. "But I need some mistletoe."

Jennifer gave him a clump, then ushered Cody inside. "There's sandwich stuff in the refrigerator. Use the counter over there, and I'll get the kitchen table cleared off in a minute." She added a sprig of mistletoe to her wreath and stepped out on the back porch to collect the winterberries she'd left there. Michael was just coming out of Ruth's garage.

"I'd like to start on the journals," he called.

"You're going to like her even more after you read them," Jennifer said. "How about a sandwich?"

"I'm coming for supper, remember?" he said.

"That doesn't mean you can't have lunch, too. Come on in and we'll show Cody yesterday's work."

They carried their plates to the den, as they had the day before.

"Hey, the tree's up," Cody exclaimed. "Looks like Santa's already come. Anything for me?" He put his plate on an end table and stooped to look at the packages, then abruptly turned back to Jennifer. "They're from Grandma."

"I found them in the storage room this morning. She shopped early again this year."

"A present from Grandma," Cody said softly and shook his head in disbelief, then in a stronger voice, "Well, the tree looks great."

"Thanks. Michael and I decorated it yesterday." Jennifer filled him in on Michael's career and Ruth's homecoming while they ate. "We have to go through Grandma's belongings. Room by room," she said.

"That can wait until Kenneth gets here," Cody said.

"Then we'll get to work."

"I'd better get to work now," Michael said. "May I take these journals with me?"

Jennifer nodded. After he left, she finished the wreath, and she and Cody hung it on the front door.

"Just like Grandma would have done," Cody said. "It's odd not having her here. I guess that makes you the head of the family now."

"Yes, I'm in charge now, and I say we have to start through Grandma's things."

"Not yet," he said as they walked back into the house. "Let's talk about that when Kenneth gets here. Tell me about Michael Shannon."

"I told you about him."

"Yes, you told me he was an author, but there's more. I can tell by the way you look at him and the way he looks back at you."

Chapter 6

W e're old friends. I'd forgotten how many good times we'd shared together. And I've seen Beth, too, and Sarah. You'll have to run over and see her. I've asked Mr. Elliston to Ruth's party. Remember how I used to be afraid of him?" Jennifer chattered on, her voice quick and light, trying to divert Cody from Michael.

Cody gave her a knowing look, but at least she had succeeded in avoiding the issue of Michael Shannon and what was between them.

And what was between them? Childhood memories, three kisses, and a feeling of rightness and security—but they were stolen kisses and feelings. She had no right to them. They were just as stolen as the roses she'd taken from Mr. Elliston's yard all those years ago. A week from this very moment she'd be flying back to Chicago and a different life—a fast-paced world. Still, nothing could stop her from taking the memory of those feelings with her, and in quiet times alone at her apartment, she could take them out and feel the warmth and security of being held by Michael.

Security. She kept coming back to that. She'd always felt secure until Grandma's death. Jennifer was head of the household now, just as Cody had said. It was not a position she wanted.

To get her mind on another subject, she showed Cody the journals and told him about the poetry.

"Maybe she mentioned where she kept them in her journal," Cody said. "Hey, what's for supper? I was thinking of looking up Joe Bob and seeing if he wanted to come over."

"Do you think of much besides food?" Jennifer said and laughed. "Ask Joe Bob to supper. Phone's on the desk. I'm headed to Luttman's."

When she returned from the grocery store, she found a note from Cody saying he and Joe Bob would be there by five-thirty. Plenty of time for her to delve back into Grandma's journals before she needed to fix supper.

She pulled several notebooks from the bookcase and traveled in time to 1957 and a slower life in Mulberry. Ruth and Grandma had developed a strong friendship and did many things together. They started the library in the old American Legion hut. Jennifer remembered spending time there in the summers. The books were all donated by people in town, since there was no library budget, and the workers were all volunteers, but it well-served the town's population of 466.

The next few years were filled with day-to-day living as Grandma spent time in PTA at Robert's school and life settled into a routine. She fought the consolidation of the high school with other small towns around, but Grandma lost that fight, so when he reached ninth grade, Robert took the bus to Gravette to school.

In "1965" Jennifer found another mention of poems.

"March 8. Today I saw a redbird in the bush outside the kitchen window. It must be the same cardinal I saw in that bush in January when big flakes of snow were falling. The bird stood out like a flame against all that white. But today, although the redbird was just as brilliant as before, the brown of leaves caught in the same brown-colored branches somehow dimmed its color. There must be a message there. Maybe I could write about it in a poem. I've been trying my hand at little verses lately, and I like the feeling I get when the words are just right. I used to write poetry in high school. Guess it's come back to me."

The next few years were years of change. Robert went to the university where he met and married Donna, Jennifer's mother. They moved to Missouri, but came to visit frequently.

"October 15. Robert called. I'm a grandmother! Donna's doing fine and little Jennifer Marie has my middle name. I could hardly wait for Orey to come in for lunch to tell him. He says he can't take off work to go see them, so we'll have to wait until the weekend. Imagine, a grandchild. I have such hopes and dreams for her."

"Jennifer? Cody?" Jennifer heard the door slam shut and marked her place in "1969." She rushed to the living room and hugged her other brother. Beside him stood a young blond-haired woman.

"Kenneth, how was your trip?"

"Great. Jennifer, this is Emily."

Jennifer smiled, hoping she had hid her surprise at seeing the woman Kenneth had been dating for several months. She hadn't known Emily would be accompanying him to Mulberry. "I've heard a lot about you, Emily," she managed to say pleasantly, swallowing her disappointment that she would have to share Kenneth's attention.

"I wanted to talk to you, well, we wanted to talk to you," Kenneth said. "Is Cody here yet?"

"He's out with Joe Bob. They'll be back for supper."

"Oh, well. It can wait."

Jennifer glanced at Emily's ring finger and she smiled, excitement washing away her earlier feeling of disappointment. "I don't think it can. Does this mean what I think it means?"

Kenneth grinned. "I was going to tell you and Cody together. We're getting married."

Jennifer hugged Emily. "Welcome to the family. When? And why didn't you tell me on the phone?" She shook her finger at Kenneth.

"We've set the date for June fourteenth, after school's out. Emily says she can't concentrate on a new husband and her fourth graders at the same time."

"I should have suspected something," Jennifer said. "We haven't had a conversation in months that he didn't mention you," she told her sister-in-law to be.

After they'd unloaded the car, Emily and Kenneth joined Jennifer in the kitchen, where she'd started supper.

"Please let me help," Emily said. "I love to cook. I have an old family recipe for spaghetti sauce that's out of this world."

Jennifer held up a jar of spaghetti sauce she'd bought and grinned. "You picked a winner, Kenneth. We could use a cook in the family. Why don't you two plan tomorrow night's fare?"

Although not gourmet, the meal was a grand success. Michael came over, carrying Grandma's journals, and Cody and his friend showed up a few minutes later. The six of them sat around the table and talked and laughed and feasted on Jennifer's decorated sugar cookies.

Kenneth and Emily volunteered for cleanup, Cody and Joe Bob opted for a movie in Gravette with some of Joe Bob's friends, and Michael ushered Jennifer to the den, where the lights sparkled on the Christmas tree. He pulled her down beside him on a small couch.

"What do you think of Grandma's journals?" Jennifer asked.

"She was very insightful and saw beauty in everyday things. From the few poems in these journals," he motioned to the ones he had returned, "I can tell she has real talent, and those were the work of a teenager. I wonder what she wrote later when she'd learned from life."

"Here's another stack for you. I just finished reading about the day I was born. Tonight I'm going to read more," she said and sighed. "We haven't started cleaning out the house yet. The boys aren't anxious to do it, and I thought we needed some normal family time." But what she'd foreseen as a time for the three of them to sit around the fire reminiscing had proved to be purely a fancy in her mind. The Faucett children had different lives now.

She'd wanted everything to be like old times, but it couldn't be. Life had to move on. These were new times and her family was changing: Grandma was gone, and Emily had come into it. Jennifer was truly glad for Kenneth and Emily, but somehow she felt lonelier and more insecure than ever.

"Let's go for a walk," Michael suggested. "It's nippy out, but if we bundle up, we'll be okay."

They strolled arm in arm down the sidewalk, admiring outside lights on houses, and turned toward Main Street. There really wasn't much to the two-block downtown—one café, which was only open for breakfast and lunch, the post office, Luttman's store, a real estate office, and the lot where a boardinghouse had been before it burned in the seventies. There were two empty buildings with "For Sale" signs in the windows. One was the old bank, and the other had housed the meat locker. On the far corner was Berley's garage, which was now a gas station/convenience store and the only business open at night. It was the gathering place when Luttmann's closed for the day.

"It's changed," Jennifer said softly. "This town is dying. Grandma's gone, Ruth's ill, Mr. Elliston's on a walker." She shivered.

"Not exactly dying, but things never remain the same. Did you know Luttman's is now run by old Tom's nephew?"

"No. When did that happen?"

"A couple of months ago. Tom said it was time he took that cruise he's talked of for years. The only family member willing to take the store was Jimmie. So, he's the new storekeeper."

"I didn't see anyone I knew when I've been in there."

"Probably his kids were working."

They crossed the street and wandered through the park. "Tell me about your life in Chicago," Michael said.

She described her typical day at work and the people she worked with. She mentioned how important her work was to her, but neglected to mention that sometimes at night, when she was alone in her apartment, just her and God, her life seemed not empty, but lacking something. She told him about the city and the lights and the action.

"It's exciting. Like New York, the city never sleeps. Something's going on all the time. Much different from Mulberry. If Trevor, my boss, saw this place, he'd think it was Hicksville."

"Do you think that, too?"

"Oh, no. I love Mulberry. It's peaceful here, and the people aren't hicks. On the whole they don't have the education of the people I deal with regularly, but that doesn't mean they aren't smart folks."

"I'm glad you feel that way," he said and escorted her up the steps of the hexagon-shaped bandstand on the edge of the park. They sat on a corner bench and looked over to the small lake which served as the town's swimming pool. "I've met more genuine people here than anywhere I've traveled." He put his hands in his pockets and did not look at her. "I've decided to stay here."

His statement took a moment to register. He'd come as a favor to Ruth, to keep her house up while she stayed with his folks. And now he was going to stay? Forever? "Can you write here on a permanent basis?"

"Sure. All I need are a post office box and a telephone. The internet lets me research anything I need for a book. I'm not saying I wouldn't take side trips. I always visit a site before I set a book there, and I'm ready for another trip out West to reacquaint myself with wide open spaces for my next western. I'm in New York once a year to meet with my editor, and that's enough to let Sam Morgan wander the streets and see what's changed for my mysteries."

"You've got it all figured out."

"Almost." He took her hand in his. "I'd like to buy Jessie's house."

"You want Grandma's house?"

"If it's for sale. It's twice the size of my grandma's house, and I've always admired it."

"Why do you need more room? You have a writing room at Ruth's."

"True. But that den with the fireplace and the bay window would make a much better office than that small bedroom I'm in now. Besides, I'd like to have a family."

"A family? You're involved with someone?" She felt

as if a fist had grabbed her heart and squeezed it. How could he kiss her as he had if he. . . She couldn't finish the thought, and she pulled her hand away from his.

"No, I'm not involved with anyone, but that could change." He stood and walked to the railing. "Lately I've come to some crossroads in my life, and it's decision time. I'm going to settle down here. I've done a lot of praying about it, and it feels like the right thing to do."

"In Mulberry?"

"Yes. Like I said, it feels right—and something else feels right, too." He pulled her into his arms. "You're so beautiful, Jennifer." He kissed her. After a moment, she kissed him back.

"Mikie," Jennifer said at last. Reluctantly, he ended the kiss but he still held her close. "We're friends, aren't we?" Her voice was breathless.

"I hope so. But there's something here that wasn't here before." He gave her a sideways grin. "A certain chemistry, shall we say?"

"Maybe some sort of chemical imbalance," Jennifer said and Michael laughed.

"I think we'd better be getting back." he said. "You're shivering."

"It is cold," she said, but she knew she wasn't shivering because of the freezing temperature. She was shivering from his touch; funny, though, because she could have sworn his hands were burning hot.

The walk home wasn't as companionable as the stroll downtown. They still walked arm in arm, but there was an awareness now that hadn't been there before. Some thing had been said, hinted at really, and it made Jennifer both happy and uncomfortable.

By the time they arrived home, they'd planned Ruth's homecoming party. Michael told her he'd called several others on the block that afternoon and asked them to drop in on Christmas Eve. Jennifer suggested a few others she knew were Ruth's friends.

"Shall I get those other journals now?" he asked when they reached her front door.

"Sure." She hesitated. "Would you like some coffee?" she asked out of politeness. She really wanted him to go. She couldn't think with him beside her, and she needed space to consider what had happened tonight.

"I don't think so," he said. "I'll just take these and read them tonight. See you tomorrow?"

She nodded.

He obviously wasn't as bothered about what had transpired between them as she was, for he bent to kiss her, another special good-night kiss, and then he left with a wave.

"Ah-hum."

She turned to find Kenneth standing in the doorway to the den.

"What's going on?" he asked.

"I'm just going to take some reading to bed," Jennifer said.

"That's not what I meant. What's going on between you and Michael?"

Jennifer colored. "I don't know," she answered. "I don't know."

Chapter 7

Sunday morning quiet reigned in the household. Jennifer had the kitchen to herself for half an hour before Emily joined her.

"Another cup?" Emily asked as she poured herself some coffee.

"Yes, please," Jennifer said. She handed over part of the newspaper she'd already read. She'd heard the plunk of the newspaper on the front porch at five-thirty and had glanced out the bedroom window in time to see Michael jog on to Ruth's house. He must have gone to Burley's station and picked up the Little Rock paper. *What a thoughtful man.*

That thoughtful man had occupied most of her waking hours—and there had been many through the long night. She'd wanted to read Grandma's journals, but couldn't concentrate. Instead she tried to sort out her feelings for Michael.

Of course she was attracted to him. She'd known that from the moment she'd laid eyes on him. And being honest with herself, she had to admit she'd had a crush on him in the summers. Because she saw him so seldom, that one week in the summer, she'd put that attraction out of her mind. But now she remembered all the fun they'd had, all the thoughts they'd shared, especially that last summer together when he'd had a car and they'd been allowed to go all over town and even to Gravette, too. She knew Grandma had been concerned. After all, Jennifer had only been fourteen, and Mikie was three years older. Was their growing friendship why their visits were scheduled for different times the following summer?

Through her high school and college years, Jennifer had dated several guys, and Mikie's memory had moved to the back of her mind. In Chicago, she didn't lack dates when she wanted them, but there was never one special man. Now she realized that Mikie had always been in the background of her heart and mind, waiting. She just hadn't known how big a piece of her heart he owned.

She wanted to be with Michael. Seeing him again was a homecoming. She felt so right being in his arms, strangely incomplete when she wasn't with him. Yet the thought that their relationship might develop into something more than a reunion of old friends had caught her off-balance. Her heart told her it was what she wanted, but her mind told her it wouldn't work.

Her life was in Chicago, not in Mulberry. How could she possibly live here? A writer could live anywhere, but not a financial advisor. Her clients in Chicago depended on her. And she liked her life.

She'd prayed about it last night, asked God to help her see what direction her life should take. Was she at a crossroads, too?

"Are you all right?" Emily asked.

"Sorry. Just lost in thought."

"About your next-door neighbor?"

Jennifer glanced up from the spot in the paper she'd been staring at for the last five minutes. She raised her eyebrows at Emily, and Emily smiled.

"Kenneth mentioned that there was something between you two."

Jennifer nodded. "There might be, but Michael has decided to live here, and I live in Chicago."

"Ah, the old ultimatum."

"It's not really like that. I mean, he hasn't said anything definite. He is just making a few plans for himself. Something about a crossroads, and he's had to make decisions."

"And you're not a part of his life now, at least not a definite enough part to be included in the decision making," Emily said.

"That's exactly right," Jennifer said. "How did you get to be so smart? I'm going to like having you in the family."

Emily laughed, a nice tingly sound. "I've been through it with Kenneth. We were dating when he was offered that promotion, which would mean traveling a great deal. He had to decide what he wanted in life. And I wasn't in a position to help him with the decision or even weigh in it. He had to decide what he wanted. And he decided a family would be nice, but if he had one, he wouldn't want to leave St. Louis every week to go on the road. And how would he get a family if he was always on the go?"

"So he made the decision that let you fit into his life."

"Yes, but at that point, he had no way of knowing I'd be the one for him."

Jennifer smiled and lifted her coffee cup in a salute. "But you knew."

Emily grinned back. "Of course. Don't we always know what's going on before men? We're more perceptive."

"In this case, Michael could be the more perceptive. After all, he's a writer. He looks within himself to find meaning for his writing. I seem to spend my life going down a written list. Checking off tasks. We're different types of people."

"Opposites attract," Emily said.

"Opposites attract what?" Kenneth asked from the doorway.

"Do you always hang around eavesdropping?" Jennifer asked.

"If I'm in the right place at the right time." He leaned down and gave Emily a peck. "Good morning. Have you been up long?"

"Not long. Coffee?" Emily asked.

"Yep. And some bacon and eggs would be good, too. Remember those Sunday breakfasts of Grandma's?" he asked Jennifer.

Cody ambled into the kitchen. "Grandma's Sunday breakfasts were the best. Biscuits and gravy, eggs, hash browns. . ."

"Pure cholesterol, and we all loved it," Jennifer broke in. "But today we settle for a bowl of cereal. We'll have to hustle to get to church on time."

"What kinds of cereal?" Cody asked.

"Kind. I only bought one kind."

"Odd—having no choice of cereal at Grandma's," he said. "Sorry, just thinking aloud. I miss her."

"I know," Jennifer said.

The foursome made it to church with only a minute to spare. Jennifer glanced around to see if she recognized any of Grandma's friends. She didn't get past the row to her left, where Michael sat beside old Mr. Elliston. He nodded to her and she mouthed "Good morning."

Reverend Swink opened the traditional Christmas service with a prayer, then the Sunday school teacher directed her students to the front of the small church. Some carried scenery and props, and they put their loads all together until they had erected a cardboard stable with a wooden manger.

The children sang a few traditional carols before Mary and Joseph, carrying a real live baby, took their places in the stable. Mary laid the sleeping baby in the manger. A processional of shepherds and kings arrived next.

When the baby whimpered, the young Mary, with dismay in her eyes, looked at a woman in the front pew, who must have been the mother. Mary patted the baby, and he quieted down while the wise men presented their gifts.

By the time the choir of children of all ages began "Silent Night," the baby was wide awake. He whimpered, then cried at the top of his lungs, while Mary did her best to hush him. She picked him up and jiggled him, but it didn't help. Finally the mother took the baby, and he calmed down instantly.

The congregation applauded loudly when the twenty-some children concluded the Christmas pageant. Maybe this town wasn't dying. Perhaps Jennifer had judged too hastily. Children were the hope of any town. If it didn't provide opportunity for them, though, then they had no avenue but to escape. Would these children stay in Mulberry?

Reverend Swink, who had been in Mulberrry as long as Jennifer could remember, stood to give announcements. In his remarks he welcomed Jessie's grandchildren back to the town.

"Mike Shannon has asked me to share the news that Ruth will return to Mulberry for the holidays. Drop in at her home on Christmas Eve, but don't forget the Christmas Eve service here at eleven-thirty," he said.

Jennifer wanted to be there—just like old times. She'd said that phrase over and over in the last few days. What she hadn't said was "for one last time," but it had been lingering in the corner of her mind.

Now what did she feel? Was there a niggling of hope that she wouldn't leave, that this wouldn't be her last children's Christmas program? Had it always been there —that hope?

As they stood for the conclusion of the service, she sneaked a look at Michael. He must have felt her glance, for he looked her direction and smiled.

Once the service was over, he appeared immediately at her side. "What's on tap for today?" he asked.

Kenneth answered. "The best cook this side of the Mississippi will be fixing dinner tonight. Care to join us?"

Michael cast a doubtful look at Jennifer.

"Not her," Kenneth said with a laugh. "Emily. My fiancée."

"What time should I be there?" Michael asked.

Others crowded around Jessie's grandchildren, welcoming them to the community. Jennifer spoke with several and heard a few ask Michael about his grandmother's return.

Once home and back jeans, Jennifer presided over another lunch of sandwiches. "We have to start going through Grandma's things," she said. "We've put it off and put it off, and we're going to run out of time."

"Emily and I are going to the grocery store, then I'll be back and help," Kenneth said.

"Bring back some empty boxes, please. Cody, shall we start in the bedrooms?"

Cody and Jennifer trudged upstairs, carrying empty boxes that Jennifer had gotten at Luttman's. They started in Grandma's closet. Soon both boxes were filled with clothes to give to charity.

"This is going to take forever," Cody said from the floor of the closet. He tossed out shoes and shoe boxes. "Are you sure I need to be here for this?"

"You're not getting out of this that easy. What about the furniture?" She pointed across the room. "That brass bed is probably valuable. That's the type of thing we really should decide on."

"Where would I put furniture? The athletic dorm isn't a place for nice things, even if my dinky room had space, which it doesn't."

"Would you object to Kenneth and Emily having it for their house?"

"No, but what about you? Wouldn't you like Grandma's bed?"

"I don't have room, either," Jennifer said.

"Hey, look at this." Instead of more shoe boxes, he pulled out a wooden box. He lifted the hinged lid.

"Letters!" Jennifer exclaimed. "Maybe the poems are in there, too."

When Kenneth and Emily returned, Jennifer was seated in front of the fireplace on the den floor reading letters from Grandpa Orey to Grandma.

Cody looked relieved to see his brother. "We need to talk. This project will take forever, especially with her reading every slip of paper in the house."

Kenneth looked at the box. "I agree with Cody. This is going to take forever. Why don't we keep the house open and come back every couple months to take a few more things out?"

"We can't do that," Jennifer said. "We need closure." At least she did. "Besides, Michael wants to buy the house if it's for sale."

Kenneth sat down hard on the couch. "Sell the house?"

"What did you think we'd do with it?" Cody asked.

"I didn't want to think about it," Kenneth admitted.

An hour later, they had a new plan. This week they'd

clean out all of Grandma's personal items, let Jennifer take home all important papers, then come back during Cody's spring break to divide up the furniture.

"We can't put this off much longer, boys. You may not want to face this, but it's something we have to do."

That night at a feast of roast beef à la Emily, Kenneth turned to Michael and said, "We can't clean the house out this week. We're going to give some of Grandma's things away, but the furniture will remain. Jennifer says you want to buy the house."

"Yes," Michael said. "I've lived in several places in the last ten years and traveled to many others for research. Now I'd like to settle down. So I asked myself—if I had my choice of anyplace, where would I like to live? And the answer is this house. Where would you like to live, Kenneth?"

"The sky's the limit?"

"Sure."

"Somewhere on the Lake of the Ozarks, right smack in the middle of Missouri. I like the changing seasons, but I like to sail, too. What about you, Jennifer? If you had your choice of anywhere."

"Anywhere. . . ," she mused, then straightened up in her chair as the thought hit her. "Of anywhere in the world, I'd live here."

Chapter 8

Everyone around the table stared at Jennifer, and she looked at Michael. He was grinning and leaned toward her.

"I knew you loved it, too," he said in a low voice that only she could hear.

"Well, well," said Cody. "This is interesting. You both want the house. Maybe, Mike, we ought to keep it in the family."

"Maybe we'd better not make any rash decisions," Jennifer said and changed the subject. "This is delicious roast, Emily."

❧

On Monday morning, Emily busied herself with preparations for Ruth's homecoming party and Christmas dinner.

"What would we have done if you hadn't brought her home?" Jennifer asked Kenneth.

"Probably had raw turkey for dinner," he said.

Jennifer grinned. "That's enough of that talk. It's nearly Christmas. You'd better be good or Santa won't come." She surveyed the growing pile of presents under the tree. "Actually, I guess Santa's already come. Okay, break's over, let's get back upstairs to work."

In record time they cleaned out the closet and dresser drawers in Jennifer's room. Then they moved to the next bedroom. When the phone rang, her brothers shouted with glee for the unscheduled break.

"Good morning, Jennifer," Trevor said. "Did you survive the weekend in Blackberry? I'll bet they don't even have a movie theater in that town."

"No, they don't, and it's Mulberry."

"Have you checked your e-mail?"

"Not yet, but I will. This system is working out very well." And it was. She could almost work out of her home—no matter where it was. She felt as if a light-bulb had gone off over her head and forced herself to give her attention back to Trevor.

"Mrs. Wedell followed your advice on that pyramid scheme and called the police. They've made a couple of arrests, and she thinks she's a hero. She wants to talk to you."

"I'll call her. Anything else?"

"Well, how are you?" Trevor asked.

"Wonderful. But my brothers are helping me clean out Grandma's things, and they're waiting for me. If there's no other business, I'd better go."

"All right. Take care of yourself. Oh, what about Shannon Barnes? Is he helping, too?" His voice had changed subtly when he asked about Michael.

"No, he's not here right now, but I won't forget the autographed copy of his latest. It's on my list."

"If you don't see him again, that's all right," Trevor said.

"Oh, I'll see him," Jennifer said.

"I was afraid you might. I'll talk to you later," Trevor promised and hung up.

Jennifer stared at the phone. Even Trevor seemed to sense there was something between her and Michael. It was time she admitted to herself the strong connection between them that was growing ever stronger. She sighed and returned to the bedroom to find the boys in a somber mood.

"I'd like some of Grandma's handkerchiefs," Cody said. The big football player held a dainty white lace cloth. "She always carried one in her pocket," he said softly.

"She'd like you to have one," Jennifer said. She looked at the loose handkerchiefs lying in the drawer, and she thought again of the packages downstairs. Obviously, Grandma had used her handkerchief boxes to wrap whatever treasures she had found for them.

In record time the threesome cleaned out Grandma's remaining personal effects from the other bedrooms.

"What about the linen closet?" Kenneth said as they hauled boxes downstairs.

"Let's leave it for now. Once you and Emily set up housekeeping, you may need more towels and sheets. And of course there are Grandma's quilts, and we each should take a couple of those."

Her stomach was full of butterflies for some reason, and she longed to curl up somewhere and dream. She knew all too well the direction her dreams would take, though, and she forced herself to check her e-mail, call

Mrs. Wedell, and make transactions for her clients. But when that was finished, she rewarded herself by popping next door.

Michael greeted her, then leaned down and gave her a peck on the cheek. The casual gesture surprised her, but somehow it felt right.

"How's the cooking going?" she asked.

"We're set," Emily said from the kitchen table where she was checking off a list. "All hors d'oeuvres are planned. We can throw this party together in a matter of two hours. That's if your brothers don't help us. If they do, we can do it in what, five hours?"

Jennifer laughed. "And Christmas dinner?"

"Groceries are in those bags. Turkey and all the fixings."

"Great. Well, I'll take them over to Grandma's." She turned to leave and saw a large ball of mistletoe hanging in the back door frame. How had she missed that before? "What's this?"

"A kissing ball," Michael said. "I read about it on the internet. It took another trip to Mr. Elliston's tree to get all the mistletoe I needed."

"I'll take some groceries," Emily said and grabbed one sack, "while you two discuss this." She disappeared out the back door.

"I'll show you how this works," Michael said and walked Jennifer to the door. He bent down, and this time his kiss was no peck on the cheek.

"It works very well," Jennifer said when she came up for air, her heart singing. "You should get a patent on it. And I'd better get these groceries home." She didn't think her senses could take another kiss like that one.

"I'll carry the turkey. You want to get those journals? I finished that batch last night."

Jennifer picked up the journals and made a dash for the door, but she wasn't quick enough to escape without one more kiss, although an awkward one since they were both holding heavy loads. Michael pulled the door closed behind them.

Emily was putting away groceries, and Michael dumped his load on the counter and followed Jennifer to the den.

"I don't have any more journals for you," she said as she put away the ones he'd read. "But I'd like to read more this afternoon."

"Me, too," Michael said. "Shall we read together?"

After lunch, they sat close together and read the journals through the afternoon.

Jennifer cried when she read the account of her father's death when she was ten. How hard it was for Grandma to give up her son, but she was philosophical about it.

"Ruth told me there was nothing I could do to bring him back. That wasn't a choice. My choices were to go on living a happy life or be unhappy all the time. You cannot live for the dead. Orey agrees, and we're working on being happy without Robert here. After all, we know we'll see him again one day when our own time comes."

Jennifer and Michael got as far as "1986" before the others demanded they quit and play Scrabble with them.

"What does 'I'm discouraged about CW' mean?" Jennifer asked as she marked their place. "Who is CW?"

"Beats me. Shall we read more tonight after I take all of you to dinner? There's a great pizza place in Gravette."

❧

That night, Jennifer and Michael settled down to more journals "Here it is again." Jennifer remarked. She flipped back through the journal and marked places with her fingers. "Grandma wrote 'CW back again' every four or five weeks."

Michael shook his head. "Beats me."

They continued reading, their heads bent over the handwritten journals. Michael returned a stack to the bookcase and brought a new bunch to the couch. "Look! 'I'm sick of CW—discouraged.' What does that mean?" Michael asked. "Who is CW? What's Cody's middle name?"

"James. Who else in town. . .no, it has to be someone out of town since he or she pops in every month or so." Jennifer tapped the journal. "I can't think who it could be."

They didn't find out that night, and Michael made Jennifer promise not to read further without him. "It wouldn't do for you to solve the mystery alone," he said.

"We need Sam Morgan for this one," Jennifer said. "Can you bring his analytical mind with you tomorrow morning?"

"Right," Michael said. "I'll be here at nine."

❧

Early Tuesday morning, Jennifer and Michael, with coffee cups in hand, resumed their places from the night before and took up "1991." Jennifer felt as if she were looking at Grandma's soul when she wrote about her feelings when Grandpa Orey died.

"I guess I'm head of the family now. But how can I possibly manage? Will the grandkids turn to me for answers I don't have?"

So, Grandma had felt the very same way as Jennifer did now. But Grandma had managed beautifully. And with God's help, Jennifer vowed that she would do a good job as head of the family, too, now that it was her turn. She read on.

"I may have put too much store in his words at times, but a man as wonderful as my Orey only comes along once in a lifetime. I've had my great passion. I hope my grandkids can find the special ones meant for them."

Jennifer blinked back tears. Kenneth had found his great passion in Emily. Had she found hers in the man who sat beside her? She leaned her head on his shoulder and sighed, then turned the page.

In "1996" Grandma wrote, "CW will be here next year! I can't believe it and I can hardly wait!"

"CW again?" Jennifer exclaimed.

"Who is he?" Michael asked.

They finished the last journal that night. There was no mention of poems, but plenty of talk of her hopes and dreams for her grandchildren. "CW is here at last. I'll tell the kids everything when they're here at Christmas,"

255

she'd written three days before her death. Her last entry was about picking ripe red tomatoes from the garden. "Their homegrown Arkansas flavor can't be beat" was the last sentence she recorded in journal "1997."

"We'll never know," Jennifer said.

"The Mystery of CW," Michael said.

"Well, I know Grandma a lot better now, and yet there are even bigger gaps in her life that I'll never be able to fill in."

"Perhaps we should all have parts of our lives that are private," Michael said. "Parts known only to God and ourselves."

Jennifer nodded. "I suppose you're right. We'd better call it a night. Tomorrow's a big day."

❧

The next morning, as they'd planned, Jennifer, her brothers, and Emily marched to Ruth's house and helped Michael with last-minute details. The boys carried extra chairs into the living room.

"I'll bet neighbors will show up long before seven," Jennifer said. "Sarah will be here ten minutes after Ruth gets here."

"I'd better start the simpler hors d'oeuvres," Emily said and headed for the kitchen.

Shortly after eleven, Michael's dad pulled the car to a stop close beside the front steps. Michael rushed outside and gingerly carried Ruth to the porch, then set her down while Michael's mom brought the walker from the trunk. The others stayed inside while Ruth made her way slowly into the house.

"Oh my," she whispered in awe when she saw the decorated living room. "It's so good to be home."

"Merry Christmas, Ruth," Jennifer said.

Ruth looked startled. "For a minute there I thought you were Jessie," she said. "You look just like her."

"So I've been told."

The doorbell rang and Sarah popped in. Emily served everyone tea and finger sandwiches, then Michael's mom insisted Ruth take a nap before the party.

The rest of the afternoon, Jennifer, under Emily's direction, worked in Grandma's kitchen making party foods.

"These trays are gorgeous," Jennifer said as she tucked another one in the refrigerator. "Are we almost done? Oops, I almost forgot to get out the special glasses for tonight's Christmas toast. They're shaped like angels, and Grandma had a tradition that they were only used once a year." She started for the cupboard in the storage room, but the phone rang.

"Merry Christmas Eve, Jennifer," Trevor said. "We're missing you at the office party."

Jennifer glanced at her watch. Wall Street had closed, always the signal for the annual office party. "Merry Christmas, Trevor."

"How are things in Mulberry?" he asked.

"You got it right!" Jennifer exclaimed.

"You like it there, don't you?"

"I love it here. The people are real, the scenery is gorgeous, the weather—"

"Okay, I get the picture. You're not coming back, are you?"

"Of course I'm coming back." She hesitated for a long moment. "But I'm not going to stay." There— she'd said the words aloud and they sounded so right. "I belong here."

"With Shannon Barnes?"

"I don't know. It's too early to tell about that."

"It'll work out. He'd be a fool not to want you." Trevor's voice was gentle.

"Thanks, Trevor. Merry Christmas."

So, now she was committed to starting a business in Arkansas, but perhaps she could continue to work via the phone line, even though it was long distance. A computer modem was an incredible invention that would allow her to keep in touch with clients like Mrs. Wedell and still be at home. Well, she'd talk to Trevor about that when she went back to work on Monday. And tonight she'd tell Michael she was staying in Mulberry.

"Jennifer," Emily called from the kitchen. "We'd better get dressed for the event."

Later that evening, Ruth beamed when Michael escorted Mr. Elliston into the house. Christmas music played softly in the background and laughter drifted from every corner as visitors came and left.

"The only thing that would make this more perfect would be for Grandma to be here," Jennifer told Michael.

When Ruth looked worn-out, the last of the guests departed.

"Can you come over for our Christmas toast?"

Jennifer asked Michael. "Then I'd like to talk to you, alone."

"Intriguing," he said. "And I'd love to be there for the toast." They walked hand in hand across the yard to Grandma's house.

Once inside, Jennifer grabbed a tray, and Michael followed her to the storage room. "I've never been here for the Christmas toast, but I've heard Grandma talk about it," he said.

"And I've never gotten the angel glasses. That was always Grandma's job. But I know they're kept here," she said as she opened the cupboard, "in a place of honor." She handed two glasses to Michael who set them on the tray. Then two more, then another of the special glasses that were molded in the shapes of angels, each one slightly different from the others.

Jennifer filled the glasses with eggnog, and Michael carried the tray to the den where they all gathered around the Christmas tree.

"This was Grandma's part," Jennifer said, "but as the oldest, I guess I have to step in now." She cleared her throat and they held up their glasses. "This Christmas is very different from any other we've known. Grandma is gone, but she must be watching from heaven and lifting a glass with us. So, here's to our love for each other and for Jesus, whose birth we celebrate tomorrow." That was the part that Grandma always said. Then Jennifer added more, a departure from tradition, but she'd learned that traditions change.

"And this year we toast Grandma, who has deeply

touched our lives and whose influence we will always feel." They clinked glasses and drank.

"What about opening our presents from Grandma tonight?" Cody asked. "I know that's not our custom, but it seems right."

As an answer, Jennifer picked out the special gifts from under the tree and handed one to Kenneth and one to Cody. She sat down with her own, holding the slim package between her hands. This would be the last gift from Grandma she would ever open, and she sat still, treasuring the moment a little longer.

Cody, however, wasn't bothered by sentimental thoughts. He got the paper off first and lifted the lid of the handkerchief box, then held up a thin book. *The Christmas Wreath* by J. M. Tapp. Kenneth's and Jennifer's gifts were also copies of the same volume.

"It's a book of poetry," Jennifer said as she leafed through the pages. She turned back to the front and read the inscription in Grandma's hand.

"For Jennifer. I feel I've put a lifetime into these verses. Hope you enjoy them as much as I liked writing them. With love, Grandma."

"These are her poems!" Jennifer exclaimed. She looked thoughtfully at the cover again. "J. M. Tapp," she whispered. Then she turned to the dedication page. "For my grandchildren, Jennifer, Kenneth, and Cody, with love."

"Well, Jessie did it," Michael said with a catch in his voice. "Jessie Marie Faucett is J. M. Tapp. And CW is *The Christmas Wreath*."

"Why did she mention in her journal that CW kept coming back?" Jennifer asked.

"My guess is the book was rejected by several publishers before it was finally accepted. That's the way the business works. Rarely does a book sell to the first publisher it's sent to."

"Why Tapp?" Kenneth asked.

"A pen name," Michael said. "A faucet is a tap. She used her own name in code."

Jennifer read the title poem, "The Christmas Wreath." The poem described how every house in town had a different type of wreath. Most started with a fragrant evergreen ring representing the circle of God's love. Some had frosted pinecones or reindeer moss or ornaments. Then Grandma told about the part that made hers special—the mistletoe hidden within.

❧

Love is secreted away in all of us, and
If you'll look closely, you'll see.
Next year I may be more daring and
Put doves in a nest or a bell that clangs
And reveal what is inside of me.

In the distance Jennifer heard the ringing of the church bells, a reminder of the Christmas Eve service.

She glanced at her watch and laid down the book. "We'll have to read the rest later." They put on their coats, and Michael took her arm as they walked out the door toward the church three blocks away.

"That's quite a Christmas present from Jessie," he said once the others had walked ahead, out of hearing range. "Now what did you want to talk to me about?"

"Um, I don't want you to misinterpret this, but I've decided I'm at a crossroads in my life, too. I'm going to live in Mulberry."

He stopped, put his hands on her shoulders, and turned her to face him. "You're sure?"

She nodded. "I've discovered this is where I want to be."

"But you don't want me to misinterpret that to mean you're staying here because of me?"

She nodded again.

"Couldn't I hope that I'm a little part of it?" Michael's voice was hesitant.

"You are a part of it. But I don't want to put any pressure on you or me."

The bells pealed again.

"I don't know about you," he said huskily, "But I feel no pressure. I already love you." He bent and kissed her, a sweet, tender kiss that made Jennifer's eyes sting with tears.

"I love you, too," Jennifer whispered, her voice shaky.

He hugged her close. "We'll take it as slow as you need," he said and put his arm around her as they hurried their steps toward the church. "Our relationship, I mean. Slow—like life in a small town. To savor, enjoy, cherish."

"I can tell you're a writer," Jennifer said.

"Yeah," he said with a grin. "And I may cross over to romances."

Veda Boyd Jones

Veda writes romances "that confirm my own values," including the award-winning *Callie's Mountain*. She has also written several books in the American Adventure and Sisters in Time series for boys and girls ages 8–12. Besides her fiction writing, Veda has authored numerous articles for popular periodicals. A sought-after speaker at writers' conferences, Veda lives with her husband, an architect, and three sons in the Ozarks of Missouri.

Christmas Baby

Melanie Panagiotopoulos

Chapter 1

"It's Christmastime!" Christina Rallis sang out, just as she did every year when the Santa in the Macy's Thanksgiving Day parade passed by her parents' Central Park West apartment. This year, she thought, she would like to give her parents something really special for Christmas, to show them how much she appreciated them. She could never think what to give them, though; they always seemed to have everything they wanted. When Christmas Day arrived, she knew they would shower her with gifts, like always, and she would give her mother a blouse and her father a pen set or a tie, something they already had. If only this year she could think of something they really needed.

Her dad chuckled, a good-natured sound that Santa might have made.

Smiling at him, Christina left her real-life view of the parade to join her father in front of the television to watch as it was telecast live from Harold Square. With his white hair, matching beard, and blue eyes, Christina thought her jolly father could have easily played Santa.

"It might be Christmastime," her mother said as she walked into the room, "but the most important thing of

267

all is that our 'Christmas baby' will be celebrating her twenty-third birthday this Christmas day." She placed a sterling tray, the same color as her shiny silver hair, on the coffee table, and glanced fondly at Christina.

Christina's father's eyes swung toward the baby grand piano where a group of framed pictures recorded most of those birthdays. He shook his head, "Twenty-three years. . .it's hard to believe. . ." His voice trailed off and he looked at his wife with an intensity that sent a familiar unrest to Christina's soul.

She had seen that fleeting, almost haunted look pass between her parents again and again down through the years. Something about the way they looked at one another always sent pinpricks of uneasiness over Christina's skin. But it was too brief a look, too dubious a sensation to even form into a question.

Wanting to defuse that vague feeling that hovered like an unwanted odor around them, Christina reached over to the table and picked up her mother's most recent woman's magazine. "Well, I certainly feel twenty-three and after only two more finals I will have my Bachelor of Science degree! So I'm very glad to be turning twenty-three and not twenty-two." She shivered slightly. "I wouldn't want to repeat this last year of university." She laughed. "I like graduating—even though I'm not sure what I'm going to do with my chemistry degree!"

"Here! Here!" her dad cheered, his jolly self once again, and he held his steaming mug of coffee high in the air. "To our almost-graduate!"

Christina nodded her head pertly in appreciation and

then held up the magazine toward her mother. "Does this have any interesting articles?"

"I don't know, dear." Her mother motioned for them to have some chips and dip. "I haven't had a chance to read it yet."

Christina nodded, understanding that her mother had been too busy putting together a new daytime drama to have had a chance to read a magazine. Her parents worked together; both were producers and writers of daytime TV, a very talented team, as the numerous Emmys on the mantle attested.

"How's the new soap coming along?" Christina asked, skimming through the glossy magazine.

Her mother expelled a breath of impatience. "The actress we want for the lead is playing the role of sensitive artist—"

"And she wants us to play the role of sensitive psychologists," her father finished with a grimace. "I think I'm getting too old for this."

Christina smiled as she continued to flip through the magazine, and her mom and dad went back to the parade on the TV. She had heard these complaints before and she wasn't worried. Practically every season one or both of her parents threatened to quit. But she knew that neither ever would. They loved their work. They loved dealing with people. They loved—

As if stung by a bee, Christina froze, her thoughts interrupted. Her eyes widened as she stared at a picture in the magazine.

It was a picture of a baby. But not just any baby.

Dark brown happy eyes, silky brown hair to match, a perky little smiling mouth with a dimple on the left cheek. . .She didn't need to look at her baby picture that sat on the piano to know the picture in the magazine was a picture of herself!

She looked anyway. And then she looked back down at the baby in the magazine. No doubt about it. It was the same child. It was her.

Christina's blood ran cold. Her shock deepened as she read the caption next to the picture of the baby, the picture of herself. But as she read she finally understood that haunted look which she had seen cross between her parents so often through the years. She felt as though she had fallen into a nightmare.

With the happy sound of the TV heralding Santa's arrival in front of Macy's Department Store, a sound that mocked her dread, she read out loud, " 'Have you seen this child?' "

"What, dear?" her mother asked absentmindedly, not taking her eyes off Santa as he waved to the expectant children.

Christina licked her lips and repeated the caption. " 'Have you seen this child?' " Her throat felt dry and constricted as she read the history of the missing baby. " 'Christina was born on Christmas Day twenty-three years ago. . .this year. . .' " Her voice faltered and she looked up at the people she had always thought were her parents. They had both turned to her. She had their attention now.

And they both wore that haunted look. But only for a

moment. Quickly, the haunted look turned to one of horror. And Christina knew that she had stumbled upon their worst nightmare. Their faces had gone as white as paper, and she knew, there was absolutely no doubt in her mind, that she was the baby in the magazine. She was as certain that she was the smiling baby in the magazine as she was that she was the baby who smiled from the pictures on the baby grand piano. The two people before her were silent, as silent as the tears, the tears of guilt and love, that coursed down their suddenly old faces.

Christina shook her head slightly, as if by so doing she could erase the last two minutes, and then she forced herself to look back down at the magazine and continue to read, feeling as if she had stumbled into the set of one of her parents' soap operas. " 'Her mother hopes and prays. . .' " she read out loud.

Mother? Christina's brows came together, a hurt and confused line that slashed across her face. She had always thought that Barbara Rallis was her mother. She shook her head again, then licked her lips and continued to read, " '. . .that the woman her baby has grown into would please contact her if at all possible. . .' " Christina shut her eyes for an instant, then continued, " 'She has never stopped loving her. . .' " She looked up at the people she had always thought were her parents and whispered the last two words, " 'stolen daughter.' "

"No!" Barbara Rallis jumped to her feet, and for the first time Christina saw that she was no longer an elegant older woman but. . .an old lady. "We didn't steal you! We didn't!" She shook her silver head, denying the black

271

letters written in her favorite magazine, looking both frightened and frail. "We didn't steal you," she repeated, as if denial could make it true. Her husband slowly stood and wrapped his arm around his trembling wife.

"Of course not. . . ," he soothed, "of course not." But Christina wondered if he were trying to convince his wife or himself.

"What. . .is going on?" Christina ground out between lips that refused to move.

Peter Rallis, the man Christina had always thought was her father, closed his eyes for a moment before answering. "If I were a praying man, Christina, I would pray right now. . .pray for you to understand—"

"Dad!" She cut him off. "Please!" Her life had changed irrevocably and he was talking about praying. For a moment, though, a part of Christina wished that she did know how to pray, that they all knew how to pray. It would be a comfort, she thought, if there were Someone beyond themselves, Someone they could turn to with this terrible thing she had discovered. But if awards were given for praying, like they were for TV shows, Christina knew that her family would never win any.

"Christina," Peter Rallis continued and his eyes were grave with misgiving, no longer jolly at all, "we adopted you when you were four months old. Perhaps we should have told you before. But we didn't steal you."

The thought boiled in Christina that they most definitely should have told her sooner, and feelings of betrayal, hurt, and anger rose between her shoulder blades. She clamped down on the stew of feelings with the force of a lid on a pressure cooker. The force of these alien feelings frightened her, and she knew she had to control them.

"Ho, ho, ho," mocked the jolly Santa on the TV. She swiveled her eyes between the two people she loved more than any others. "Tell me," she commanded.

Peter Rallis nodded, but before he spoke he helped his wife back into her chair. Christina noticed something she had never thought of before: Her parents were actually old enough to be her grandparents. They had always been so vivacious, so successful, so strong, so admired by so many people, that she had never really noticed how old they actually were. They had both passed seventy but until this moment, they had always made that age seem so young, so youthful.

"Your mother—" Peter Rallis motioned toward his wife, and the fact that he felt he had to clarify who her mother was felt like a knife slashing Christina's heart. She raised her hand to her mouth and pressed her knuckles against her lips to keep from crying. "Your mother," continued Peter, "was too old to have children when we married. We tried to adopt a child here in New York but. . .because of our age, we were told that it would be next to impossible to adopt a baby. We were becoming desperate—" His voice faltered, and his wife reached out and squeezed his hand. They exchanged a look, and Christina understood that her mother was silently assuring him that she was capable of continuing the story, the story which they had dreaded to tell for nearly twenty-three years.

"When we learned that it was quite easy for Americans of Greek ancestry to adopt children in Greece," the older woman said, her voice sounding as if she had just lost something very precious, "we traveled there in the hopes of finding a child." She paused and smiled into Christina's eyes, a small smile that hoped for forgiveness. Christina read the love mixed with the yearning, the same love Christina had never doubted once in her life. Not even now. "We found you."

"We—" Her father's voice broke again but he continued, "We loved you the moment we set eyes on you."

"You smiled at us," her mother continued and Christina could tell from the light in her blue eyes that she was looking back to that moment in time, "and your little fingers reached out for ours. . .almost, we thought, as if you were begging us to take you home with us."

Christina could only shake her head. So many questions, so many thoughts raced around her mind like balls in a pinball gallery. She glanced back down at the picture of herself in the magazine, then looked up once more at her parents. "But—" Her voice broke. She tried again. "Didn't you ask about my. . ." The question trailed away.

Barbara Rallis picked it up and supplied, "Mother?" The only mother Christina had ever known bit her lower lip. Grateful she had said it first, Christina nodded.

The older woman sighed, a heavy sigh Christina knew she had carried around inside her for nearly two and a half decades. "We did," she admitted. "We asked and we were told that she had violated her contract and had left you for longer than the agreed-upon four months at the orphanage."

"And since she hadn't come for you. . .well, everyone assumed that. . .she didn't want you. . . ." Peter Rallis spoke the words as softly as he could, but still, Christina flinched. *Why should I care?* she wondered. After all her natural mother was a total stranger to her. But somehow her father's words hurt her.

She looked down again at the magazine and reread the emotional appeal written there. Her natural mother had wanted her, Christina realized, otherwise she wouldn't have considered her daughter to have been stolen.

" 'Her mother hopes and prays,' " Christina softly reread as tears gathered in the corners of her eyes, " 'that the woman her baby has grown into. . .would contact her if at all possible. . .' " Christina tried to catch the first tear with her finger, in order to dam up the rest. But it was useless. She gulped and sniffed. "I think this proves. . ." she spoke as softly as the tears that ran down her cheek, "that she did want me after all. . ."

The silver head of her mother nodded as she wiped at her own tears. "I think this means. . .that we should have investigated. . .further. . .especially when," she looked over at her husband and he nodded for her to continue, for her to tell the entire story, "the people at the orphanage asked for—" Her voice broke.

"For what?" Christina softly urged, but there was steel in her eyes and a maturity that hadn't been there before.

"A contribution," her mother whispered the word as

if it were a sentence of guilt.

Her father's head bobbed up and down and his lips moved a moment before any sound came out. "A rather large contribution," he amended. "As though we were paying them to keep a secret. We never wanted to admit that, though. . .not even to ourselves." His face creased. "We were just too scared of losing you, Christina."

Christina shook her head from side to side again. Suddenly, the whole scene seemed as unreal to her as a bad dream. The change in her parents made the nightmare sensation even stronger. Her parents, who had always been as tough and hard as Manhattan's granite, suddenly looked weak and old and vulnerable.

Christina's life flashed before her eyes. Her life with them had been wonderful, full of love and fun. They had never been too busy to spend time with her, never so busy that they missed anything important in her young life. She knew she had to meet her natural mother and maybe even her father—the need to see them was almost overwhelming—but she also knew that she wouldn't change the life she had lived for anything in the world. She loved these people, and in spite of their revelation she still loved them and she felt honored to be their daughter. For the first time in her life, she realized that not only did she need them, but they needed her. For once she could give to them, truly give to them. It was a heady feeling, a grown-up feeling. She was the only one in the world who could give them exactly what they needed.

As they had done for her a million times before, she

held out her arms to them. They came to her, their faces wet with tears, and the three of them held each other and cried, a strong family that wouldn't be torn apart by the keeping of a secret that should never have been kept.

"Why didn't you tell me?" Christina whispered a few minutes later as she held their hands.

"We wanted to. . ." Her mother's eyes implored her to believe her.

"But we were too afraid," her father finished. Looking at these strong people, Christina knew that telling her this was probably the only thing they had ever been afraid of in their entire lives.

Christina sighed. And then she smiled, a smile that mirrored the forgiveness both her parents had given to her numerous times in her life. "Well, you don't have to be afraid. You have been my mom and dad for all but four months of my life and I love you both dearly. Nothing and no one could ever change that, but—" Her eyes landed on the picture of herself in the magazine. There was a need in her to meet the woman who had given her life, a need that was growing stronger and stronger by the second.

Her mother saw it, and cleared her throat, once again the woman of substance and action she had always been. "Call the phone number in the magazine, dear." She looked over at her husband, and at his encouraging nod, she continued. "We will do everything and anything we can to help you find—"

"Your real parents," her father finished.

Christina shook her head, and her parents regarded her in confusion. "You don't want to contact your real mother?" her mother asked, ironically disappointed to think that Christina would ignore her birth mother's appeal, an appeal that traveled through time to reach her daughter.

Christina smiled, a smile that brought out the deep dimple in her left cheek. "No. I do want to meet her but . . .you're wrong when you say my 'real' parents. Don't you know, Mom and Dad, that you two are the most real parents in the world to me? Nothing could ever change that."

"Find your birth mother, dear," her mother encouraged. "At this moment," she laughed shakily, "I don't know why I was ever afraid of telling you the truth. I should have known that there is enough love in you, daughter, to love two mothers."

"And two fathers." Her dad smiled that jolly smile Christina loved so much.

Tears of happiness filled her eyes, and she was glad now that she had clamped down on the stew of bad emotions that she had felt just moments earlier. Her parents' faces were lit up with the same wonder and joy that shone from the children on TV as they looked at Santa. Christina smiled. She had given her parents exactly what they needed this year: love.

❧

The following Monday, she called the number listed in the magazine, which in turn gave her a number to call in Athens, Greece. She learned from the agency there that her birth mother had put ads in newspapers, magazines, milk cartons, and bulletin boards around the world for two decades.

Christina took her last two final exams and with her parents' blessings flew to Athens. As she waited at the airport, she shivered with excitement, hardly able to believe how much her life had changed in just ten days.

Chapter 2

"hat a wonderful surprise!" exclaimed Christina's friend Kristen Andrakos as she opened the front door of her home. She spoke first in Greek, then switched easily to English and repeated herself.

Looking down at Kristen's very pregnant stomach, Christina gasped. "It looks like you're the one with the surprise!"

Kristen placed her hand lovingly against the child that was growing within her and tilted her head to the side. "A good surprise?"

"The best!" Christina and Kristen hugged. Their parents had been long distance friends for years, until Kristen's had died in a boating accident. But even though the two girls hadn't seen one another often, there had always been a bond of friendship between them, one which had easily extended into womanhood.

"I couldn't believe it when I heard your voice on the phone," Kristen said, as she ushered Christina into her home, "but when you said that you were coming to Athens—what a gift!"

From behind them, Paul Andrakos, Kristen's husband, chuckled as he placed Christina's luggage next to the wooden banister leading upstairs. "I thought my wife might have our baby then and there, what with all the jumping around she did."

Christina's eyes narrowed with concern. "If I had known about the baby—I wouldn't have accepted your invitation to stay with you. I can easily go to a hotel close by and come and see you every day—"

"Don't you even think of such a thing," Kristen warned, her soft southern accent making the words sound almost like a threat.

Paul chuckled, but understanding and appreciating the concern Christina felt, he turned to assure her, "Kristen has been very much looking forward to your arrival. We've just recently moved from my mother's home into our own so she wants to chance to play hostess. Plus, we have a big house, a wonderful and dear housekeeper who is pampering Kristen beautifully, and we would love your company."

For the first time Christina turned to look at the house. It was big. Big and absolutely beautiful in an old-world, almost Victorian sort of way. It was decorated for Christmas like something out of a magazine—except it was better than any magazine because love seemed to be wrapped around every post along with each twist of garland.

Christina sighed and feeling a bit like Anna in *The King and I*, she reached up and removed her traveling hat. Kristen clapped her hands. "Good. Now that that's settled." She looked up at her husband with a teasing gleam in her brilliant green eyes, then leaned close to

Christina and in a stage whisper asked, "So, tell me, what do you think of my Paul?"

Christina laughed and with a conspiratorial whisper of her own responded. "I think any man who fights holiday traffic at an airport to pick up a person he has never met must be a saint!"

"Ummm. . ." Kristen nodded her head and smiled up at Paul as if they carried a secret. "You're right there—he is a saint. . . ."

Christina felt something pass between the husband and wife, something special and wonderful. Whatever it was, it didn't make Christina feel uncomfortable and left out, as she sometimes did with married couples. Instead, their happiness seemed to cast itself like a blanket over her, sharing with her the warmth of their love. "Well. . .I thank you, Paul, for coming for me," she repeated. "So tell me, when is the blessed event?"

Kristen motioned Christina to a soft chair and then eased herself onto the sofa. She lovingly rubbed her belly and replied, "Christmas Day."

"Christmas!" It was on the tip of Christina's tongue to tell them that it was her birthday, too, but something held her back. She wasn't sure whether it was because she didn't want to usurp their baby's day of birth in any way or whether it was tied up with the woman she had traveled to Greece to meet. Whatever the reason, she remained silent.

"The day of our Lord's birth," Kristen continued, and reached for her husband's hand as he sat on the sofa next to her. "I think only He could understand how much that means to us."

Christina brows drew together in question. "What do you mean?"

Paul and Kristen exchanged knowing glances. "We fell in love while we were both searching for something more in life."

"And together we learned," Paul continued, his dark eyes showing the love he felt for his wife, "that that something more was a personal relationship with Jesus Christ. What could be a better day for our baby's birth than the day we celebrate His birth?"

Christina's lips curved into a thoughtful smile. She found herself remembering her father's wish that he knew how to pray. She was certain Kristen and Paul knew how to pray. She had never given religion must thought before, but now she found herself thinking that prayer would be a very beautiful and intimate thing for a husband and wife to share. . . .

Later that evening, after both women had napped—Kristen because of pregnancy and Christina because of jet lag—the three sat in the living room, sipping home-made eggnog while gazing at the blue and silver orna-mented Christmas tree. Christina's eyes moved to the *Caique* that was set beside the tree. The *Caique*, a traditional Greek Christmas decoration, was a model of a Greek fishing boat, colorfully painted and strung with lights. Christina liked it as much as the Christmas tree. She had a hard time differentiating, though, where the lights of the huge city shining in through the window ended and those of the tree and the boat began.

Paul and Kristen's house was located high on the last road before the cliffs of the Acropolis, that most historic of hills and home of one of the most photographed buildings in the world, the graceful Parthenon. Christina had found she had a view of the cliffs from her bedroom window and if she tilted her head, she could even see the walls of the Acropolis above.

But the living room looked out over the city of Athens with the three tall mountains to the east, west, and north of the city, fencing in the modern sprawl. The high and pointed hill of Lykavittos could be seen in the near distance, with a star made out of streaming lights topping it for the Christmas season.

Traditional carols filtered into the room from Paul's elaborate entertainment system, filling the air with Christmas cheer. The love and welcome she felt in the atmosphere, she knew, however, did not come as much from the music and decorations, as it did from Paul and Kristen's air of joy and peace.

The thought occurred to Christina that the prayer going on inside this house might be what made this house so different from any place she'd been. She wasn't sure—but the sight of the well-worn Bible lying in a place of honor under the tree made her think so even more. Christmas—the true meaning of Christmas—was obviously celebrated in this home. For the first time in her life, she found herself thinking of Christ's birth as a real event that still had power to bring joy and peace to human hearts.

"So tell me," Kristen asked, after a few moments of

companionable silence, "was there any particular reason why you chose to visit Athens so suddenly?"

Christina turned away from the twinkling lights of the city to face Kristen. She had been expecting the question. She knew that she could prevaricate and explain away her trip as a graduation gift from her parents, but in that split second before she answered, she also knew that she didn't want to do that. She didn't want to lessen the importance of her visit by giving a flippant answer. But neither did she want to explain everything; she needed to meet her birth mother before telling anyone else about her reason for coming to Athens.

Before she could think of an answer, the door chime interrupted her. As if he had been expecting someone, Paul quickly stood. "That must be Dino—a working associate of mine," he explained to Christina, as he walked toward the entrance hall. "A fantastic shipping lawyer, but also one of my very best friends."

As Paul disappeared into the hall, Kristen further explained. "Dino's been away on business for the past month and we've really missed him." She rolled out and up from the sofa. "He's a wonderful man, an even better Christian—" Kristen stopped, and her emerald eyes lit up as the two handsome men came into the room. "Dino!" She reached out her arms for the man who was even a bit taller than her own tall husband. "We missed you!"

Dino hugged Kristen. He seemed not to have noticed Christina yet, but when he spoke, something in Christina's heart jumped to sudden life. "It looks like that little baby has been doing some growing while I've been gone." His voice was deep and slightly gravelly, the English words accented with the inflection of Greek.

Kristen rolled her eyes and laughed. "A lot of growing!" she corrected, and turned to Christina.

The man named Dino turned with her and that thing within Christina's heart that had pulsed to life at the sound of his voice started pounding when his blue eyes looked at her. Christina didn't think that she had ever seen such beautiful eyes before. They shone with a light that seemed to reach out from his inner being to touch her, to touch a part of her that had never been touched.

"Dino Mathis, I would like for you to meet my very dear friend Christina Rallis—"

From her peripheral vision, Christina saw her hand reach out for his, to be taken by his. But from the periphery of her mind, she felt something she had never felt before. She wasn't sure what it was—magic, hope, love? All three—or something else entirely. She wasn't sure. The only thing she knew was that she felt alive in a way she had never felt alive before. As if. . .as if a part of her that had lain dormant slept no more. . . .

"How do you do?" she heard her voice respond, glad of the manners that came automatically to her rescue.

His eyes seemed to sparkle more as he smiled at her. "I do very well thank you." His words were softly accented. "Even better now than I did a few minutes ago," he admitted, still holding her hand, still smiling at her, still making her feel. . .magic.

Christina thought what she felt was magic—but

Dino knew that what he was feeling for the woman with the doe eyes and the dimple on her left cheek was a feeling he had never before had. A feeling, in fact, that he had always teased his friends about. But the joke was on him now. The logic and precision of his profession had no place in his being now as strong, self-assured Dino Mathis knew that what he felt for the woman before him was the proverbial love at first sight. A love that he knew was God's answer to his prayer.

Dino had always thought the bachelor's life was for him. But watching Paul and Kristen together during the two years of their marriage had changed him. While he was away, he had finally admitted to himself that he wanted what Paul had, the gift of a lovely woman like Kristen to share his life with him. All the while he was gone, he had poured out his dreams and longing to God. And now he was quite sure that he was looking at her. . .a woman named Christina.

"What brings you to Athens, Christina?" he asked, but he was certain that he already knew. God had brought her to Athens so that they could meet, fall in love, marry, and live happily ever after.

"I. . ." She ran her tongue over her lower lip. "That was what I was just about to explain to Kristen and Paul when you rang the bell," *and changed my life,* she finished mentally. Although she didn't say the words out loud, in the moment before she turned to Kristen, Dino saw the message in her eyes. His heart sang.

"I came to Athens because I have to meet with a—" Christina paused as she scanned her mind for a vague word to describe meeting her mother. Her face brightened when she found it. "A relative, actually." That's what her birth mother was after all. A relative. "I don't really want to explain everything but—"

"Oh, Christina," Kristen interrupted her and motioned for them all to take a seat. "You don't have to explain a thing."

Paul nodded his head. "You are our friend and welcomed here for as long as you wish."

"Thank you," Christina whispered. "I need good friends right now," she admitted.

"You've got them," Kristen assured her and Paul nodded his agreement.

"I, too," Dino spoke from her side and Christina turned her brown eyes to meet his blue, "would like to be your—friend." The way he said the word made everyone in the room, probably even the baby in Kristen's tummy, know that what he really meant was that he wanted to be a whole lot more than friends.

Kristen and Paul glanced at one another, and that part of Christina's heart that had come alive when Dino had walked into the room nearly skipped a beat. Her lips wouldn't let her even try to deny the pleasure his declaration brought to her. Of their own accord, they curved upward.

"In fact," Dino continued, "I would be honored if you would let me show you around my city."

His city, Christina thought and her smiled deepened. Little did he know, did any of them know, that it was her city, too. "I'd like that."

"Starting tomorrow?" he inquired. Dino sensed, with a lawyer's skill, that it was all right to push for something definite.

Christina wanted to agree. But until she met with the agency that was representing her birth mother she didn't feel she could plan anything. "I have a meeting to go to in the morning." She didn't have to say anything more, she realized, and she could see by their faces that they would wait until she was ready to tell them more. "After that, I'll be able to let you know."

"Good enough." He smiled.

She smiled back. Athens, she realized, had a lot more to offer her than just a mother. A lot more. . .

Chapter 3

W hile nervously making her way to the agency that morning, Christina hadn't noticed how gaily decorated Athens was for Christmas, but on her return trip to the Andrakos', she noticed. Strung with lights and garlands, with either Christmas trees or the traditional boat, the *Caique*, decorating every house and shop window and with manger scenes filling many of the squares, the city reflected her mood—happy, wondrous, almost carefree.

The woman at the agency had been kind and helpful, and after comparing her information with Christina's, she was certain that Christina was her client's long-lost daughter. The only reason Christina could not meet her birth mother immediately was the fact that her mother was out of the country and not due to return until Christmas Eve. That meant that Christina would have to wait until Christmas Day, her birthday, to meet her.

Christina had smiled. What better time to meet the woman who had given her life than on the anniversary of her birth? And surprisingly, Christina hadn't felt at all impatient that she would have to wait another week before meeting her; instead, she felt relieved, as if granted a reprieve. So much had happened during the last few weeks, that Christina discovered she was actually glad her birth mother was unavailable. It gave her a chance to gather all the changes in her life and to ponder them without having the pressure of having to do something about them. From the moment she had seen the picture in that magazine on Thanksgiving Day, she had been in motion, and now she found she was grateful to be able to sit back and let her thoughts settle.

She looked out the cab window as it passed by the huge Parliament of Greece and she smiled as she caught a glimpse of the tall Evzones, the Greek soldiers, as they stood in ceremonial guard in front of the tomb of the Unknown Soldier. Her smile deepened as she sank back into the rich seat of the taxi.

She had never thought much about her birthplace, readily accepting her adoptive parents' explanation that they had been in Greece when her mother had gone into labor with her. But now, as she rode the taxi back to the Andrakos's home and she looked out at the vibrant city that pulsed around her, she knew that she wanted to get to know the city of her birth as well as she could in the week before she met her mother. She wanted, in fact, to be a carefree tourist and let the wonders of this city sink in, this city that had seen so much of recorded history. And. . .she knew that she wanted to see it on Dino's arm.

She had never before met a man whom she had felt as attracted to as she did Dino. With Dino, everything was different. She felt as though a magic button had been switched on in her, a button she hadn't even known she possessed.

When she walked through the door of the Andrakos's home a few minutes later, Dino was there waiting for her. His smile told her that he felt the same about her. Again, Christina rejoiced that she had a week free before meeting her mother, a week in which she could concentrate on getting to know Dino. She was even more glad when Dino told her he had the next week off as well.

Winking at Kristen, he said to Christina, "My boss," who Christina knew was Kristen's husband Paul, the owner of the shipping company, "knows how deserving I am of a holiday. So," he turned to face Christina, "I am at your beck and call, my lady." He bowed slightly with old-world charm. "How best may I serve you?"

Playing along, Christina tilted her head imperiously. "By showing me this beautiful city of yours, my lord," she responded, and happiness rose in her like water from a tap rises in a glass.

His blue eyes looked into hers and Christina felt her heart do a flip-flop. "That I will be honored to do," he finally responded, and Christina knew it was true. He wanted to be in her company every bit as much as she wanted to be in his.

Kristen clapped her hands together, and Christina and Dino turned to her. "Well," Kristen's eyes danced in merriment. She knew what was going on between her two friends, and it had been a subject of discussion between Paul and herself the night before, a subject that had delighted them both. "I don't think you could have chosen better weather for sightseeing."

"I know!" Christina exclaimed, glancing pass the

sparkling Christmas tree and out the window to the sunny and bright day that lit up the city. "I can't believe it! It's so hot! When I left New York it was snowing and here—" She motioned to her double-breasted suit jacket. "I was too warm with this on."

Kristen laughed her agreement. "That's Athens weather for you. However," she felt the need to warn, "it's highly subject to change. One day it might be like late summer, and the next, wintry, with the mountains around the city so covered with snow that you'll think you're in Switzerland and not in Greece."

Looking out the window again at the bright Mediterranean sun, Christina was skeptical. But at Kristen's insistent nod that it was true, she quirked her lips and asked, "So you mean we might have a white Christmas?"

Dino laughed. "Anything is possible in Athens." The timbre of his voice and the way his eyes slanted toward her told Christina he was talking about a lot more than just the weather. Smiling boldly back at him, she was glad.

Christina liked it when possibilities were endless.

And as that day wore on, and then the next and the next, and they spent every moment together until late every night, Dino not only showed her the wonders of the ancient city but he also showed her that her first impressions of him were correct. Christina knew that he was a man she could easily spend the rest of her life with. There was something special about him, and Christina soon understood what it was. He was quite simply a man who believed in God, a praying man, a

293

man who wasn't confused about who he was or where he was going in life like so many of the men Christina had met. He wasn't offensive in his beliefs but rather giving and tolerant, and he slowly whetted Christina's appetite for the knowledge he possessed; a knowledge he freely gave.

And while telling her about the God he loved, Dino showed her the city. He showed her the Acropolis, he showed her the ancient Stadium where the first modern Olympics took place, and he showed her the old town of Athens, the Plaka.

They walked and talked, and they laughed and held hands as they traveled from one end of the Plaka to the other. From the oldest known theater in the world, the Theater of Dionysus, from which Aristophanes, Sophocles, and Euripides saw their plays performed, to the site of Plato's famous Academy they went, falling more deeply in love with every step they took.

The Acropolis shining overhead, little domed chapels popping up in ever direction Christina looked, shops selling anything from leather goods to copies of Byzantine icons and Greek dolls, rose bushes still spilling out their fragrance even in December; all of it blended together to make Christina feel as though she had stepped into a totally different life from that of a month before. Not only had she discovered that she was adopted and that her birth mother lived in this amazing city, but she had discovered the love of a good man, a complete man.

As they walked they stopped off at all the little churches along the way and talked to the friendly caretakers who loved the American woman who was interested in their little chapels, who was amazed by their history. Out of all of Athens' multitude of treasures, Christina discovered that it was the Byzantine churches she loved the most. They were so unassuming as they sat in the middle of busy streets several feet below the modern level, or with restaurants in their courtyards or even modern buildings built above their domes. Every one of the little Byzantine churches would have been considered a national treasure in any other capital of the world, but in this city, this city of such concentrated history, they were almost forgotten, like a king's forgotten gems. Most had been built at least five hundred years before Columbus sailed to America, but even more amazing was that many still held church services.

When Dino told Christina that the beautiful Parthenon had been converted into a Christian church in the fifth century, when the building was already nearly a thousand years old, she insisted that they trek back up to the Acropolis's windy height for her to look at it again. They stood on the ancient windswept hill with the blue of the sea shining in the one direction, the three tall mountains of the city surrounding them in the others, and Christina looked up into Dino's eyes, sharing her joy and exhilaration with him. He leaned close, and she thought for a moment he would kiss her. Her heart beat fast, but then he drew back, as though something had stopped him. She frowned, but the smile he gave her was as warm as ever.

The wind played a song around the golden columns above them and looking up into his eyes, eyes that were as deep and as blue as the sea that sparkled to the south of them, she had no doubt that he loved her, though he had not said the words. She sensed that the love she read in his eyes was rooted in something much greater than mere human love. The knowledge gave her a sense of security and joy that she had never felt with another man. She smiled, showing the dimple on her left cheek. *I love you, too*, her own eyes answered him. She knew that she did. With Dino she was alive in a way she had never been alive before.

He gathered her close to him and whispered, "I long for so much—but for the moment," his accent gently bathed his words with love, "this is enough, I think." She wasn't sure she understood, but she nodded her head against his shoulder.

Dino felt her breath like a feather against his skin. He closed his eyes and forced himself to draw back just a little. Even though Christina still hadn't told him the real reason behind her coming to Athens, he knew that it was something that she had to see to before they could make any plans for the future. More important, though, he knew they couldn't plan a life together until she came to the same personal relationship with God that he had. A marriage between them wouldn't work without it. They would be unequally tied together. . . . *Dear God, if Christina really is the woman You want me to marry, then please bring her to You. Soon.*

Christina shivered slightly inside the circle of his

arms "I think the weather is about to change," she murmured, blaming the weather for the feeling of dread that had suddenly swept through her.

Dino held up his hand to catch the direction of the wind. "Northerly winds," he commented. "They quickly bring the arctic chill with them this time of year."

Just a cold draft of air, she told herself, *that's why I shivered.* She smiled up at him. "So you mean we just might have that white Christmas after all?" She had to admit, she liked the idea.

He chuckled and leaned toward her. "Like I said before —anything is possible in Athens." She waited for his kiss on her lips, but it fell lightly on the tip of her nose instead. She smiled, hiding her disappointment. Anything was possible here. . .even the start of a lifetime of love.

By the time they returned to the Andrakos' house, not two hours later, the air had cooled considerably and the blue sky had turned into a steely gray. Paul had left a message asking if Dino could help him out at the office that evening, so for the first time in days, Christina and Kristen were left alone.

The long look Christina and Dino had shared before he left didn't escape Kristen's happy notice. When Christina turned away from the door, Kristen didn't give her a chance to say a word before she sang out, "You're in love!"

Christina ran to Kristen's side and took Kristen's hands in her own. She squeezed her eyes shut and admitted, "I never realized that it could happen so fast. . ."

Kristen patted her tummy and remembered back to when she had first met Paul. "All it took for me was one afternoon to fall in love with Paul."

"One afternoon. . ." Christina murmured. *It took me one moment*, she thought. "You've never told me how you and Paul met and fell in love. I always thought it sounded a bit like a fairy tale."

Kristen laughed as she remembered back to the joy of falling in love with Paul, but then a cloud crossed over her face as she remembered the times of agony, too. Christina saw the shadow and she knew then that Kristen's romance had not been the easy one she had believed it to be. "Tell me," she gently encouraged. "If you want to," she amended. She didn't want to be pushy; it was just that, with her own love so new, she really did want to know.

Kristen told Christina how the thing that first drew her to Paul was that they both knew that there was something more in life than the empty social scene and the endless climb to make money. They searched and learned together, while falling in love with one another, that that something more was a personal relationship with God.

"That was an amazing time." She looked down at the baby that was hidden within her flesh. "And it all happened here in Athens. . ."

Christina looked out the window at the ancient city that had grown so gracefully into a modern one. "Something about this city. . .it makes one consider. . .God," she admitted.

Kristen simply nodded her head but her heart rejoiced

to hear her friend's words. "Well, it's little wonder that people think about God here in Athens. So many of the early Christians visited here, the New Testament was originally written in Greek, and—" She motioned out the window at the domes that dotted the skyline. "Christ has been worshiped in this city from when Dionysius and Damaris accepted the truth St. Paul brought to them in his famous speech to the Athenians."

"Amazing. . ." Christina whispered, looking out over the city which was lighting up for the winter night. She turned back to Kristen. Although she wanted to ask Kristen more about her belief in God, she also wanted her to finish the story of her romance. "But," she thought back to Kristen's letters a few years ago, "didn't you leave Athens. . .and Paul. . .for a while?"

Kristen held her palm protectively over her unborn baby. She knew, if not by the grace of God, that this little human would never have been made. Taking a deep breath, she nodded. "We had some serious struggles. To make a long story very short, we spent three long months thinking that we would never be able to have a life together." She fingered the beautiful antique emerald ring on her left hand.

"Oh, Kristen. . .how horrible for you. . ." With the intensity of her feelings for Dino, Christina could empathize with the pain her friend must have felt. "I don't know if I could stand something like that happening to Dino and me."

"Well," Kristen looked thoughtful, "I have to admit, my new faith was sorely tested then. But you know—I appreciate the love Paul and I have more because of that time."

"But still. . ." A shudder like a cloud passed through Christina, and she felt the same cold foreboding that she had felt earlier by the Acropolis. "How hard it must have been for you, for both of you."

Chapter 4

C hristina awoke the next morning, Christmas Eve, to the sweet clear notes of children's voices drifting over the city in song. Stretching, she looked out the window and blinked as she saw groups of bundled-up children running from door to door, caroling to the accompaniment of little silver triangles they clutched in their mittened hands. Her lips curved into a happy smile.

When she glanced upward, she saw the reason the children were wearing heavy ski parkas and stocking hats, and she squealed in delight. Rolling clouds of cotton wool sheets, clouds that held the promise of snow, marched above the city like a Christmas fantasy.

Christina was glad that the weather had changed. She loved snow, but never more than at Christmas! Scrambling out of bed, she hurriedly dressed in woolen pants and a plush sweater of soft honey that brought out the golden lights in her dark hair.

She dialed the agency to confirm her appointment with her birth mother and was told that her mother was anxious to meet her. Their appointment was all set for ten the next morning, Christmas morning. Christina declined the agency's offer to escort her, wanting instead to meet her mother in private. Jotting down the address, she hung up the phone and paused for a moment. Here she was going to meet her natural mother the following day and yet, amazingly, she couldn't muster up the least bit of excitement, nor for that matter, trepidation. Nothing.

She wanted to meet her natural mother, but her feelings toward the woman were just a great big blank, as blank as a chalkboard that didn't have anything written on it. She thought that maybe that was good, but she wasn't sure. Not wanting to dwell on it, she pushed all thoughts of her upcoming appointment out of her head and thought instead about Dino.

Dino. . . Thoughts about him made her smile. He had promised to take her somewhere special today and glancing out the window, she hoped that it would be somewhere outdoors—and that it would snow. To walk through the falling snow with the man she loved had to be one of the most romantic things. . . .

She descended the stairs just as Kristen swung the door wide to welcome a group of children. Pausing, Christina watched as with frosted breaths they politely asked Kristen if she wanted to hear them sing. When Kristen assured them that she did, they smiled and swirled the metal stick around their triangles. To its tinkling notes they merrily sang out one of the prettiest tunes Christina had ever heard. She translated the words in her head as they sang, glad for the millionth time since coming to Greece that her mom and dad had insisted she learn to speak Greek, as they did themselves.

❧

"Good Morning m'Lords,
   and if it is your will,
it's Jesus Christ's birthday.
    May I come into your fine home?
Jesus is being born today in Bethlehem!
    The sky is happy,
and nature is happy,
   for in a cave,
He is born in a stable of horses,
   the King of the skies,
and the maker of everyone."

When they finished, Kristen clapped her hands and after offered them each a *kourabiede*, a Greek Christmas cookie made with butter and piled high with confectionery sugar. Then she gave them a nice amount of money to share among themselves. They went on their way, smiling at the powdered sugar that had stuck to the tip of the youngest nose.

"That was lovely!" Christina exclaimed, and Kristen turned to her with a thoughtful smile.

"I think that *kalanda*, the children's caroling," she commented as she half walked, half waddled into the livingroom, "is one of the nicest Christmas traditions in Greece."

Christina followed her. She warmed her hands before the gently burning fire in the fireplace and remarked softly, "The song has such meaning." The simple beauty of the lyrics had struck the same cords in Christina's soul that Dino's soft words about God had touched upon during the last week.

"Ummm," Kristen agreed as she sank carefully into her chair. "This is getting difficult!" she admitted ruefully, while lovingly patting her tummy. "The carol is beautiful, isn't it? A beautiful way to remind people that it's the birth of God's Son that we're celebrating tomorrow and not all the secular things people have made Christmas into."

Christina's eyes went to the porcelain manger scene that sat on the mantle. She looked at the baby, the Christmas baby, that had been lovingly tucked into His makeshift manger bed by His mother, and Christina knew that she had to agree with Kristen. The song did remind people about the true Christmas Baby, the Christ Child. It had reminded her and she hadn't thought about Him, really thought about Him at Christmastime. . .ever . . .until now.

❧

She and Kristen were sharing companionable cups of coffee and eating kourabiedes. The weather was blustery and the two friends sat in the living room watching the winter show from its window. As yet undetected by the women, Dino stood in the hall for a moment and watched them.

A fire in the fireplace gave forth a cozy heat, and the colorful lights from the Christmas tree and *Caique* fell upon their faces like starlight from on high. Dino thought that seeing these two women he loved so dearly, one as a sister and the other as a man loves a woman, was one of the most beautiful scenes he had ever beheld. It was as though they were posed for a Christmas card. Two friends happy with their lives; happy with Christmas coming, happy with all the changes soon to take place.

Dino fingered the velvet box he carried in his pocket. He knew that all his hopes and dreams were contingent upon things that were out of his control; on Christina coming to know God, on her mysterious reason for coming to Athens, and last, but certainly not least, on whether she loved him enough to give up the life she had always known to make his home her home, his city her city, just as Kristen had for Paul. He shook his head slightly and reminded himself that God had already overcome physical geography and human emotions to bring them together. He would be obedient and trust God for the rest.

He fingered the soft box in his pocket again. That she was the women for him he was absolutely positive. He just had to be patient and let the Great Designer work everything out according to His plan. He smiled. God wouldn't mind him pushing the situation along a little bit by taking her to the place he had planned to go to today. A hushed place, it was a place where God's voice seemed easier to hear, a place where he himself had heard God speak many times, a place where he hoped Christina might hear Him, too. And maybe, just maybe, she would ask God to be a part of her life. He rubbed his fingers against the box in his pocket; only then could he ask her to share her life with him. . . .

He cleared his throat as emotions threatened to clog

it, and two pairs of bright shining eyes, one brown, one green, both beautiful, regarded him. "Dino!" The pregnant woman with the green eyes exclaimed. "I didn't hear you come in!"

"Neither did I!" The woman with the soft brown eyes and deepening dimple confirmed. She leapt to her feet. Dino loved the sureness in Christina's steps as she came to him, the way her hand automatically found his and the way their fingers intertwined together just as he hoped their lives one day would. But most of all, he loved the way she looked at him, as though he was the most important man in the world to her. He felt cherished, loved, and all he wanted at that moment was to lean toward her, to kiss her, to hold her close to him, to—

Kristen cleared her throat, breaking the spell and reminding Dino of where he was and who he was. A smile touched the corners of his mouth as he and Christina turned their faces to her. Kristen didn't think that she had ever seen either of her friends look happier. "I wish Paul could see the two of you now," she commented, and her green eyes sparkled with humor. "Is it possible though that you two are in need of. . .a chaperon today?" she teased.

Dino's eyes touched Christina's but he spoke to Kristen. "Don't worry." He picked up Christina's navy peacoat and ivory cashmere scarf and matching hat and placed the coat around her shoulders, letting his hands linger there a moment longer than necessary, "Your friend is safe with me, Kristen. Besides, where we're going God has been the chaperon since the fifth century."

Kristen laughed. "That could be practically anywhere in Greece, Dino!"

"True," he conceded to Kristen. "But we're only going a few miles away." Leaning close to Christina, he spoke for her ears only. "But it may as well be a thousand."

A few minutes later, Christina thought that it was more like a million miles or maybe even an eon away, with time and distance seeming to merge. Athens sparkled in the wide valley below like a toy city in a glass ball.

Dino had driven her through the bustling avenues and up a road that was like a beltway around the eastern part of the city. When he had turned off the road toward Athens' east mountain, Hymettus, it was as if they had not only traveled back through time and gone a million miles away but had gone into a remote world of reaching cypress trees standing like the very guardians of time. Christina had never driven through a cypress forest before, but she decided that it was a forest unlike any she had ever seen. The narrow evergreen trees shot straight up, proud and sure, optimistic somehow, into the snow-ladened clouds that hovered just above their reaching tips.

She waved her hand toward the trees. "It's like they're sentinels standing at attention!"

"Then they would have to be Christian sentinels guarding that," Dino said, and pointed to several stone buttresses that extended down to the edge of the road.

"A fortress!" Christina exclaimed as she looked up at the stone walls the buttresses supported. "What is it?"

"It's called Kaisariani—and I guess you could say it's one of God's fortresses."

She tilted her head to him. "What do you mean?"

"It used to be a monastery."

"A monastery," she repeated in wonder. They got out of the Jeep and walked down a stone path, passing an ancient ram's head spring that still ran with water, before reaching a long wall that led to the monastery's entrance. The peace, the solitude, was a part of the very air around them, with the rock walls not an intrusion but rather, a welcoming part of the land. It seemed to have grown right out of the earth and was totally at peace with it.

The west enclosure wall held the kitchen and the refectory, the north wall, a tower and the monks' cells, while directly across from the entrance was a Roman bath. But what captured Christina's attention was the beautiful little church that was the focal point of the well-kept courtyard. She walked toward the little domed building of stone. Even though it was very similar to those she had seen in the old town of Athens, she felt there was something special about this church.

"It's enchanting," she whispered and Dino squeezed her hand. He had known she would like it. They were too much alike for her not to.

"Tell me about it," she softly commanded, knowing that he would know its history as he had many of the beautiful churches they had seen in the Plaka.

"It was built in the eleventh century," he began but stopped when he caught a wry twinkle in her eye.

She smiled, a smile that matched the look in her eyes. "It's new then. . . ?" She was beginning to understand how a hundred years in American history could be likened to a thousand in Greece.

Dino chuckled, a low sound that Christina loved. "Compared to the ruins of the original fifth-century basilica which I'll take you to see in a little while—yes," he rubbed his thumb against the soft wool that covered her hand, "I guess you could say that it's new."

They stepped through the narthex and into the hush of the sanctuary. The church was light and airy, though cold enough to frost their breath. But it was the beautiful paintings of Bible stories that caught Christina's attention.

Dino waved his arm toward the icons. "When people couldn't read, as the majority couldn't back in the Middle Ages, these told them the amazing stories of the Bible."

"They're beautiful." Christina walked into the main sanctuary and looked up at the dome and its painting of Christ the Pantocrator, the Almighty, holding a Gospel.

Pointing up at the Book, Dino commented, "But I think, in the literate world in which we live today, that God prefers for all who can read to read His Word rather than to rely only on paintings."

Christina nodded her head, and she felt something like conviction wash through her at Dino's words. "I hate to admit it, but. . .I practically never read the Bible." She walked from one painting to another along the walls of the little church. "But these. . ." she held her hand out, "they make me wonder what I've been missing. They make me want to read the Bible. . .to know God. . .and His Son. . . ."

Dino smiled, and within his heart, he breathed a prayer of thanks. "Then I believe they are fulfilling their purpose," he responded after a moment and she could hear the emotion in his deep voice. She knew that Bible reading was a daily part of his life, and she loved him more because of it.

Turning to him, she shyly admitted, "I've always admired people like you and Kristen and Paul. . .people who have strong religious feelings toward God. . ."

Gently, lovingly, he corrected her. "What we have, Christina, is a personal relationship with Christ."

Kristen had said the same thing. Christina hadn't wanted to ask Kristen about it then, but today, in this building, built and adorned to honor God, she wanted to know more. "What do you mean?"

Dino was ready for the question, had been ready for it since the moment he'd met her. "We who have made a commitment to God," he explained, "have been born into His kingdom. We've been given the right to become His children."

"Born into God's kingdom. . ." She shook her head. She didn't understand. She might have if he had said adopted into God's kingdom. But born? She had been born of one woman, raised by another. . .but still, only one birth. "What do you mean? How can a person be born. . .more than once?"

Dino smiled and guided her over to the painting that depicted Jesus' birth. "There once was a man named Nicodemus, a very smart man, who asked

Jesus that exact question."

"Really?"

Dino nodded and continued speaking while looking up at the painting that showed Jesus born in a cave. "He came to Jesus late one night to talk and when Jesus told him that no one can see the kingdom of God unless he is born again, Nicodemus asked, 'How can a man be born when he is old? Surely he cannot enter a second time into his mother's womb to be born!' "

Christina's quick intake of breath stopped Dino. Looking at her he saw that she had gone white, that the blood seemed to have left her face. "Christina—what is it?"

Her eyes swiveled around his face, a frenzy of movement. *What is it? What is it?* She wanted to scream back his own question, but she didn't. She knew what 'it' was. Tomorrow, the very next day, her birthday, she was to meet the woman from whose womb she had emerged. She was to meet the mother who had birthed her, and somehow, out of all the stories in the Bible—and looking at the painted walls surrounding her she knew there were many stories—they had had to stumble onto the one that told about a man asking about birth and mothers' wombs.

She realized then that the actual reason why she hadn't told anyone her reason for being in Athens was because, in spite of what she had told her parents, in spite of what she had intellectually believed, she was hurt, deeply hurt, to learn that she was not the person she had always thought herself to be. The lid of that symbolic pressure cooker she had clamped onto her emotions blew off. It sprayed all the emotions that had been simmering there for the last month—hurt, betrayal, anger—over her heart.

Her personal history, her genetic history was not what she had always believed it to be. It bothered her, it bothered her profoundly that her parents hadn't been honest with her from the beginning. And she couldn't understand how her birth mother could have lost her baby. People, responsible people, just don't lose their babies.

"Christina?" Dino repeated.

Wanting to get away from him and the question she heard in his voice, she turned and ran out the door of the church. But once outside she stopped and blinked. She pulled the gloves off her hands so that her sense of touch could confirm what her sense of sight was telling her, and her face relaxed.

She smiled. Then she laughed. Her delight cooled the heat of her thoughts, as snow, glorious, refreshing snow floated from the sky all around her. "Oh, Dino!" She held out her hand to him as he joined her. "Look!"

Dino smiled at the snow and silently thanked God for this perfect gift. He knew that this snow was a healing snow for Christina. He had known through the days of their being together that Christina's reason for being in Athens dealt with something traumatic. The knowledge wasn't anything he had been able to put his finger on, just a vague feeling of unrest, of denial even, which he had sensed in her. If he had needed confirmation, though, she had just given it to him in the church.

He didn't realize how intense his eyes were as he regarded her, but Christina knew that it was only because he loved her that they had turned black with questions. And she knew, too, that she owed him an explanation. Her smile froze on her face, a smile that couldn't hide the hurt within her soul, as she reached up to rub her hand across the roughness of his cheek. "Oh, Dino. . ."

He grabbed her hand and pulled her close. "Tell me, Christina," he demanded, wanting to protect the woman he loved.

"I can't," she whispered into his shoulder.

"I want to help you," he ground out, and his breath melted the snowflakes that had fallen on her hair.

"I know."

"Won't you let me?"

"Oh, Dino. . .until right now, I didn't even know I needed help."

"But I have known it," he said, surprising her.

Of course he would know, she realized. He cared enough about her to notice all the nonverbal, unconscious messages she herself had ignored.

The fog from his lips enveloping her, he said, "It has to do with your reason for coming to Greece." He didn't ask, he stated, and looking up at him she didn't even try to deny it.

"It has everything to do with it."

"And with your appointment tomorrow?" He had been surprised when she'd told him that they wouldn't be able to spend all of Christmas together. Surprised and suspicious, and he watched as she again nodded her head. "I love you, Christina," he ground out, the gravelly tone of his voice mixed with his soft accent.

"I know, Dino. And I love you," she whispered.

He nodded his head. He knew that she did. "Promise me. . .that if you need me. . .you will call me."

She bit her bottom lip and whispered, "I promise."

It was all he could ask of her. But it wasn't all he could ask of God. He would uphold her in prayer. "I'll pray for you," he stated, and the peace which she felt flood her at his words showed on her face.

"I'd like that. . .no one's ever prayed for me before."

"How do you know, darling?" His thumb rubbed the sensitive spot on her wrist. "Maybe someone you've never even met has been praying for you for your whole life."

His words made her think. Hadn't the magazine article said, "Her mother hopes and prays that the woman her baby grew into would please contact her"? Maybe her mother—her birth mother—had been praying for her all these years.

The thought brought a warm glow to her heart. She smiled and suddenly, as when she had first found out about being adopted, she was again looking forward to meeting her natural mother. "You know, you may be right, Dino. You just may be right."

Silently, he took her hand and wound his fingers around hers as they walked out of the monastery and through a winter wonderland toward the ruins of the fifth-century basilica he had promised to show her. The walk through the falling snow with the man she loved was even more romantic than Christina had thought it would be. It wasn't just a dream fantasy, but real life, the type of life she hoped she'd always have.

Chapter 5

C hristina found out the next morning, Christmas morning—a day that glowed with sunshine and snow-covered mountaintops—that Dino had been right. Someone had been praying for her all her life. Her mother, her birth mother, had been praying for her throughout all the years of their separation.

A little before ten o'clock Christina stood before her mother's home, surprised to discover that it was close to the Andrakos' home in the old town of Athens. With citrus trees naturally decorated for Christmas with their own yellow and orange fruit, the road was one of the most picturesque she had seen, and she wondered why Dino had never shown it to her.

The house was by far the biggest and most elegant home in the area. She stood for a full five minutes across the narrow street below a sweeping eucalyptus tree, just gazing at her mother's home. *Her mother's home. . .* The thought echoed inside her mind. The woman who had given her life was sheltered within.

The house was neoclassical, the same time period as she had learned the Andrakos' to be, but this one was even bigger, more like a mansion than a house. Tiny white Christmas lights outlined its edges, and a huge live Christmas tree decorated with glass balls and ribbons was on the balcony above the front door. But it was the warmth of the golden light that spilled out through the unshuttered windows that most filled Christina with Christmas cheer.

She glanced at her watch and discovered that the moment set for her to meet her mother had arrived. The radiant light that shone out like welcoming banners gave her a sureness of movement as she crossed the narrow street and reached out to press the doorbell.

The bell had hardly stopped ringing when the door swung open. A beautiful woman with blond hair, hair that softly brushed her shoulders, with eyes that were as giving as they were gray, stood before Christina. Christina knew she was looking at her mother, and an unexpected love flooded her.

The other woman knew the moment she looked up into the soft brown eyes of the young woman at her door that she was looking into the eyes of her little baby once again, her baby grown into splendid womanhood. With a mother's knowledge, she was certain of it; and with a mother's heart, she loved her daughter.

Silently, the two women reached for one another. They both knew that words would never convey this moment's depth of emotion and meaning, and so they remained quiet as they held each other close. For the first time in nearly twenty-three years the beating of their hearts merged together once again.

Christina felt as though some primitive part of her remembered her mother, remembered the way she smelled, the way she breathed, the way she felt, and that blank chalkboard of her mind started filling up, filling up with good emotions. This woman was familiar to her, known to her, and Christina didn't need papers nor certificates to prove that she had been born of her. From deep within her being she knew it to be true.

Christina's birth mother felt the same. Christina might be a grown woman now, taller even than herself, but to her aching arms Christina was her little baby once again. With fleeting wisps of thoughts, thoughts that only mothers can have, she noticed that her daughter's hair was the same silky chestnut brown, her skin the same pale olive, and that even the way the nape of her neck smelled like fresh toast was the same.

Standing back, with tears of joy swimming in her gray eyes, she looked at the woman her baby had grown into and her smile deepened. She shook her blond head, her professional training the only reason she was able to push her voice through the clog in her throat. "Welcome home. . .Christina. . .my Christmas baby. . ."

" 'Christmas baby'. . . ?" Christina murmured, her eyes traveling around her mother's beautiful face. Her mom and dad, her adoptive parents, had always called her that. Had her mother, her birth mother, thought of her in the same way as well?

Her mother nodded and explained, "That's how I've always referred to you. You were born this day. . .twenty-three years ago. I named you 'Christina' in honor of the One whose birthday you share." She squeezed her eyes together. "It was the happiest moment of my life. Happy birthday, my daughter."

Christina rubbed her mother's hands, hands that were as long and tapered as her own. "Thank you. . .Mother. . ."

Her mother, a woman who looked young enough to be her sister, made a sound that was half laugh and half cry as she dabbed at the corners of her eyes. "I've waited longer than half my life to hear you call me 'Mother.' " She tucked Christina's hand beneath her arm as if she didn't ever want to let go of her again. "You know, you are the image of your father."

"I am?" It seemed unreal to Christina that they should be having this conversation, unreal but nice, too. The Rallises had never talked much about looks. Christina now understood why.

Her mother nodded as she guided her into the house. "Come. . .I'll show you."

On a grand piano in the elegant, second-floor living room sat not only the picture of herself, the one Christina had seen in the magazine, but a picture of a man Christina knew could only be her father. The coloring was the same, the eyes and the hair, even the dimple was the same. Christina ran her fingertips over the face of the man who had fathered her, letting them rest upon the deep dimple on his left cheek. "I've always wondered where I got my dimple from. . ."

"Your dimple, your forehead, your eye coloring, your smile. . ." Her mother's eyes traveled over each of those areas on Christina's face. Taking the picture of Christina's father from the piano, she motioned Christina over to the sofa in front of the silver-and-gold clothed Christmas tree.

319

Sitting together and holding the picture before them, Christina knew from the way her mother looked at the picture of her natural father that she had loved him very much. Christina felt glad somehow, glad and warm all over.

"You are so much alike. I saw that even when you were a baby. . ."

"Really?" Christina was surprised at how badly she wanted to know more about him. "Please tell me about him," she encouraged.

Her mother nodded. "He was my best friend. We were both orphaned at quite young ages and we were both raised by elderly godfathers who were next-door neighbors and best friends themselves. We grew up together, we were family to one another even before we married and made it official."

"You were married to my father?" Christina interrupted. That had never occurred to her, but when her mother sighed, as if hurt, she wished that she could have kept the incredulous surprise out of her voice. Her mother softly, almost reverently, placed the picture of her husband on the coffee table and then turned to face Christina squarely. "You don't know anything about me, do you?"

Christina shook her head. "Nothing." She smiled wryly. "I don't even know your name. They wouldn't give it to me at the agency."

"That's probably my fault," she admitted. "I asked that my name not be given."

"But why?"

Her mother held her hands together in front of her as though in supplication before answering. "I think we had better start at the beginning." She smiled, a smile that lit her face with joy. "My name is Aliki Pappas. It's a rather well-known name in Greece, and I wanted to avoid publicity."

"Aliki. . . ," Christina repeated, as if to taste the name, and her eyes roamed hungrily around her mother's face, trying to make up for all the years of not seeing her. Her mother had exceptional good looks, like the movie sirens of the early Hollywood years, and somehow the name fit her perfectly.

Her mother nodded and continued. "Your father and I were very much in love and when he died—" She paused and looked into the warmth of the gently burning fire in the marble fireplace. Christina knew that she wasn't seeing the glow of the embers, but rather, she was seeing that difficult time. "I almost didn't want to go on," she admitted. Turning back to Christina, she took her hand and smiled. "But your father had left me with a part of himself. I was pregnant with you, my daughter, and it was because of you that I knew that I had to go on so that in you, a part of him would live."

Her mother's love seemed to hover in the very air around her. "Did he. . .did my father. . .know about me?"

Aliki nodded, her fair hair brushing her shoulders. "He knew." Tears swam in her mother's eyes. "And he couldn't wait for you to be born. We had planned on having a houseful of children."

Christina squeezed her mother's hand. Learning that

321

not only had she been wanted but that siblings of hers had been wanted as well, was like a gift, a most fantastic gift. It told more than a million volumes ever could about the love her natural parents had had for one another.

Aliki ran her slender fingertips over the smoothness of her daughter's face. "He used to rub my tummy every night with lanolin and talk to you, telling you—" Her voice broke. She swallowed and continued, "Telling you about all the wonderful things the three of us were going to do together. . ."

Christina looked at the handsome young man in the picture, a man who couldn't have been any older than she was now. "I'm sure that I would have liked—and loved—my father very much."

"He was. . .one of the best," Aliki said, and Christina's heart was gladdened with pride. Her mother shook her fair head and continued, "After you were born, reality stepped in. I had no one to help me and—no money."

"No money?" Christina couldn't help casting her eyes around the house that told an entirely different story.

Aliki smiled in understanding. "I've since changed that condition," she admitted. "I'm an actress."

Christina could easily believe it. Her mother was stunning. Suddenly Christina was certain that her mother was a very famous actress, at least in Greece.

"But back then, I was only nineteen and very poor," Aliki continued, "and I had to turn to social aid to help me. I was allowed to leave you in a home for children for six months before you would be given up for adoption."

"Six months?" Christina frowned. Her adoptive parents had said it was four months.

Her mother nodded her head. "Not the four they were telling people who adopted babies from there."

"So my—" She licked her lips and tried to continue, but she wasn't sure which words to use. "That is. . .the people who adopted me—"

"Your parents, Christina," her mother stated emphatically, startling Christina with the fire that was in her eyes. "Don't ever do them the injustice of taking that away from them. What happened wasn't their fault any more than it was mine and they are every bit as much your parents as Costas," she motioned to the picture of Christina's natural father, "and I are." She stopped speaking and smiled at the picture of Christina's father before she softly continued. "Besides, if you are anything like your father, I think that your heart must be big enough to have two sets of parents, isn't it?"

Slowly, Christina smiled and nodded her head. Her mom—Barbara Rallis—had said something similar. Looking at the picture of the handsome young man who had been her natural father, she knew she could easily love both sets of parents. She already did.

"Anyway," her mother continued, and Christina understood that she wanted to tell her everything. "I visited you every week, sometimes two times a week. I didn't have money for the bus so I walked, during the winter, to and from my little one. A twenty-mile round-trip walk during the darkest days of winter." She looked out the window at the blue, cold sky and the gleaming snow-covered mountains in the distance. Her lips curved ruefully. "I don't remember any sunny days that winter. They were all rainy and cold." She shivered, and Christina understood that her mother had very little to smile about that long-ago winter, regardless of the weather.

"But I didn't mind the walk." Aliki's lips curved into a smile of remembrance. "I saw my little Christina—and in you," her eyes searched Christina's brown ones, "I saw a bit of your father." She fell silent, and Christina squeezed her mother's hand, wanting to give her the courage to go on. Her mother took a deep breath and said, "Well, I finally found a job working in a movie theater as an usher and, most important of all, a grandmotherly woman who offered to look after you for money I could afford to pay. After only four months and three days of your being at the children's home, I went to bring you home."

Her voice changed. It became hard, formidable almost, and yet it quivered with the despair she had felt as that young widow. "I was informed. . .that you had been adopted by a loving, capable couple and that I was no longer legally your mother."

Christina felt as though she were the girl who had been told that her baby was lost to her forever. A girl who was four years younger than what she was this very day. But despite Christina's feeling of oneness with that girl, a question had been on her mind and she needed an answer to it, even though she might hurt her mother by asking. "But. . .didn't you try to get me back?"

Aliki looked at Christina with both anguish and fire

in her eyes, and her voice shook as she went on. "I tried!" She implored Christina to believe her. "I asked a lawyer to help me find you and we tried. For years. . .but nothing. That it was a scam was certain. That we couldn't prove it was equally certain." Her mother squared her shoulders. "But through the years, I have made sure that it never happened to another young mother. No woman should have to go through the agony that I went through. No one!" Christina was certain that her mother had spared many the heartbreak she herself had experienced.

They were silent for a moment as their mutual history settled around them. A medley of church bells rang out over the city, bringing another question to Christina's mind. "Mother. . ." She was surprised by how easy the word rolled from her lips, and she was glad that she had used it when she saw the light that jumped into her mother's eyes. It was something, one small something, that she could give to her birth mother.

"Yes?"

"Have you ever. . ." Christina paused and licked her lips, before softly continuing. "Have you ever blamed God for what happened?"

Her mother sighed deeply, a sigh that traveled back through the years. "Well. . .I didn't know Christ when all this happened." Christina gave her a look that was full of questions, and she quickly explained, "What I mean is, I was only a traditional Christian, someone who went to church occasionally and believed in God—but that was like possessing a lamp without knowing how to turn the switch. I had never accepted Christ as my Savior and

Lord. So I suppose I did cry out to God. Remember, not only had I lost my baby, but I had just lost my husband a few months before that." She turned her eyes to the smiling youth in the photograph. "And I loved him very much."

"So—you did blame God?" Christina pressed. She wasn't sure why the thought of her mother blaming God made her feel as though shackles were being clamped upon her.

Aliki turned back to her. "No." She shook her head emphatically. "No, I didn't. How could I?" She raised her palms questioningly before her and Christina felt lighter as those symbolic shackles fell away from her. "If it wasn't for God, I would have gone insane worrying about you," she explained. "As it was, because I lost you, I knew that I had to depend on God to keep His eyes on you. I couldn't see you. . ." She looked off into that time that was years away from her, before turning her gray eyes back to Christina, "But I knew that God could still see you. Not a day passed that I didn't ask Him how my little baby was. In fact, it was your loss that brought me to a deep personal relationship with Him. I couldn't have survived without my faith." She smiled. "Quite simply, *agapi mou*, my love, I learned how to switch on that lamp."

"You. . .learned to trust God?"

"Totally."

"Even though He had allowed your little baby to be taken from you?"

Her mother sighed. "I guess I should answer something

like Joseph in the Old Testament did when he reassured his brothers that he didn't hold a grudge against them for selling him into slavery. What someone—the people at the home for children—meant for evil, God meant for good. And it was God who led me to put ads around the world in whatever form I could—newspapers, magazines, milk cartons. He led me to believe that when you were old enough, that you would find me. . . just as. . .you would find Him."

"Oh, Mother. . ." For the first time since Christina was a little baby, she fell into her mother's arms, and rested her head against the warm comfort of her mother's shoulder.

Chapter 6

ave you, darling girl," her mother asked after a moment as she smoothed her daughter's hair, "have you found God?"

"I. . ." Christina sat back, and as she looked into the hopeful, gray eyes of the woman who had given her life, she knew that she wanted to have a relationship with the God who had led her to this remarkable woman. She nodded her head. "I want to." And she knew that she really did. "Can you show me how. . .to turn on that lamp?"

Emotion, happy, glad emotion played across Aliki's youthful face. "Darling—leading you to birth into Christ's kingdom will be even more wonderful than when I gave you earthly birth."

Christina's smile froze on her face. She felt confused. After finally meeting her birth mother and after witnessing the joy Paul and Kristen had over the soon-to-be birth of their child, she didn't think anything could be better than giving life to another human being. "How can that be?" she finally asked.

"It's simple really," her mother said as she reached for her Bible. "In physical birth you had no choice in being born. But in spiritual birth—the choice is entirely your own. It's not dependent on anyone else." Aliki's smile deepened. "Spiritual birth is based on the decision you, Christina Rallis, make and on that alone."

Like a light being switched on in her soul Christina suddenly understood perfectly what her mother was saying. The choice to be born into God's kingdom was hers, just as the choice had been her mother's, Kristen's, Paul's and. . .Dino's.

Dear Dino. . . Christina smiled as she thought about him and at how happy all this would make him. Turning a thousand-watt smile on her mother, sure of her decision, she asked, "What do I have to do?"

Bowing their heads, mother and daughter prayed a prayer of salvation. Twenty-three years after the birth of Aliki's Christmas baby, on yet another birthday of the true Christmas Baby, Christina accepted Jesus Christ as her Savior. From now on she would have three birthdays to celebrate on Christmas Day: the birth of Christ, her own physical birth, and now her spiritual birth.

After a moment of silence, a silence filled with the very spirit of God, Christina felt a need to share with her mother what Dino had told her the previous day at the monastery. "I have a friend," she smiled, a smile that told her wise mother that this friend was a special one, "who told me about a man named Nicodemus. My friend said Nicodemus asked Jesus how a person could be born more than once."

Obviously familiar with the story, Aliki quickly flipped to the passage found in the third chapter of John and read, " 'How can a man be born when he is old?' "

Nicodemus asked. " 'Surely he cannot enter a second time into his mother's womb to be born!' "

"That's it!" A new excitement and thirst to know more about God filled Christina's soul. "Does it say how Jesus answered?"

Her mother nodded and read Jesus' answer. " 'I tell you the truth, no one can enter the kingdom of God unless he is born of water and the Spirit. Flesh gives birth to flesh, but the Spirit gives birth to spirit. You should not be surprised at my saying, "You must be born again." The wind blows wherever it pleases. You hear its sound, but you cannot tell where it comes from or where it is going. So it is with everyone born of the Spirit.' "

Christina's eyes were wide. "It's all so amazing—but I think that the most amazing thing of all is how I," she touched her fingers to her chest and gave an amazed little laugh, "I understand it now and—I believe it!" She shook her head, "I wish I had let my—friend tell it to me yesterday."

With a sparkle in her eyes and in her voice, Aliki commented, "I think I'm going to like this—friend."

Christina nodded thoughtfully. "You will." She was glad that she could share her love of Dino with her birth mother. "He's a Christian and a wonderful man. In fact . . .I think that I'm going to marry him!" They hadn't said anything to one another about marriage but somehow Christina knew it to be true. She was as sure of this as she had been about their love for one another.

She was rewarded with her mother's cry of joy. "Praise God! I've missed so much of your life—but

330

at least I won't miss your wedding day!" They hugged one another tight.

"I'm glad, too," Christina murmured.

"Mamma!" The deep gravelly voice called out from the front door, and Christina frowned. She knew that voice. They heard the man shut the door and then his footsteps on the stairs to the living room. Christina shivered, overwhelmed with the sense that something was terribly wrong. Surely, that voice belonged to. . .

"Mamma, are you—"

"Dino!" Christina gasped his name and their eyes collided.

"Christina. . .?" Confusion played across Dino's face at seeing her there and his eyes bounced back and forth from one woman to the other. "What are you—" He froze when his eyes saw the framed picture of the man sitting on the coffee table behind Christina. And then he understood.

He understood why Christina had traveled to Greece. Understood why she couldn't spend Christmas morning with him. Understood even why his mother had asked for a couple hours alone this morning. The only thing he couldn't understand was how he had been so obtuse as to not realize who Christina was from the very beginning.

He turned to Aliki. "Mamma? Christina is your 'Christmas baby'?" He didn't need the confirmation of his mother's nod, but he wanted it anyway.

Christina swiveled to Aliki as realization dawned on her. "You're Dino's mother! Then—that means. . ." *No!*

331

Her brain refused to consider the words that came next. *That means Dino and I are brother and sister.* She wouldn't let this nightmare be true. She wouldn't! "No!" she moaned out loud, knowing that no matter what she did, the nightmare was already real. She and Dino were brother and sister. "No!" Her moan was like a wounded animal's. She grabbed for her coat. She had to get out of the house before she broke down. Already she felt faint and her vision was fuzzy.

Dino grabbed her wrist and pulled her to him, knowing the agony she must be going through and knowing that he had to explain everything to her and quickly. "Christina. . .listen to me."

"No!" she wailed, shaking her head from side to side, her hair whipping against her cheeks. "I've got to go. I've got to. . ."

"Christina!"

The urgency in his voice made her pause, despite the tears that coursed their way down her cheeks. "Dino. . ." Despair filled her voice. "There's nothing you can say. . ."

"How about this? I am Aliki's adoptive son."

Her tears stopped flowing, her head stopped shaking, her very breath even seemed to still. "What?" It was more a sigh than a word.

"I am your mother's adoptive son."

"Adoptive?" Her voice squeaked up an octave as she spoke the word.

He nodded and smiled that wonderful smile she had fallen in love with. He repeated the most fantastic word in the world to her. "Adoptive."

"You mean. . ." She pointed her finger between the two of them. "We aren't related in any way?"

He shook his head. "I'm not related by blood to Aliki." He smiled. "And I'm not related to you either."

"Oh, Dino. . ." His name was a relieved wisp of air as she fell against him. "I thought. . ."

"Shh. . ." He rubbed her neck, trying to relieve the tension of the last few minutes. "I know what you thought."

Aliki had been caught unaware at first, but she hadn't needed more than a moment to understand that Dino was Christina's special friend. Putting one hand on each of her children's shoulders, she explained, "Christina, I adopted Dino when he was seven years old." She looked from her handsome son to her beautiful daughter and smiled. "That and giving birth to you were the best things I've ever done."

"Oh, definitely." Dino laughed and rolled his eyes. "If you're someone who happens to like mean, incorrigible, dirty street urchins."

Eyes twinkling, Aliki remembered back to that time. "I'm an actress—I recognized an act when I saw one. You were as lonely as I. You had lost your mother and father, and I," she squeezed Christina's shoulder, "had lost my husband and my baby."

Dino regarded Aliki, and Christina could see he loved her dearly. "She took me in and made me her son," he explained, and even after so many years Christina could hear the wonder of it all in his voice. She was coming to admire her mother more and more with each passing moment.

Turning to her, she commented, "So that's why you understand the position my adoptive parents are in?"

Aliki nodded. "I understand and empathize. And I would like to ask them to come and visit. I'd like to get to know them."

"I'd like that, too." Christina was certain that her mom and dad would want to meet Aliki as well.

Aliki nodded but then, after a thoughtful pause, she commented, "You know, Christina. . .in a way, a spiritual way, you are related to Dino—you are both members of God's family, so—" Dino's indrawn breath interrupted Aliki, and she smiled. She knew that everything would work out just as God had ordained it now.

Turning sharply to Christina, Dino scanned her eyes with his own. Seeing the joy there, he whispered, "Alleluia." He knew now that all his hopes and dreams of a life with her could come true. The happily-ever-after could be theirs.

"Alleluia," Christina whispered back in confirmation, just before his warm lips finally came to meet hers in the kiss they had been wanting to share from the first moment they had met. For them to kiss was the most natural thing in the world. For them to love was a gift from God, the perfect gift, a gift they would cherish forever.

After a moment, Dino reached into his jacket pocket for the velvet box he had been carrying around, patiently waiting for just this moment. With their foreheads

334

touching, he said, his voice even more gravelly than usual, "So . . .it's your birthday today. . ."

"Ummm. . .I was born of the flesh twenty-three years ago today—and of the spirit, only a few moments before you walked in."

"So much to celebrate," he murmured and stepped back from her, pulling the little box out of his pocket. "It's a good thing that I have a birthday present for you."

"A birthday present?" She didn't understand. How could he have a birthday present for her? He hadn't known that it was her birthday.

He tilted his head to the side and glanced over at his mother, who was watching the exchange with the concentration she might use at a dress rehearsal. She nodded her head and smiled encouragingly. She knew what was on her son's mind and nothing in the world could have made her happier.

"Well. . ." He turned back to Christina and held out the box to her. "Maybe it's more of an engagement present."

"Engagement. . . ?" Christina lifted the lid and gasped at the diamond solitaire. Sunlight caught the angles of the gem and it flashed up at her.

Taking the ring from the box, Dino held it before her. "Christina—will you do me the honor of becoming my wife?"

She smiled, and Dino saw reflected within her soft eyes the inner light that had been turned on in her when she had accepted Christ as her Savior. That light was the best Christmas gift he could have, because it meant the woman he loved was safe for eternity.

"Dino. . .the honor will be mine," she murmured.

"No, mine," he refuted as his mouth lowered to hers.

"No, mine," she argued.

But just before their lips touched they whispered together, "Ours," and their kiss told their love to each other, a giving love based on the very love of God, the love that had become incarnate on this day two thousand years earlier when the Christmas Baby had been born.

Chapter 7

O ne week later, Christina stood on the balcony of her mother's home, gazing out over the city of her birth. After a week of cold weather, the air had again turned warm, melting all the snow on the mountains and making the first day of January feel more like Easter than New Year's. The diamond on her left hand flashed in the strong Grecian sun, and she smiled, still amazed at how God had taken all the events of her life and worked them out so perfectly.

Behind her in the living room, she could hear the happy sounds of the people she loved—her adoptive parents, her birth mother, and Dino. Aliki had been genuine and eager in issuing an immediate invitation to the Rallises, asking them to join her for New Year's.

While watching the birds that frolicked over the rooftops of the city, Christina remembered back to those first few tension-filled moments when her adoptive parents had arrived at Aliki's home. Aliki had defused the tension immediately in the gracious way Christina was coming to learn was an innate part of her mother. "I wish to thank you both for taking such good care of Christina and for being wonderful parents to her," Aliki had said.

"We. . ." Barbara Rallis had licked her lips and looked over at her husband for support. He nodded for her to go on. "We didn't know that she was taken from you falsely." She lowered her silver head before continuing, looking to Christina like a very old lady, a lady old enough to be Aliki's mother in fact, and Christina wanted to go to her and wrap her arms around her and tell her that everything was all right. But she didn't. She knew that had to come from Aliki this time.

"We should have checked into the adoption more thoroughly," Barbara admitted, before speaking the only words Aliki needed to hear. "We're very, very sorry." Peter Rallis nodded his head in grave agreement.

Aliki's lips trembled between crying and smiling as she arose from her chair and walked to where the two older people sat. She held out her arms in a welcoming and forgiving embrace, an embrace which Peter and Barbara Rallis gladly accepted. After a moment, while tears were shed by all, Aliki whispered, "I have to say to you the same thing I said to Christina the day that we were reunited, the wise words of Joseph in the Bible—'What someone meant for evil, God meant for good.'"

"I think," Peter Rallis nodded his head while swiping at the tears that had gathered in the corners of his eyes, "that I have to get to know some of those Bible sayings again. It's been a few years," he admitted. "Although," he looked at his wife and whispered words that were like gold to Christina's ears, "during the last few weeks Barbara and I have been praying again. . .praying that we wouldn't lose our little girl to her birth mother." His eyes pled with Aliki's, asking a question.

Aliki took a deep breath before walking over to Dino. She touched his face before turning to Peter Rallis again. "As you know, Dino is my adoptive son—so I know the position of an adoptive mother every bit as well as that of a biological mother."

Peter and Barbara hung onto her words as if they were a lifeline. In a way, Christina knew that they were.

"I'm sad of course that I missed my daughter's growing up years. But more than that sadness is a gladness, a joy, that she finally found me and that we will have many years ahead of us, years from which I will not exclude you. I won't try to diminish your role as her parents in any way whatsoever."

A cry escaped Barbara Rallis, a cry of relief and of joy, and Christina couldn't restrain herself any longer. She ran to the older woman and held her tightly in her arms. "See, Mom," she whispered into her ear, "where there is prayer, there is joy."

Barbara nodded her head against her daughter's chest. "I guess mothers can learn from their daughters," she whispered, smiling up at Christina through tears that had been turned from bitter to happy.

"And God did work everything out!" Aliki exclaimed as she held her son close to her. "I'm sure that our lives are just as they should be because of the events that have gone into their making. I probably wouldn't have adopted my son if I hadn't lost my 'Christmas baby'— and that would have been a tragedy." She jabbed Dino good-naturedly with her fingernail. "Even if he doesn't tell his girlfriends about his mother," she said, and they laughed, knowing that Dino hadn't told Christina about his famous mother because too often, girls had wanted to date him just because of her.

The flutter of the birds around Christina's head as they darted back and forth across the ceramic roof of her mother's home brought Christina back to the present. She felt Dino's strong arms wrapping around her waist. "Here you are," he whispered into her ear, "I missed you," he admitted, just before he lowered his lips to nibble the sensitive spot on the side of her neck.

Christina smiled and brought her palm up to rest against his face. "I was just thinking."

"About what?"

"About how blessed we all are."

Dino squeezed his eyes together in thankfulness. For him the biggest blessing of them all was hearing Christina talk with the understanding of God's wisdom in her words.

"Ah. . ." Aliki joined them on the veranda. "So this is where you two lovebirds have escaped to." Her eyes twinkled. She was thrilled that her adoptive son and her biological daughter were going to marry.

"Is there a convention going on out here?" Peter Rallis's booming voice asked as he and Barbara joined them. Christina was happy to see he was once again the jovial man she had always known and loved.

"With this weather, who wants to stay inside?" Barbara commented and breathed in the warm air. "I love Athens' weather," she stated emphatically and they all laughed because she had made it very clear over the last few days just how much she loved the warm winter. Even Athens' cold days seemed warm to her.

"Then you are going to have to visit often," Aliki encouraged.

"And you," Peter Rallis spoke to Aliki, "are going to have to think seriously about acting in our new show."

Christina and Dino glanced at one another and smiled, the smile of a man and woman who can communicate without words. God had certainly worked everything out—even to Christina's three living parents having similar and complimentary careers.

At the sound of a car pulling up in front of the house, they all looked down. A new excitement buzzed between them when they saw who it was.

"It's Paul and Kristen!" Dino exclaimed.

"And the baby!" Christina caught a glimpse of a pink blanket through the windshield before they all hurried down to meet the newest member of the Andrakos family.

"We're on our way home from the hospital," the proud father said as he stepped out of the car. "But we just thought we'd stop by and wish you all a Happy New Year and. . ." Paul looked into the car where Kristen cradled their new little girl in her arms, "introduce you to Aphrodite."

"She's beautiful!"

"Look at all that hair!"

"And those gorgeous eyes!"

They all cooed and smiled over the alert infant.

Kristen smiled the happy smile of a new mother, a Madonna-like smile. "She was born on Christmas Day." She softly kissed the infant's downy head. "She's our Christmas baby."

"Christmas baby. . ." Aliki murmured, her eyes meeting Barbara's.

"Christmas baby. . ." Barbara whispered back, and Christina's two mothers smiled at one another easily, sharing the love they both felt for their own Christmas baby.

Dino looked at the baby in Kristen's arms as she waved her little hands around. "To think that Christ was once so small and so dependent on earthly parents. . ." His voice was full of awe.

"And that He grew up to bring us Easter." Kristen instinctively tightened her hold on her precious little baby as she thought about the agony Christ's mother was to go through on that day thirty-three years down the road.

But Christina smiled. "Easter is the biggest miracle of them all." Her voice rang with confidence and joy. Resting her head against her soon-to-be husband's chest, she glanced up at him.

He smiled down at her, and Christina knew that the inner light radiating from his eyes was the light the Christ Child had brought to his heart. It was the same light Christ had brought to her, too.

He had brought the light to the whole world. On Christmas Day nearly two thousand years ago He had been sent to earth so that all humans everywhere, down through the ages, could have eternal life.

God gave His own Son for us all to cherish, adore, worship, believe. . .our Christmas Baby.

Melanie Panagiotopoulos
Born and raised in the United States, Melanie now makes her home in Athens, Greece, with her husband, a cardiologist and intensivist, and their two teenagers. Melanie enjoys studying all kinds of history—biblical, ancient, and medieval. She writes about her surroundings in her contemporary romance *Odyssey of Love* (Heartsong Presents).

A Letter to Our Readers

Dear Readers:

In order that we might better contribute to your reading enjoyment, we would appreciate your taking a few minutes to respond to the following questions. When completed, please return to the following: Fiction Editor, Barbour Publishing, Inc., P.O. Box 719, Uhrichsville, OH 44683.

1. Did you enjoy reading *Christmas Dreams*?
   ❑ Very much—I would like to see more books like this.
   ❑ Moderately—I would have enjoyed it more if_____

   _____

   _____

2. What influenced your decision to purchase this book?
   (Check those that apply.)
   ❑ Cover   ❑ Back cover copy   ❑ Title   ❑ Price
   ❑ Friends   ❑ Publicity   ❑ Other

3. Which story was your favorite?
   ❑ *Evergreen*   ❑ *Search for the Star*
   ❑ *The Christmas Wreath*   ❑ *Christmas Baby*

4. Please check your age range:
   ❑ Under 18   ❑ 18–24   ❑ 25–34
   ❑ 35–45   ❑ 46–55   ❑ Over 55

5. How many hours per week do you read?_____

Name_____

Occupation_____

Address_____

City _____ State_____ Zip_____

E-mail _____

If you enjoyed

CHRISTMAS
Dreams

then read:

LONE STAR
CHRISTMAS

Someone Is Rustling Up a Little Holiday Matchmaking in Four Delightful Stories

The Marrying Kind by Kathleen Y'Barbo
Here Cooks the Bride by Cathy Marie Hake
Unexpected Blessings by Vickie McDonough
A Christmas Chronicle by Pamela Griffin

Available wherever books are sold.
Or order from:
Barbour Publishing, Inc.
P.O. Box 721
Uhrichsville, Ohio 44683
www.barbourbooks.com

You may order by mail for $6.97 and add $2.00 to your order for shipping.
Prices subject to change without notice.

If you enjoyed
CHRISTMAS
Dreams
then read:

PATCHWORK
HOLIDAY

*One Heirloom Quilt Comforts
Four Couples in Search of True Love*

Twice Loved by Wanda E. Brunstetter
Everlasting Song by DiAnn Mills
Remnants of Faith by Renee DeMarco
Silver Lining by Colleen L. Reece

If you enjoyed
CHRISTMAS
Dreams

then read:

Simply Christmas

TWO HUMOROUS MOTHERS, TWO LONELY WIDOWS,

FOUR STORIES OF REGAINING CHRISTMAS PEACE

All Done with the Dashing by Pamela Dowd
No Holly, No Ivy by Wanda Luttrell
O Little Town of Progress by Wanda Luttrell
My True Love Gave to Me. . . by Christine Lynxwiler

Available wherever books are sold.
Or order from:
Barbour Publishing, Inc.
PO Box 719
Uhrichsville, Ohio 44683
www.barbourbooks.com

You may order by mail for $6.99 and add $2.00 to your order for shipping.
Prices subject to change without notice.

HEARTSONG
PRESENTS

If you love Christian romance...

$10.⁹⁹

You'll love Heartsong Presents' inspiring and faith-filled romances by today's very best Christian authors...DiAnn Mills, Wanda E. Brunstetter, and Yvonne Lehman, to mention a few!

When you join Heartsong Presents, you'll enjoy 4 brand-new mass market, 176-page books—two contemporary and two historical—that will build you up in your faith when you discover God's role in every relationship you read about!

Imagine...four new romances every four weeks—with men and women like you who long to meet the one God has chosen as the love of their lives...all for the low price of $10.99 postpaid.

To join, simply visit www.heartsongpresents.com or complete the coupon below and mail it to the address provided.

Mass Market 176 Pages

✂- -

YES! Sign me up for Heart♥ng!

NEW MEMBERSHIPS WILL BE SHIPPED IMMEDIATELY!

Send no money now. We'll bill you only $10.99 postpaid with your first shipment of four books. Or for faster action, call 1-740-922-7280.

NAME_____

ADDRESS _____

CITY _____ STATE _____ ZIP_____

**MAIL TO: HEARTSONG PRESENTS, P.O. Box 721, Uhrichsville, Ohio 44683
or sign up at WWW.HEARTSONGPRESENTS.COM**

ADPG05